About the Author

Leah Curtis was born in Essex in 1997 where she now works as a childcare provider. From the age of nine, Leah has been writing books and never finishing them, this one has been completed so that her nan will stop telling her off!

Seven

L A Curtis

Seven

Olympia Publishers
London

www.olympiapublishers.com
OLYMPIA PAPERBACK EDITION

A CIP catalogue record for this title is
available from the British Library.

ISBN: 978-1-78830-961-5

This is a work of fiction.
Names, characters, places and incidents originate from the writer's
imagination. Any resemblance to actual persons, living or dead, is
purely coincidental.

First Published in 2021

Olympia Publishers
Tallis House
2 Tallis Street
London
EC4Y 0AB

Printed in Great Britain

THE BEGINNING AND THE END

After sitting in the drab, frosty waiting room for what seemed like forever, an unfamiliar voice broke the silence, 'Brooke, Dr Daw will see you now.'

I followed the plump receptionist down the corridor until we reached the oh-so familiar office of my counselor.

I wondered what had become of her old receptionist, dreamy Daniel.

The only reason I would turn up half an hour early to my sessions was so that Daniel and I had an excuse to talk for a while. And when I say talk I mean passionately kiss in the storage cupboard for twenty minutes.

That was until I met the love of my life of course. Dreamy Daniel was just a distant memory now.

The room itself was simple; mint green and light with potted plants placed perfectly along the bottom of the floor to ceiling window, I suppose it was decorated in a way that would make people feel calm.

I slumped down on the cream leather sofa, opposite Dr Daw, who sat royally in her arm chair.

She was a skinny lady with bright blonde hair twisted neatly on the top of her head, held there with a very sparkly jeweled clip. I had observed over the years of seeing her that not a strand of hair on her perfect little head was ever out of place, it was kind of irritating.

'Hi, again.' I smiled half-heartedly.

'Brooke, it must have been over a year since our last session.

What brings you back?' She asked in her song-like voice.

'It's pretty fucked up,' I stated, 'I wouldn't know where to start...' I shuffled in my seat, the thought of explaining what had happened that day all over again was enough to make me want to hurl.

She chuckled at my brutal honesty. 'Well we can only start at the beginning...'

I breathed in, still unsure whether I wanted to delve into the deepest darkest parts of my life, to tell her the whole painful, horrendous truth, but I was sitting in that room again and there was no turning back now.

'Right, the beginning...'

I

It was Christmas Eve and I had two hours left of work before I had been gifted with one whole week off.

That was one of the perks of being an apprentice, we weren't seen as relevant enough to stay working over Christmas so to get us all out of the way we'd been given paid holiday.

I knew this was just a ploy to convince us to stay there once our training was complete. The department was very understaffed. I was beginning to understand why as I sat in the bleak, somber briefing room and listened to the latest heart-wrenching discovery of yet another house full of depleted and defiled women who had been harbored there to then be sold onto disgusting men for unimaginable reasons.

The constant photographs, recordings and statements that I had to listen to day in day out was enough to make me want a career change, but the fact that we were finding some of these women before they were exploited was enough reason as any to carry on soldiering through the job each day.

'We received another anonymous tip…' Mr. Daniels — the big boss of the Organized Crime Unit — was addressing everyone in the room whilst standing in front of a board filled with possible suspects, photographs and post it notes of questions.

'…Which led us to this house.' He pointed to the picture of the crumbling house in which the women were being hidden in.

I shuddered.

'This address is registered to a Mr. Andrew Spence, forty-five years of age,' he said as he pinned the picture of Andrew next to the house on the board. 'This is who we put all of our focus on now, we need to find him and bring him in for questioning as soon as possible. Before any more innocent people have to die or suffer.'

I gulped nervously as I examined the photo he had pinned up.

Andrew Spence had a face that looked much senior to that of a forty-five-year-old. His dark brown eyes added a hellish look to his withered face which was framed with what appeared to be a very greasy, matted head of jet black hair.

Mr. Daniels paused for effect as everybody in the room hung onto his every word, writing notes as he spoke and nodding in agreement.

'This department has raided thirty-five houses this year, *thirty-five.*' He paused again, making sure he stared at each and every one of us in the eye.

'In those thirty-five houses we found over five hundred women and children. Two hundred and seventy-six of those were dead on the scene or died later in hospital. This is too many, we must act faster or the figure is going to reach its thousands. And this is just in our area, in London alone.

Modern slavery is becoming an even bigger issue than in previous years. Millions of people around the world are being subjected to this wrongful exploitation and if our little team here can contribute to stopping one major organized crime group then we can sleep well knowing that we are helping in some way, yes?'

Everyone nodded in unison.

'So Andrew Spence, we find him and we find out who else is involved.

Trainees, I know you're off for Christmas now, but whilst

you're at home filling your bellies with mince pies and pigs-in-blankets please spare a thought for all those millions of people who are spending their Christmas being sold, exploited, used for organs, raped, need I go on?'

Well this got a bit unnecessarily depressing. I thought to myself as I glanced around the room at my fellow apprentices, squirming uncomfortably in their chairs as the officers looked at them with a hint of judgment on their faces, or was it jealousy because we could go home for Christmas and they couldn't?

Either way, I'd had enough of this deep and dismal lecture. Yes, I understood the severity of the situation, but I also didn't want to be made guilty for enjoying a pig-in-blanket or four.

'Anyway,' Mr. Daniels continued, 'have a lovely Christmas, trainees. And the rest of you I will see you here tomorrow bright and early.'

The room buzzed with murmurs of pointless chatter, people saying 'have a lovely Christmas' and 'I'll see you in the morning' as they collected their things and made their way out of the door.

I didn't speak to anyone as I hurried out of the building without a second look. I jumped into my car and made my way to my auntie and uncle's home where I had spent every Christmas since I could remember.

'Merry fucking Christmas,' I said to myself as I breathed a huge sigh of relief.

As the only conscious soul in the otherwise sleeping house, I made a prodigious effort to keep it that way as I crept across the lustrous floorboards which bounded the upper story of my aunt and uncle's home.

As I snaked down the grand staircase I glanced at the many family photos held proudly by the walls.

My thoughts departed back to a time when I would slide down the steel arms of the staircase to be caught by my then doting father at the bottom.

I often wondered where that happy, loving, care-free father had disappeared to. Nowadays he was an emotionless robot who only seemed to care about pleasing my pompous mother.

As I reached the large kitchen I smiled as I peered out of the frosty window. Snowflakes glided peacefully downwards from the early morning sky, settling on the beautiful garden that lay miles ahead of me. I trembled as my bare feet touched the tiled floor, sending a visible chill up my spine.

'What are you doing up so early, darling?' My auntie whispered gently from behind me.

I tensed at the unexpected company, 'I'm sorry, did I wake you up?'

I watched her glide into the kitchen; she did not make a noise as if she were an angel floating inches above the ground.

'Merry Christmas,' she beamed as she kissed me on the cheek — ignoring my question. The warmth that travelled off of her made my goose bumps disappear.

'You too, Veronica,' I replied as I wrapped my arms around her petite neck.

Auntie Veronica — my mother's older sister by ten years — and I had always been very close, she would repeatedly tell me that from the minute I entered the world she knew we would be the 'best of friends.'

Auntie Ron and Uncle Jeremy had taken me in when I was seven years old after my parents couldn't handle my constant breakdowns with their, and I quote, 'busy work schedules.'

Veronica had lived through the worst times with me. The debilitating sleep paralysis and night terrors, the constant being sent home from school after being sick and not being able to breathe being just a few of those times.

She was the person who pestered the doctors for months to help me after they insisted it was a stomach bug, or something in my diet that was causing the constant illness.

All the while my mother had to escape to holistic retreats and extensive therapy to help cope with her, and yes here's another quote from the witch herself, 'out of control child.'

For this reason, along with many others, I had always had a much better relationship with Auntie Veronica than I did with my own mother.

'Would you like a coffee?' I glanced up at her as I flicked the switch on their very fancy coffee machine.

'Do you even have to ask, dear?' she beamed again.

Veronica and I perched on the cushioned barstools and gazed out of the frosted window in admiration as we hugged our steaming mugs of delicious smelling coffee.

Despite the frost, the day dawned into a blue and cloudless sky.

Dawn had always been my favourite time of day, so much so that 'Dawn' had been her nickname for me throughout my childhood.

There was something peaceful about waking up with the sun and hearing nothing but the birds singing in the sky.

I must have had my usual dopy look painted across my face

13

as Veronica was grinning lovingly at me, 'Are you in Brooke land again?'

I grinned back at her, 'I was indeed, romanticizing life in my head as always.' I blushed.

'Promise me you will never stop doing that.' She sighed as she sipped on her creamy coconut latte.

I couldn't even if I tried. I rolled my eyes inwardly at myself; I knew one day I'd have to live in the real world.

The patter of tiny footsteps echoed down the stairs, breaking the peaceful silence of the morning, before my excitable twin siblings Riley and Ruby burst through the door, running straight over to the huge Christmas tree and gasping at the tower of presents piled underneath, followed by my parents.

Their angelic emerald green eyes — filled with wonder and magic — twinkled against the beautiful lights wrapped neatly around the tree,

'Merry Christmas sweeties,' I whispered, planting a kiss on their tiny foreheads before heading upstairs to dress for the day.

They were the only reason I hadn't packed up and left home by now.

Or the fact that you're too scared to live, anxiety reminded me.

'Aha!' Veronica resounded from the other side of her vast living room.

Her voice echoed as she jumped up from the chair she was perched on. 'I know what it is!'

Everyone's bewildered expressions turned to face her, the lights from the towering tree reflected against her chandelier earrings, blinding us all in the process.

'What? How in the world could you know what *that* is?' My uncle exclaimed from the long dining table behind her between mouthfuls of homemade chocolate cake.

He squinted across the room at my mum — obviously misplacing his glasses again — she was standing in the center of the room fluctuating her arms around in a drunken attempt to play charades.

'What am I acting out then, Ron?' she slurred, still waving her arms above her head as if she was performing a rain dance.

'I believe it is *Grease!*' she cried delightedly. She took an elongated gulp of her wine before standing up and executing an exaggerated bow as the twins cheered gleefully for her.

My mother staggered back to her seat on the floor besides my dad who attempted to give her a high five, but they both completely missed one another's hands. I rolled my eyes and giggled.

'What?' she looked up at me sternly whilst tucking her short, blonde hair behind her ears. Her exorbitant sparkling diamonds dazzled against her pasty skin.

'Nothing,' I snapped.

Here we go again.

I stared straight into her bright, blue eyes. She glared daggers back at me.

'Well, don't laugh at me then, laughing at people doesn't do well for their self-esteem does it?' she snarled.

'Your self-esteem could never be damaged, mum,' I retorted sarcastically.

With that remark she briskly stood up, tipping her glass of wine to the side so that it spilt on her deep purple dress, 'now look what you've made me do!' she screamed.

'Claire! She didn't do anything,' Veronica jumped in. Her villous eyebrows tightened on her face.

'Stay out of it, Ron! She always ruins everything!' she huffed, stamping her feet like a turbulent child, 'I'm sick of you and your horrible comments. After everything we have done for you!' She stomped out of the room. The clicks of her heels echoed throughout the house.

'Brookie, please don't argue with mummy, not on Christmas day,' Ruby pleaded in a high pitched whine.

'Don't listen to her, darling,' Veronica comforted as she placed herself next to me. Her long fingers brushed up and down my arm reassuringly. 'And don't you worry about it either you two, go and play with your new toys before bed time!' she ordered, nodding her head towards my uncle.

Jeremy immediately jumped up from his seat. 'The tickle monster orders you to play with your toys!' he roared as he chased them in a circle.

They soon forgot about my mother's outburst.

I wished it could be that easy for me.

'I'm not, when do I ever listen to her?' I turned my attention back to auntie Veronica who was watching me worryingly.

My dad looked up at me with a disappointed expression painted across his un-ironed face.

'Go and apologize to your mother,' he ordered.

'Are you joking? I didn't do anything wrong!' I hissed so

that the twins wouldn't hear.

I promptly stood up, towering over him as he still lounged on the floor. 'She can't handle her drink.'

'If you are going to be disrespectful, then you can get out. She's right, we have put up with too much from you and you can't even give us a break on Christmas day!'

I looked down at my father sympathetically, ignoring he's desperate attempt to disquiet me before lumbering into the hallway, shivering as my shorn feet met the bleak temperature of the marble flooring. My hair faintly patted against the bottom of my spine as I did so.

I grabbed my coat off of the rangy coat hook before swiftly leaving the now very tense house.

I knew there was a reason I hadn't joined in on the drinking, it was so I could make a quick getaway.

I relaxed into the soft chair of my *BMW* and breathed in a huge sigh of relief.

I was abhorred with the constant feud between my parents and me. I couldn't for the life of me think of anything I had done to them that was as terrible as they repaid me with.

It used to be just my mother that acted like the spawn of Satan, but over the years my father had begun to chime in with the hopes of receiving a gold star.

I knew that my mushy, lovey-dovey dad was only trying to 'stick up' for my mum, but it wasn't a good look for a man of nearly fifty-five.

As I cruised down the countryside roads I contemplated what to do about the situation. Although I pondered this a lot, I never seemed to find a conclusion.

Because you're stuck in a rut, anxiety reminded me.

Ignoring her, I switched on the radio and flicked through the channels until I eventually found a channel reporting the news.

The polished voice of the news reporter interrupted the conversation between the car engine and the silence of the frosty evening.

'...thank you, John. And if you want to get involved in John's bee charity so that they do not become extinct by 2020 then visit our website,'

I rolled my eyes and leant towards the button to scan through the channels again, 'and in other news the remains of an unknown woman have been accidently dug up by a group of young paleontologists.

Here's Rupert with the details.'

I leant back in the chair and listened to the news report as I studied the road ahead of me, trying to determine where I had transported myself to.

'...The remains seem to be around twenty years old so police are currently looking at all cold cases and testing to see if there is any DNA or trace that can help them find out who this woman is. It has been confirmed that they are treating this as a murder case due to suspicious markings on the woman's remains. There will be more updates on this story as soon as we receive new information.'

I knew there was only one place to go, so I steered the car in the direction of Jamie's, knowing that she too was probably having a miserable Christmas.

'Hello there, fitty!' Jamie giggled childishly as she glanced up to the television I had just switched on.

Looking up at the news channel I noticed there was a posh, balding man in a grey suit that seemed as though he was executing a speech, but he had been interrupted by a young boy who was shouting riotously at what looked like a member of the bald man's security team standing powerfully behind him.

'Thanks for letting me crash here, babe.' I sighed, thankful that I didn't have to spend the rest of Christmas with my brat of a mother. I positioned myself comfortably on Jamie's feathered mattress and studied the TV further.

The security man had moved in front of the bald man to protect him as he was escorted from the scene.

His firm position did not change — yet his facial expression looked panicked, but not shocked I noticed. I wondered if he knew the boy.

Suddenly, some police stepped in, pulling the boy to the ground. His brown curly hair bounced as they tackled him to the concrete.

He managed to pull his head up far enough to look at the camera. His big, brown eyes were the only thing I noticed. At that moment the screen flickered and then the news reporters were on the screen explaining a slight technical hitch.

'Wonder what that was about,' I muttered to myself.

'He is probably stoned or something,' Jamie replied quietly as she hunched on the floor, delicately painting her perfectly square toe nails a deep ruby color.

'No, I think there's more to that. He seemed really upset. And it's Christmas day, why isn't he at home with his family?' I pondered.

Jamie rolled her eyes. 'You're so dramatic,' she snapped

before changing the subject. '*Anyway,* you're very welcome. Thank god that we have each other right, B? Otherwise this Christmas would have been like any other day.' Her bold eyes rolled dramatically again as she spoke.

'At least one good thing came of our families being total failures,' I agreed.

Jamie's parents were on another extravagant holiday, celebrating Christmas together and leaving Jamie, yet again, at home alone.

Jamie and I had grown up together as our families were very close.

My mum had met Jamie's dad, Mike before any of us were born, they had a brief relationship after meeting at the local *Sainsbury's* one night where their trolleys had collided.

Mike and my dad had been best of friends ever since secondary school.

Mum would bring up the story of how she met my dad at any given opportunity — equally as cheesy and sickening each time she blurted it out.

'We met at a pub one night where Mike and I were having a quick dinner before heading back to our own home, not planning to stay the night together; we were going through a rough patch.'

She would always start, emphasizing the 'rough patch' so she didn't look like a tart who jumped from one guy to his best friend, which was exactly what had really happened.

'Jerry (my dad) strolled in through the door dressed in skinny jeans, a white shirt with the sleeves rolled up and a smile that would make any girls heart flutter. Mike noticed him and introduced us; he had me from the first cheeky wink after that.'

She would gush, at this point she usually planted a sloppy, inappropriate kiss on my dad's lips as everyone 'awwed' at the happy couple.

'Mike could see that me and Jerry had instantly hit it off and he pulled me over to a quiet corner to talk, saying that he knew we were better as friends and that I could go for Jerry — he thought he would like me.

I then dragged Mike to the bar and tried setting him up instantly with a gorgeous girl; he couldn't find any one of taste so he insisted that he left us to it.

Jerry and I sat at the bar talking and having one too many drinks until the pub closed; I felt like I had known him for years after that night — so romantic, it was like fate brought us together I always say.'

I usually left at this point making up a silly excuse like I needed to use the toilet or I thought I had left my T.V switched on in my room, but I would always be back down to the crowded room in time to catch the end of the story.

'Mike met Lisa (Jamie's mum) at the library, he was scanning for a gardening book, and funnily enough so was Lisa. They both reached for the same book and *bam!* Sparks flew.

We all became very close friends after that, and have been ever since.'

She would end the story by raising a glass to 'love, happiness and friendship' before she would be flooded with personal questions and admirable looks, everyone wishing they had the 'perfect life of Claire Hamilton.'

Jamie laughed. 'One year we will be in our own homes, with our own families, you never know, I might be married to Luke,' she winked.

'Remind me, which one is Luke again?' I frowned; I couldn't always tell the difference between her numberless queues of good looking men.

'Keep up, B,' she snapped.

'Asking me to keep up with the amount of men you open your legs for is not an easy task Jamie,' I retorted.

Jamie wasn't offended easily, but that comment touched a nerve, just like I knew it would.

'EXCUSE ME?' she screamed, 'you can be such a bitch, B. And not that it's any of your business, but I haven't slept with him, we've been on ONE date. Just because the only time you get any is when you go to get mental help don't take it out on me! Daniel is a head case too!'

'Too? What do you mean by *too?* I don't go for mental help, I go counselling, it's nothing to be ashamed of. Maybe you need some counselling, shall I book you in? Can you get off of your knees for five minutes to go to a counselling session with me?' I exclaimed.

This wasn't a rare occurrence, us two arguing over petty nonsense. We knew how to dig where it hurt.

Jamie creased over laughing. 'That was a good one,' she howled. 'Anyway, that's enough now, it's Christmas, Jesus Christ, peace and love and all that crap.'

'Merry fucking Christmas.' I exhaled wistfully.

II

'Why haven't they been arrested?' I wondered out loud as I observed the woman across the street serving another happy customer a bag of drugs as her little boy watched from the cracked window at the front of their house, 'she should have that kid taken away from her.'

'Oh here we go.' Jamie rolled her eyes at me. 'Here comes police officer Brooke, the Brooke that is *so* annoying,' she complained as she glissaded a large brush through her lengthy hair. 'Brooke!' She shrieked at me as I continued to stare past her.

I jumped out of my oblivious state and turned to her. 'What?'

'They're none of your business. *Me* on the other hand, your best friend of *seventeen years* should have your full attention at all times, yes?' She moaned, shaking my shoulders franticly. 'And anyway, isn't the whole point of you working in the police now that you can just go all Miami Vice on her arse?'

I laughed, 'Jamie, for the millionth time, I'm *not* a police officer. I have reported them so many times though…'

I stopped talking as I noticed her blank expression. It wasn't that she didn't support me, but Jamie could never understand why I didn't take the easy route and work in my mum's beauty business like she had.

Yes, the money was good. And yes, I'd learnt how to do pretty much everything during my work experience in school. I could give anyone an amazing spray tan, a big bouncy blow dry, lashes to die for and be finished by five pm every night.

But working with my mum was my idea of hell.

'I'm so excited for tonight! Everyone's going.' Jamie quickly changed the subject. She pouted her rouged lips into the mirror.

'By everyone, you mean Luke, right?' I answered half-heartedly, still keeping one eye firmly on the child in the window opposite.

'Luke, who's Luke?' she grinned. She was probably one of the prettiest people I had ever met.

Her perfectly straight teeth seemed to glisten against the lights of her Hollywood mirror.

I shot her a disproving look. 'But I'm not allowed to forget who he is?' I sighed as the child's mother yanked the curtains across the window and decided to turn my attention into looking even half as good as my best friend did without even trying.

I ran a nude lip-gloss over my puckered lips and swished my long hair over to the other shoulder.

Jamie looked at me through the mirror, knowing that I was probably being internally self-critical to myself in that moment she nodded at me reassuringly. 'You look really pretty.'

As we wedged our way through avid crowds of teenagers, I began to question why I had agreed to join Jamie that night.

It was not the right place for a girl with crippling anxiety to be spending her time. I could feel my chest becoming tighter, and my vision turned blurry-those two were always the first signs of a panic attack.

Not now please body. I begged.

'Oh my god, it's so good here isn't it?' Jamie grinned, holding my arm and leading me towards a tall stand at the far end of the Christmas fair.

'Yes,' I reluctantly agreed; trying to sound at least a tiny bit enthusiastic in an attempt not to hurt her feelings. 'Where the hell are you taking me now?' I wondered.

As we drew closer to the stand, I noticed that there were not as many people over this end of the capacious circus tent, I had been dragged through for the past three hours.

My chest felt a bit loser, I inhaled and exhaled a few times to bring my heart beat down, just like Dr Daw had told me to do many times.

'It's a Clairvoyant!' she replied excitedly, fastening her pace as she noticed a big group of Goth-like twenty something's join the small queue to the stand.

I peered around a tall girl dressed head to toe in black to see the Clairvoyant herself. She was typical of what you would expect; dressed in a long gypsy style outfit with a scarf wrapped around her long, braided hair. I hissed in Jamie's ear. 'Why are you making me do this?'

She turned to me and frowned. 'For god sake, can't you live a little? You're becoming your mother you know that?'

I gave her a sharp why-would-you-say-that look, but stayed in the line as I did not want to become my mother in any way, shape or form.

When it came to be Jamie's turn, she pushed me in front instead. 'You can go first because I'm so nice.' she grinned.

I scowled at her as I walked towards the woman.

'Hello, there,' she smiled at me as I placed myself on the wooden chair in front of her. There was a small table positioned between us, she nonchalantly laid her hand onto it — her long, red fingernails pointed towards me as she did so.

'Hi,' I greeted her politely. 'Nice to meet you.'

'You're a lovely girl aren't you, not at all like your mother,' she said as she starred straight into my eyes. She made me feel quite uncomfortable; I fidgeted nervously as I felt her eyes bore into mine. She *must have overheard the conversation Jamie and I had about my mum,* I thought to myself.

'Now, give me your hand,' she ordered. I could hear Jamie's high pitched giggle from behind me.

I held my hand out as instructed, but instead of holding it she just stared.

After what seemed like an age of silence she whispered, 'you're nervous, why's that my love?'

'I'm not nervous,' I lied. I was always nervous.

The hand that she had sprucely laid upon the table quickly flew up, making me jerk in my seat. She seized hold of my hand and yanked it forcefully so that it was closer to her. She closed her eyes and I turned around to Jamie; at least she was amused.

'Turn back!' the woman shouted. I did as she said and watched her as she narrowed her forehead in concentration.

Her hand began to shake and then she expeditiously let go. Her face turned into a picture of panic. 'Well, there is nothing I can do for you,' she said sternly.

'What do you mean?' I laughed, but she dismissed me and

signaled for Jamie to take a seat, but I grabbed her and pulled her out of the queue.

'We are *not* wasting any more time with that psycho!' I insisted before hurrying her away.

'What the hell did she mean by that?' Jamie laughed as we sat down at a table after spending a fortune on the dessert stand.

'Don't ask me,' I answered as I stuffed in a mouthful of sugary doughnut, jam oozing down my chin. I studied her intrigued looking face. 'You don't really believe any of that crap she just said, do you?' I asked as I wiped my chin with my sleeve.

Jamie looked at me in disgust before replying, 'You hear loads of stories about them being right, don't you?' Her gaze followed a boy who was sliding past the table with a tray of food in his hands — she raised her eyebrows suggestively at me and I knew that was the end of that conversation.

I turned to look at the boy as he sat down on the table behind us, he looked up and I swiftly pivoted back around in my seat. Jamie however, smiled and waved at him flirtatiously before mouthing to me, 'I told you it would be a good night.'

I carried on eating whilst I inspected the crowd. Strangers were my favourite type of people, they didn't know anything about me and that made me feel as though I could be anyone I liked around them.

You can't be anyone you like though; you're Brooke — a useless, pathetic mess. Anxiety began to rear her ugly head again, but I swallowed her back down to the pit of my stomach where I knew how to handle her.

A young boy and girl bolted past us as they headed towards a small ghost train.

An elderly woman took a leisurely stroll as she pulled apart her candy floss, humming to herself.

I noticed a familiar figure leaning against one of the many poles that were holding the tent up.

'Harriet!' I shouted across the crowds; she didn't answer.

Harriet was one of the few trainees, including me, that were still undertaking their apprenticeships to qualify for a job at the National Crime Agency.

We were only four months in to our two-year course, but had become quite close during this time.

We had a lot in common and many things to talk about as we were both gripped constantly by the ever-growing rate of organized crime that we witnessed every day.

We would spend hours after work debating what we could do to 'make the world a better place' over a bottle of wine or two. I guess we were both dreamers, but I liked that about us.

I was about to walk over to say hello when a boy approached her, Harriet apprehensively looked around while he spoke, they looked as though they were in deep conversation. He was a lanky, disheveled looking boy; he couldn't have been much older than her.

I observed as the conversation became more and more intense. He grabbed her arm and pulled her closer to his unsanitary-looking body.

I ascended from my seat. 'Can we go and talk to Harriet for a minute?' I asked in a way that was more of an instruction than a question.

'B, me and that boy were having major eye chemistry, this Harriet girl better be important,' she whined as I pulled her along behind me.

I ignored her groans as I dodged around hordes of people. My heart began to pound in my chest again. *NO, not now!* I demanded.

As we grew closer I could faintly hear the boy's sullen voice.

I turned to Jamie and placed my finger over my mouth as I guided her a few yards behind Harriet and the boy. I still couldn't hear their conversation properly over the noise of the fair, but he seemed to be doing most of the talking.

'Is that her boyfriend?' Jamie whispered disapprovingly into my ear.

I shook my head and shrugged. 'I don't know who he is, maybe we should just go over to her.'

The boy looked as though he was becoming angry with her. I lugged Jamie along after me. 'Hi Harriet,' I smiled. She jumped as she heard me and then gave me a faint hearted smile.

The boy stared at Jamie and I before giving us a threatening look.

'Nice to meet you,' I said as I held out my hand for him to shake. He stared at it rudely and then spat on the floor.

'Could you not see we're 'avin a conversation?' He growled. His voice was deep and profound.

He glanced over to Harriet with a worried look in his bloodshot, jaded eyes.

'Don't be rude mate.' Jamie stepped forwards. 'She's only being polite. It's not really that nice to meet you.'

He strolled forwards cockily until he towered over Jamie. 'Know your place, babe.'

I watched Jamie cautiously as she stepped closer to him and looked up; she didn't look scared at all. '*Don't* call me babe.'

I had always been so jealous of the lack of fear that Jamie possessed, I would have given anything to not have my heart pounding through my chest every waking minute of the day.

He grabbed her arm and Harriet and I both jumped towards her.

'Leave her alone, Matt!' Harriet piped up. 'It's not her you have the problem with!'

Jamie and I looked at each other in a state of confusion as he dropped Jamie's arm and shot Harriet an almost apologetic look.

She was such a beautiful girl and he was, well the complete opposite. I wondered what their story was and how their paths could have crossed.

Even he can get someone to love him anxiety teased.

Go away, A! I snapped.

'Just let me talk to them for five minutes, yeah?' she asked softly as she stroked his arm. He nodded reluctantly and strolled away, kicking a Coke can across the grass as he did so.

Harriet relaxed immediately and stepped towards us shyly, rubbing her hand against her forearm.

'What are you doing with him?' I questioned her.

'Straight to the point as always.' She chuckled timidly, wincing as she did so.

'What's wrong?' I held my hand out to hug her, but she flinched and stepped backwards.

'Nothing, I'm fine. I'm sorry about Matt. He can be…' she paused to think of the correct word to describe her boyfriend, '…intense. He's just got a lot going on, we both have. He is nice really. You know I wouldn't be with him otherwise.'

I nodded, she was usually such a good judge of character that I would never have doubted her choice in anything — but there seemed to be more to the story.

'Didn't seem it,' Jamie muttered under her breath.

Harriet shot her a disgusted look. 'Well you don't know him. We're in love.'

'Love? You're in love with *that*?' Jamie sniggered.

I glanced over to him, blowing cigarette smoke out of his nostrils and pacing restlessly.

'Yes, do you have a problem with that?' Harriet seemed as though she was earnestly protecting him. 'Jamie, shut up,' I snapped at her. 'As long as you're okay nothing else matters,' I reassured Harriet. 'I don't think we've been doing the same shifts for ages have we? I haven't seen you for a couple of weeks.' I carried on the conversation, not wanting to leave her so soon.

'I-I haven't been at work actually, I've not been well,' she answered nervously. 'I'm okay now though, I'll be back Monday,' she quickly added before I could ask her what was wrong.

I looked over to Jamie and raised my eyebrows, expecting her to apologize, but instead she childishly shrugged. 'See you around, Harriet.' She muttered before strutting back over to where we had been sitting, flicking her hair over her shoulders and pulling out a cigarette from her *Chanel* handbag.

'Don't you want to go after her?' Harriet asked as she led me back to the pole she was standing at before we had interrupted. I noticed that she had lost a lot of weight since I had last seen her.

'No, she's fine.' I smirked as I glanced over and saw that canteen boy had already sat down next to her. 'Apart from being ill, how have you been? I questioned, turning back to face her.

'I've been fine, busy.' She tucked a lose strand of hair from her pony tail behind her pierced ears. 'Did you hear much about the raid they done on that house the other day?' she frowned as her eyes jolted towards where Matt was pacing.

'They found four rooms filled with girls. Some of them didn't make it; we know whose house it is now…' I informed her, remembering that she was absent at work on Christmas Eve.

Her eyebrows rose inquisitively. 'That's good, who is it? I'm going to need to be caught up before I come back.'

'His name is Andrew Spence. We should organize to go for a drink in the next few days then?' I asked hopefully, I knew after a few wines she would open up about Matt to me.

'They've been working that case for so long. I hope they find the people behind it all soon.' She sighed, blatantly ignoring my invitation.

It was true; we had been attempting and failing to find the people behind the biggest human trafficking organization they have experienced in years.

Countless anonymous tips and houses being raided later and it seemed we were none the wiser.

'You look tired.' I frowned as I noticed the big, black bags under her eyes. 'Are you sure you're okay?' I clutched the arm that she had been holding the whole time we had been speaking, she grimaced in pain. 'What happened?' I pulled up her sleeve before she could stop me, revealing several dark purple bruises scattered up her arm.

'It's not what it looks like,' she insisted.

'I think it's exactly what it looks like, Harriet, he can't do this to you!' I whispered so no one around us would hear.

'I didn't think you were judgmental, Brooke. He is stressed out; you don't know the half of it,' she rambled.

'We both know that there's no excuse for what he is doing to you,' I stated bluntly as I gently pulled her sleeve down again, clutching her fragile hand instead.

'It's not as bad as it sounds, trust me!' She pulled away from my grip on her hand and smiled at me almost apologetically. 'We will meet up for a drink soon,' she said hastily before hugging me and darting over to Matt.

'Harriet?' I called after her, but she ignored me.

I watched as he hugged her and said something in her ear; he looked down at her dotingly as he guided her away from the fair.

There is defiantly more to that story, I decided.

Frustrated, I strolled back over to Jamie and sat down opposite her and what would probably be her new flavor of the month.

He was very tall and muscular with dark hair and baby blue eyes.

I grinned at Jamie and she nodded her head in reply — she and I had always had the ability to communicate telepathically, especially when it came to boys.

'Is she okay?' Jamie asked me, 'that was *a lot.*'

'Yeah, she'll be fine.' I smiled, not believing my answer at all.

'How was your Christmas?' Daniel asked.

I laughed. 'Now we do the small talk?'

'No, I want to know.' He smiled, rolling over to face me.

We were lying in his king sized bed, the sheets intertwined between our bodies and the pillows had been thrown somewhere on the floor.

The week I'd had off for Christmas was filled with drunken nights in Jamie's living room and days spent under Daniel's covers — so not too different from my usual day to day occurrences really.

He tucked a strand of my now very messy hair behind my ear, as if that was going to help. 'My Christmas was tedious and uneventful.' I sighed, sitting up and throwing his large T-shirt on to cover myself up. 'What about yours?'

He rolled onto his back and pulled me on top of him.

'Tedious and uneventful?' he chuckled. 'You are a funny one. My Christmas was delightful actually.'

I looked down at his face; I couldn't help but become irate whenever he spoke. But I didn't call him dreamy Daniel for no reason. Besides from the irritating personality, Daniel was, well, *very* dreamy. And that, I thought, was a good enough reason as any to carry on stringing along my counselor's receptionist.

I had thought of ending the whole sordid relationship many a time, with much encouragement from both Harriet and Jamie. I had been seeing Daniel for nearly a year now, and to cut contact would mean breaking out of my comfort zone — which wasn't something that sounded very appealing to me in any aspect of my life.

He droned on about his Christmas dinner, clearly very passionate about the roast potatoes his great-aunt, whatever her name is, had served.

I smiled at him suggestively, knowing that was the only way to get him to shut up.

'What are you smiling at?'

'Just your boring stories…' I prodded.

Don't be too mean to him Brooke; he is the only guy weird enough to want you in his bed. A reminded me.

He pulled me down to his lips and I succumbed to the inevitable. It was *much* better than listening to him carry on talking for another hour.

At around four pm I made my excuses, and after many highly irritating arguments from him asking me to stay longer, I was finally freed.

I paced down the fourteen flights of stairs, the lift in his building *still* hadn't been fixed. I had been fighting the urge to grab a tool box and figure out how to mend it myself. Swiftly I pushed open the rusty doors onto the busy road outside.

The cold wind hit me like a ton of bricks, and the door simultaneously nearly hit a forty something business man like a ton of bricks too.

'Sorry, sorry,' I panted as he shot me a disproving glare. 'I'm sorry,' I repeated again, but he was already rushing off — probably to his next pointless meeting.

I decided that I didn't want to go home just yet, so began to take a stroll down the road, in the opposite direction to Mr. Angry businessman of course.

The winter sun was beginning to disappear and street lights were twinkling up and down the street. I wrapped my arms around my body tightly as I walked. The hustle and bustle of the city always made me feel weirdly at ease. Despite what some may think about the disorder, my anxiety was never quite as bad when I was around lots of people. In a way, London had always been my cure.

I pulled my tangled headphones from my coat pocket and placed them in both my ears, drowning out the noise of honking cars and angry taxi drivers, replacing them with the beautiful sound of Frank Sinatra's *Summer Wind.*

I strolled happily down the lit up streets of London for hours, imagining that the love of my life was next to me clutching my hand and keeping me sheltered from the cold.

I imagined that I was beautiful — not cute and mousy Brooke kind of beautiful — but super model, every guy falls in love with me Jamie kind of beautiful instead.

I imagined that I had a loving family who I was on my way home to see right that second.

And as always, I imagined that I didn't suffer with the crippling and de-mobilizing feeling of fear and dread throughout every day of my life.

I imagined right up until I couldn't imagine any more, and the front door of my house loomed over me like the shadow of a monster in a child's dream.

I knew once I turned the key into the lock that the imagining would stop and the anxiety would once again rear its ugly head.

Dr Daw said you can't hide from reality forever, Brooke. You have to accept me. A tapped her foot impatiently, waiting for me to let us into the warm.

'*Leave me alone,*' I hissed under my breath. She didn't like being told what to do and in reply made my stomach churn up in a ball of pain.

I sighed because she was right, turned the key and reluctantly stepped inside the madhouse.

'And where have you been?' my mother's warm welcome erupted from the top of the stairs.

Ignoring her, I closed the door slowly and exhaled, shrugging my coat off and tip-toeing into the living room.

The twins were curled up on the sofa under a blanket with Netflix asking if they were still watching.

The light was on in the 'Man Cave' outside so I knew dad had probably been hiding out there all night.

It was a Sunday, so that meant mum would have been in some lavish spa all day receiving treatments fit for the queen.

'I said, *where have you been?*' mum repeated as she burst through the living room door.

'Clearly not here,' I replied sarcastically as I searched for the TV remote. 'Have the twins had dinner?'

Mum shrugged carelessly. 'Ask your dad. I've been out with Vivienne.' I glanced up at her, noticing her glowing complexion and suspiciously tight forehead.

'Botox day was it?' I snapped at her, retrieving the remote from underneath the sofa and switching the TV off.

The twins stirred and Riley squinted up at me with tired eyes. 'Hey sleepy,' I whispered, stroking his overgrown hair off of his face. 'Are you hungry?'

'Daddy said he was going to make dinner, and then he put *Paw Patrol* on so I think he forgot.' He replied, nervously shooting his eyes in mum's direction.

She was rattling around in the kitchen trying to find a wine glass that hadn't been thrown in the I'll-wash-that-later pile in the sink.

'Okay, do you want some sausages and mashed potato?' I asked as Ruby began to wake up too.

Riley's eyes lit up, an image I would never get tired of seeing. 'With beans please, mum, I mean Brooke, oops…' Riley blushed at his mistake.

'*She* is not your mum; she will never be anyone's mum.' The delightful Claire Hamilton and her new face arrived back in the room accompanied by a glass of red wine.

'What?' I starred at her.

'You're too fucked up darling,' she snarled before heading upstairs.

'Will you not be a mummy because nobody loves you to marry you Brooke?' Riley asked innocently, but the question tore a hole right through my heart.

My eyes filled with burning tears — but I held them back for the twins' sake.

A was laughing at me hysterically, *See, even a four-year-old knows that you're unlovable.*

'I'm going to make your dinner, go and wash your hands,' I croaked, defiantly ignoring anxiety and her snide remarks.

'*I* love you Brooke, I'll marry you even though you're fucked up!' Ruby squeaked as they both followed my orders and headed out to the downstairs loo.

That night I cried myself to sleep and dreamt of an empty, loveless future.

Thanks mum.

III

I had resumed work on New Year's Day and it was like I had never left.

Every day was the same, starting with leaving my very tense household before anyone was awake. Then, sitting in the stuffy trainee's office undertaking mundane paper-work while engaging in pointless trivial chatter with the new apprentices for most of the day.

Lastly, at 7.30pm I would practically run out of the office doors, spending my evenings out with Jamie and a few of her friends from work. As much as it made my stomach knot up in pain, it was better than going home straight away.

I would return home late every night, only to check that the twins had been fed and put to bed, before setting my alarm and starting the whole mundane cycle again.

I often wondered if that was it for my life. No one to love me, no family of my own, just a lifetime of nothingness. *Sounds about right.*

Mr. Daniels had informed us in a back to work briefing that Mr. Spence had finally been located after he had fled from his home. They were close to bringing him in.

Harriet had still not returned to work, or any of my calls for that matter.

Now that I didn't have Harriet to pass the time it had become rather boring sitting by that desk day after day with no real work to do.

I guess I had thought that when I applied for the apprenticeship it would have involved a lot more action and a lot less sitting around writing reports and making countless cups of coffees for people 'higher up' than myself.

The other trainees didn't seem to mind the lack of stimulating work; in fact, I think they enjoyed it.

We worked in very close proximity to each other day in, day out and they had all become very good friends.

Every day, they spoke about their work drinks antics and how much fun they had together the night before.

They had given up on inviting me to join them, of which I was very thankful for as I had run out of viable excuses. Instead, I would receive polite, pitiful smiles from my colleagues before they headed down the road to commence their nightly routine in the buzzing streets of Camden. I didn't mind. They were nice people, but I could only deal with them for short periods of time. They were loud and sometimes obnoxious.

I missed Harriet's company immensely.

It was late January and the weather was as bleak as it had been since October.

I was thankful that I overlooked the street from my corner desk. It kept me occupied and calm.

Each day I watched as the unbelievably tall man with his well-groomed dog appeared from the housing estate on the corner at around nine am.

I'd named him Vladimir, Vladimir the giant, and decided that he'd previously worked in the circus before quitting to become a normal citizen.

After I returned from my lunch break at around 1:30pm, the running lady would 'jog' past.

Her curly hair flailed around in the wind along with her arms. She didn't seem to care about who was watching, I noticed she received many odd looks as she zoomed past judgmental passers-by. I envied her care-free attitude.

Then, there was the bus load of obnoxious secondary school children that would spill out onto the other side of the road at around 3:45pm.

The girl's skirts were rolled so far up that they may as well have not bothered wearing them, the boys would shout at them and they would giggle like, well like a bunch of annoying school children.

And every evening without fail, a boy would sit down on a crooked bench placed next to the bus stop.

He sometimes arrived around seven pm, other times he would just be sitting down as I was driving away.

He always wore a khaki green coat and ripped jeans.

He seemed to watch everyone and everything that went past him, like he was searching for something.

I thought at first he was just waiting for the bus, but it would pass him each time.

Then I thought maybe it was a girlfriend, or a friend, but no one ever showed.

I couldn't quite think of a scenario for him just yet.

It had been another slow, unbearable Friday until we had all been abruptly rushed to the department's meeting room as some new evidence had come to light.

I walked through the door and squeezed past what felt like countless bodies to reach the other side of the already filled up room.

I placed myself in a chair that was next to some people who I knew were nearly as awkward as me and wouldn't try and spark up a conversation.

I nodded at them and gave them a slight smile before slouching down in the uncomfortable plastic chair.

'Right everyone!' Mr. Daniels' voice boomed over the buzz of chatter, everyone immediately took their seats; a few taller men leant across the wall at the back of the room clutching on to cups of steaming coffee.

'We seem to have had a breakthrough at last!' He declared as he rolled in the old TV that was usually pushed to the back of the staff room.

'Here, I have Mr. Andrew Spence's interview, conducted yesterday at 5:52pm. I want you all to watch and listen carefully, we have the bastard and now it's time to get the rest of them.'

Everybody watched the tape intensely, jotting down notes and gasping at some of the rude, derogatory things Andrew Spence was mumbling.

He was defiant in revealing any information, insisting that his house was purely used as a place to hide the girls until they were shipped elsewhere.

'I never saw their faces,' he repeated for the thousandth time. 'Everyone wore balaclavas, they would drop the girls to me and leave.'

'You say you have been working for this organization for a

long time, three years to be exact… ' Katie, who was one of the lead investigators on the case stated as she tucked her short fiery hair behind her ears.

Everyone in our department knew not to mess with Ginger Kate, and I was sure Andrew Spence would figure that out for himself sooner or later.

'…In that time you must have heard something, seen something, just something little.

Do you think you could remember *anything* at all that would help us, and more importantly help *yourself*?'

Katie studied his face closely as the wheels turned around in his brain.

After a minute had passed she swiftly stood up from her chair and shrugged. 'Well it looks like you are going to be behind bars for a very long time then Mr. Spence, you are the only person we have that is linked to these crimes, crimes that will see you sent away for a lifetime.

We have substantial evidence and DNA all over your home and witness statement after witness statement of the girls you have been holding there against their will.

Without any other information, I believe we are done with you. Interview terminated at…'

Andrew interrupted her as he clearly began to panic. 'There is one thing,' he mumbled, jolting his eyes towards his lawyer who was shaking his head. 'They always said seven.'

'Seven?' Katie repeated, lowering herself back onto to her chair.

'Yeah, I remember now.

Whenever they dropped the girls off they would always say something like, *they will be here until seven's team collects.* Seven must be the person in charge, right?'

At that moment Mr. Daniels stopped the tape and studied our faces.

'We must find out who seven is,' he stated as he stuck a post-it-note with the number seven next to a question mark right in the center of the board.

'I'm afraid that's all we have to go on until we can get some more out of Andrew Spence.'

'How was work?' Mum asked me as I stepped into her car. I looked at her anxiously, taken aback by her friendly, non-argumentative question.

She probably wants something from you.

My mind began to run away with ideas of why mum would possibly be acting this nice.

My car was still at Jamie's from the night before where I had been too intoxicated and responsibly paid for a taxi home.

I had learnt that lesson the hard way at eighteen years old when I had drunkenly drove my car into a bush and nearly rolled down a very deep ditch.

Somehow, I had found the control to veer back onto the road, but it had scared me for life, that was for sure.

Luckily, mum was passing by to pick the twins up from dance lessons so I had convinced her to pick me up — very surprised that she'd agreed.

After thinking of many different reasons why she would suddenly decide to act like a normal mother to her first born child, I came to the conclusion that clearly she was experiencing some sort of brain hemorrhage that had resulted in a personality transplant.

'Boring, like always,' I muttered in reply to her question, even though I knew she wouldn't care for the answer.

Doing up my seat belt and resting my head back, I finally breathed a huge sigh of relief that the day was done and the weekend was here.

'Maybe you shouldn't go in with a hangover and it wouldn't be that bad. Do you not care about your future? Because I'm telling you now, Brooke you are not staying at home until your thirty being a drunken wreck, because that's the way you're going,' she nagged, switching on the ignition.

And she's back.

'Thank you for picking me up, but maybe we shouldn't talk,' I replied as I turned on the radio.

Mum leant over and slammed the button to turn off the music. Her long, fake nails scratched against the metal.

'Listen to me, Brooke. Don't go showing your boss what you're really like and getting sacked!'

'What I'm *really* like? What's that supposed to mean?' I rubbed my head as it began to pound increasingly with every word.

'You're a stupid, selfish cow. If you show them what you're really like then they will fire you straight away, trust me. Get out!' Mum shouted.

'What?' I laughed, bewildered by her sudden mood change.

'You heard me, get out!' She leaned across me and opened the door.

'I am not just *getting out* I have nowhere to go do I?' I attempted to refuse as I jolted upwards in my seat. 'This is over an hour's walk from home and it's like the fucking Antarctic out there!'

Mum starred at me for a second, her eyes filled with hate, before slapping me viciously around the face. 'GET OUT!' she ordered.

'Fine!' I took my seatbelt off and jumped out of the car.

I was in shock; she had never laid a hand on me before, which was one of the few things she still had going in her favor.

My bag was violently thrown after me.

'You're rude and horrible and I've had enough! Do not think of coming home ever again!' She screamed.

I slammed the door in her face and stood there helplessly for a second or two.

I watched like a deer in headlights as she pulled her bright white Range Rover out of the turning and sped down the road without a second thought for the shivering, hopeless wreck of a daughter she was leaving behind.

I waited a moment before crossing the road to sit down on the bench beside the bus stop.

I lounged there for what must have been about ten minutes, pondering to myself about what to do for the night.

Jamie was working a late shift; she usually had extra clients on a Friday who wanted sprucing up ready for the weekend.

And as much as she'd be fine with me rocking up unannounced, somehow I didn't think I could cope with Jamie's highly opinionated view of my life and how I should stick up to my mother more.

She's right, you're a pushover.

'Oh, here you are.' I acknowledged A as my chest began to tighten.

Harriet was still MIA and they were the only friends I really had.

A chuckled meanly. *Loser.*

I scrolled through my phone and sighed, dreamy Daniel it was, I sent him a text asking if he wanted to meet up. As I sent the text I noticed that a boy had quietly sat down next to me, the sudden company made me jump.

He perched on the edge of the bench as if he was attempting to not make me uncomfortable by getting too close.

More like he doesn't want to sit too close to the weird girl who is crying on a bench by herself.

I tried to act like I hadn't acknowledged him and carried on looking at the cars going past, placing my phone back in my coat pocket and wiping away any stray tears that were escaping down my face.

A strong smell of sweet aftershave blew my way in the wind, forcing me to sneeze.

'Bless you.' The boy smiled kindly.

I looked at him — only quickly — but I noticed the same green coat I had seen sitting on this bench for the last couple of weeks.

I wondered why he was so late to take his seat today, it was already nearly eight pm. Thoughts ran through my head of whom or what could have held him up.

I wanted to ask him why he always came to this spot, why was it so special? What does it mean to him?

'Thank you.' I blushed realizing I'd probably left a bit of an awkward silence.

I studied his face closely; he was rather beautiful in an un-groomed kind of way.

'You recognize me? Oh no…' He muttered as his cheeks flushed red.

Hey! That's your thing A laughed at me, or him, I couldn't tell.

'Excuse me?' I questioned, taken aback.

'Mad boy from the news.' He rolled his eyes sarcastically and chuckled. 'That's what my mates keeps calling me.' He spoke in a strong cockney accent, I liked it.

'Sorry… I… er…' I frowned. *Words Brooke! Use words!*

He watched me with raised eyebrows, leaving a moment of silence to see if I would finish that sentence. 'Sorry, I've been getting a lot of stick for that and you were looking at me so closely, I thought maybe you might have recognized me… Sorry.' He smiled again.

Wow, that smile. It was my turn to blush. 'I didn't mean to

50

stare...' *You're just so beautiful* I added internally.

I looked at him again and suddenly realized what he was referring to. I thought back to the news report on Christmas Day. So *he* was the curly haired boy who had been rugby tackled to the floor by the police.

I wanted to ring Jamie and tell her I told her so, I *knew* there was an intriguing story behind him.

'*Oh* the news...' I glanced at him. 'I recognize you more from the fact you sit here every night though,' I stated bravely.

Where did that confidence come from? A looked around, confused.

HA! I gloated internally. *I have some hidden far away from you.*

He grinned. 'So being on the news for fifteen seconds makes you famous enough to have a stalker then?' He joked.

I grinned back. I felt like I needed to know this strangers deal. Why was he acting like that on TV?

Does it have anything to do with why he never misses a night of sitting on this very uncomfortable little bench? I shifted in my seat.

'If you're waiting for a bus you'll be waiting a while,' he commented as he glanced at his worn looking watch. He looked as though he was fighting to keep his warm, chestnut eyes from closing.

Why was he so exhausted? I wondered again.

I nervously chuckled. *Why is he talking to me?*

'I was just sitting here thinking of something to do tonight, my car is at a friend's...'

He smiled crookedly. 'Come up with anything yet?'

'Nope.' I sighed.

I watched as he pulled out a cigarette box from his deep

pocket and pointed it towards me.

'Er, yeah, go on then.' I shrugged. *Why not?*

I took one out of the box, and the lighter from his hand. Our iced fingers brushed against each other briefly and my stomach whirled excitably.

I coughed as I took a long chug on the cigarette, which seemed to amuse him. 'It's been a while.' I blushed again. He chuckled. His smile made me feel strangely at ease.

I studied him further, he was dressed head to toe in dilapidated clothes, yet he managed to look so breathtakingly handsome. Realizing that I'd probably been starring at him for a little too long again I turned away, taking another long pull of the cigarette.

'My name's Liam, by the way. What's yours?' He looked at me with an intrigued expression painted across his face. Smoke whirled out of his mouth like a snake emerging from the grass.

'Brooke,' I replied as I flicked some ash onto the cracked pavement.

The cold breeze whistled past and I watched as the ash flew into the air, landing a few feet away from us in the middle of the road. Liam didn't answer; he just chastely gazed at me.

'What?' I laughed, patting my iced face with my numbed hands to check there wasn't something there.

'Oh, nothing…' his cheeks flushed red as he swiftly looked away, shaking his head as if he was cringing at himself. His visible nerves helped to calm my invisible ones.

I dropped the cigarette onto the floor and stubbed it out with my burnished shoe, before shifting slightly closer to him and his delightful scent.

We stayed seated on the bench for some time; it seemed neither of us wanted the conversation to end.

He asked me what I liked to do in my spare time.

I was taken aback by his questioning, but told him about how I loved to read books at night before bed and go for runs in the morning as they both relaxed me.

I told him about how I loved animals, but was never allowed any growing up. 'Yeah, I used to spend my weekends in the pet shop round the corner from my aunt and uncle's. The owner would let me stay there all day petting the animals. All I had to do was help her feed them and stuff.' I reminisced as he listened with a smile.

'So she basically made you work and didn't pay you.' he laughed.

'Spending a day with puppies? Is that not better than getting paid?' I argued my case.

Liam told me about his love for films, especially romance. *A fellow romance lover!* I gushed. Although my love for romance was more novel based, it was nice to meet someone likeminded for a change.

He boasted that he had memorized quotes from countless classic films, old and new.

'I have a room in my house that's just filled with DVD's and old videos,' he told me.

'Videos?' I chuckled. 'You still have a video player?'

'Yep, how else am I going to watch the first couple of Harry Potter's?'

'Buy them on DVD?'

'Not the same,' he replied adamantly. 'It just wouldn't be the same listening to Hagrid say *you're a wizard Harry* on a DVD. It just wouldn't.'

I giggled.

My chat with Liam had demonstrated yet again why I loved

strangers so much. He didn't know the depths of my past and how messed up my mind could be. He didn't know that the reason I was sitting on the bench that night was because my mother was a loveless psychopath.

What was even better is the fact that he didn't ask. Not once did we speak about work, or family, or anything of the sort. He was just interested in *me*.

He asked me about what I loved to do and what songs I played on repeat, what my thoughts were on aliens and what my favourite food was. It had been a very long time since I'd had a real conversation like that.

'God, we've been here for so long,' I stated as I noticed the time change to 8:50pm on my watch under the dim street light towering above us. 'I should probably get going, find somewhere to go tonight.' I sighed, remembering that I wasn't welcome at home any more.

He nodded as he tightened another cigarette between his lips. I watched as the flame from his lighter lit up his tanned face.

'Can I ask you something?' he frowned as he leant back into his seat placing the lighter back into his coat pocket.

'Of course,' I answered hesitantly, wrapping my arms tighter round myself to protect my hands from the brisk wind that was gushing past. At that moment my phone started to ring, it was Daniel.

'Do you want to come with me?' I looked down at Daniel's name lighting up my phone and then back up at Liam's ruggedly handsome face. 'Or do you need to answer that?' He added.

'Oh… er…' My heartbeat grew faster and my stomach tightened, but it was a different kind of nerves — a more pleasant kind.

The way he asked me was so calm, so reassuring, so

intriguing, for some reason I felt I couldn't say no.

His dark eyes starred at me as he patiently awaited my answer.

I declined the call and switched my phone to silent. 'I don't need to answer that.'

Brooke, what are you doing? A raised her eyebrows.

Oh, now you care? I scowled.

I took a few pulls on the cigarette he had just passed to me and watched in awe as he stood up and held out his hand. I noticed how tall he was, he transcended over me and I felt almost inclined to take his hand and follow wherever he wanted me to go. I blew out cigarette smoke slowly as I stood up, but through the mist I saw a smile.

It was so out of character for me, but the way he spoke, the way he laughed, the countless stories he told me as I followed him unknowingly along the winding pathways he led me down made me want to stay, I wanted to know more.

My stomach clenched every now and then as if anxiety was attempting to pull me back to reality, but I tried my best to ignore her.

We reached a shadowy high street that I didn't recognize, there were a few flickering bar signs and a group of giggly girls staggered arm in arm past us.

One of them wolf whistled at Liam and I felt a twinge of an unknown feeling deep in my stomach.

Oh, she is capable of normal human emotions A sneered at me.

'Liam!' a deep voice called from ahead, I could make out a faint figure under the neon light of what looked to be a club. As we drew closer I noticed a group of boys, all had dark, untidy hair and kind smiles, none of them as bewitching as Liam's.

I smiled nervously as we approached the group, my mouth was dry and my heart was about to beat out of my chest. But I wasn't letting my body ruin this night for me, not now I had come this far.

'This is Brooke.' Liam waved his arms towards me as he presented me to the group. I shuffled on the spot and smiled awkwardly. I felt so exposed.

'We just met, but I'm gonna marry her one day,' he joked, winking at me. I melted a little inside.

We entered the club which was entirely decorated with brick walls and shabby leather chairs, the music was deafening. The boys ushered me to the crummy looking bar and bought me a drink straight away, they seemed to know all of the bar staff and addressed them by nicknames, so I assumed this was a regular night for Liam and his gang.

I caught my reflection in the mirrored wall of the bar and realized that I was still dressed in my smart, un-exciting work clothes. I popped open a few buttons of the white shirt I had tucked into some high-waisted black trousers, my lace bra slightly revealed itself in my now lowered top. I released my unkempt hair from the messy bun perched carelessly on top of my head and shook subtly so that my long, chocolate locks fell over the ridge of my breasts and down to my waist.

I caught Liam gazing at me intensely as I took a large swig of my red wine, a feeling I didn't recognize surged through me again me as my eyes met his.

Maybe it was excitement or maybe it was danger, I wasn't sure, but I liked it.

'So Brooke...' One of Liam's friends shouted over the loud music at me. 'How do you know Liam?'

I gulped down my glass of wine, knowing from experience that it would be the only thing to help me become more confident in speaking to the strangers I was now suddenly surrounded by.

'We met a few hours ago.' I laughed, studying the slightly chubby, very spotty boy that was talking to me. 'What about you?'

'We all go way back, primary school.' He chugged down some more beer; his breath stank strongly of alcohol and cigarettes.

'Dale, what are you saying to her?' Liam's rasping voice questioned from behind me, he lightly placed his hands around my waist and I flinched as my whole body became a current of electricity. He lent forwards until I could feel his warm breath tickle the back of my neck.

I was frozen on the spot, a statue of lust.

'I don't usually ask random girls from the street out, just wanted to let you know.'

I forced myself to move, turning to face him, his hands still held their place around my waist. 'I don't usually follow random boys into dark alleys either...' I smiled up at him.

Wow.

'Smart. I'm glad I'm the exception to that rule though.' He smirked.

'I didn't have any better offers...' I smiled back.

'What were you doing there anyway?'

'I work across the street; I'd not long finished.' I sipped my drink and gazed up at his eyes, which had suddenly turned very wide.

He swiftly released his grip. 'You work at the NCA?'

'Don't panic, I'm not a police officer or anything, I'm just training, I'm quite new to it all really…' I paused as I watched him study me intently. 'Oh, are you like a criminal or something?' I took a step back, but immediately relaxed as he laughed and pulled me back towards him. I'm pretty sure my heart had lost all control by this point.

'No, I'm not a criminal or something. I'm just impressed,' he reassured me. 'You're getting better and better by the minute,' he added.

'Oh… well thanks.' I blushed.

HA! If only he knew the real you hey, Brooke?

He laughed at my reaction. 'So when you're done training do you get a police officer's uniform to wear?' he prodded teasingly.

I rolled my eyes and ignored the question, sipping more of my wine instead. I was beginning to feel a little tipsy and welcomed it with open arms.

I knew that sober Brooke wouldn't be able to handle all of these unknown feelings running through her body right now, she was going to hate me in the morning, but that was tomorrow's problem.

'Okay, random girl from the street, how would you feel about going on a date with me?'

I choked on my wine and he seemed to find this highly amusing.

'Have you never been asked on a date before?' he raised an eyebrow at me as I regained my breath.

Throat burning, I croaked out a reply. 'No, as it happens… I haven't.'

Kissing Daniel at a counselling session defiantly doesn't class as a date.

Liam looked shocked.

Oh no, now he is defiantly going to know there is something wrong with me.

Something? There's a list! A corrected me.

I wished she would shut up; her constant internal dialogue drove me insane.

Brooke, you are insane. My constant internal dialogue is YOUR constant internal dialogue. She corrected me once again. She always got like this when I was drunk.

I mean, *I* always got like this when I was drunk.

Ah, I don't know. It was busy inside my head sometimes.

'So... do you want to?' he asked again.

'I guess that would be okay.' I smiled as I shrugged my shoulders casually. Inside I was anything but casual.

I turned around and walked towards the bar to buy myself another large wine, leaving him hanging.

I couldn't wait to tell Jamie the news.

'Brooke?' A girl's voice from beside me broke my trail of thoughts. I turned around swiftly and was met by the surprised eyes of my colleagues.

'Hey! She does get out!' One of them remarked sarcastically, but smiled at me to soften the blow.

I couldn't for the life of me remember his name. Aaron, maybe?

The girl, whose name I knew was Nyema, smiled kindly from her place next to me. 'Are you having a good night?' she shouted over the music.

I nodded.

I liked Nyema. She had started her training a month ago and seemed to settle in straight away, she was friendly and very intelligent.

I had listened in awe as she'd told us about how she'd secured the trainee position and moved alone to London from Uganda, as there were more opportunities for her here.

The thought of leaving everyone I knew and travelling thousands of miles away from home seemed in-comprehensible to me. But Nyema seemed to take it in her stride.

'It's nice to see you out and about. You should come out with us one time. Now there's no excuse, we've caught you in the act so we know you're no better than us.' She laughed.

I studied her beautiful black braided hair that fell to her hips as she spoke. Her skin was a stunning complexion. 'Oh god, I don't think I'm better than any of you! It's quite the opposite actually!' I blushed, looking round at the bemused faces of my co-workers.

Is that what they all think of me?

'Good to know. Have a nice night Brooke!' she smiled as she nodded towards the direction of Liam knowingly before grabbing the tray of drinks she had just ordered. *Is it that obvious?* I blushed again, thankful for the dim lights.

The rest of the group waved and shouted their drunken goodbye's over the music before they headed towards a free booth in the corner of the room.

I strolled back to where Liam was sitting.

Legs stretched out.

Grinning ear to ear at me.

Looking perfect.

Wow.

It was around three am and Camden Town was closing its bars for the night. I felt a wave of disappointment rush over me as I was having such a good time.

Seemingly defeated, anxiety had left me alone for a few hours. Maybe it was just because of the wine, or maybe this was what Dr Daw had meant when she said 'being around good people is good for your mental health.' Even so, I knew that there was no doubt she would be back with a vengeance come the morning.

Liam grabbed my hand and lead me out of the club. 'Come with me?' he slurred drunkenly.

'Where are we going now?' I whispered as he gently pulled me along the street. I was thankful that we weren't saying our goodbyes just yet.

His friends were walking in the opposite direction waving and shouting goodbye to us.

'My favourite spot in the city.' He grinned widely.

Throughout the night I had noticed that everything and everyone seemed to fascinate and excite him.

I wondered for a moment what it would be like to see the world through his rose tinted spectacles, it must have been wonderful.

I followed him back down the street for a while until we walked through a village like area.

Liam clutched my hand and sighed wistfully. 'Primrose Hill.' He stated as we turned the corner.

'This is a good spot,' I said as we took our place at the very top of the hill which overlooked the beautiful lit up city that I call home.

I slumped myself down on the floor next to him and took in the sparkling surroundings.

'Isn't it?' He smiled, seemingly happy that I approved of his favourite place. 'When a man is tired of London he is tired of life,'

'I don't know that one?' I frowned, remembering what he had said about constantly quoting films.

'Not a film, Samuel Johnson wrote that... He was a writer...' he clarified as he noticed my blank expression. 'Don't know much of his stuff but I always remember that quote because it's so true.'

I watched in awe as Liam rambled on about writers and poets and films. His lust for life was truly contagious.

'Sorry, I talk a lot,' he apologized.

'Don't be sorry,' I giggled. 'I like listening to people who actually have something to say, you know?'

He nodded in agreement. 'Here's a question.'

He turned to face me, crossing his legs and cupping my hand in his.

My heart fluttered uncontrollably.

'If you had to die, like there was no other choice but to die, how would you want to go?'

I pulled my hand away. 'Are you about to murder me? Because this has gone from a really good night to the start of a horror film really quickly.'

I noticed that his favourite spot was lacking any human life for miles.

That's Convenient.

See, someone this hot wouldn't want to date you Brooke.

He wants to murder you. Anxiety popped up for the first time in a few hours.

'No, no. I'm not going to murder you. I promise.' He smirked. Our eyes lingered longingly for a few seconds.

I let down my guard again and A went back to sleep.

I guessed being murdered by a person as beautiful as him wasn't the worst way to go. Slowly, I relaxed into the damp, cold grass.

'I guess, if I had to, I'd go in my sleep. Peaceful, not knowing what was happening, I guess that's the least horrific way of dying,' I answered truthfully.

'What about you?' I turned to face him as he lay down next to me.

He thought for a second and then his big, brown, beautiful eyes widened. 'I'd want to die a hero. I'd want to die for a cause or for the people I loved. I'd want my last seconds to be so filled with love and purpose, you know?' He paused and tilted his head to face me. 'I'd want to die for a reason and not just slip away unknowingly. No offence.'

'None taken.' I chuckled. 'That is a very heroic way of dying, I commend you.'

'Was that a bit of a depressing question to ask a complete stranger?'

'No, it's very insightful. The answer says a lot about a person, I might ask it more,' I reassured him as I looked up at the stars.

There he was, a person who would die for the people he loved, and then there was me, a person who most nights wanted to close her eyes and slip away peacefully. Two complete opposites, but somehow the universe had made it so that in that exact moment we were lying next to each other under the stars.

It was the first night for as long as I could remember that I didn't want to close my eyes and I didn't want to sleep because reality was a lot better.

I knew once the sun rose that my mundane life would take

its toll again, but in that moment I was extremely happy that I'd met this beautiful stranger with the curly, chocolate brown hair.

'It's been very nice meeting you, Brooke.'

Liam breathed as if he had read my mind. He felt for my hand in the darkness. 'I think this is the beginning of a beautiful friendship.'

'Casablanca?' I guessed.

He grinned up at the sky.

Wow.

IV

It was the morning of my twenty-fourth birthday and I was awoken by the sound of Jamie's phone buzzing against her pillow, much like every morning since I had been staying at her house.

Her parents had returned home for a couple of days after their Christmas trip, but they travelled for work for the majority of each year, leaving Jamie to have free run of the house.

Although they were best friends with my parents they never got involved with our ongoing dispute, and like always they had both greeted me with open arms.

Jamie said it was because they didn't care, but I think deep down they knew how difficult my mother could be.

I smiled fondly as I reminisced over the times Jamie and I had slept in her bedroom as children, playing with dolls and sharing our secrets, there were photos of her and I all around the room.

I rolled over and checked my phone for any messages.

From: Mum

04/02/2018

22:46pm

I meant it when I said that you are not allowed back to this house.

I will let you know when we are all going to be out and you can collect your stuff and leave your key on the side.

You are not welcome here.

Have fun partying and drinking yourself to death.

My eyes filled with angry tears, but I swallowed them away. *She is not going to ruin your birthday.*

'Brooke?' Jamie's voice broke the silence.

'Hey,' I greeted her softly as I lay back down beside her.

'Happy birthday.' Even in the mornings, Jamie managed to look flawless. Her long eyelashes fluttered as they adjusted to the light.

'Thank you...' I sighed.

She jumped out of the bed swiftly, throwing on her satin dressing gown and ordering me to stay put.

I smiled knowingly. She always made such an effort on my birthday and vice versa.

I listened as she made her way around the kitchen, not very quietly may I add. The smell of bacon and freshly made coffee began to make its way up the stairs.

My phone pinged again.

Okay mum, I get the hint! I sighed as I glanced at the screen apprehensively.

From: Liam

05/02/2018

9:04am

Hey, random girl from the street.

How are you on this fine morning?

(It's the random boy from outside your work, in case you had forgotten)

My stomach flipped with excitement. *How could I forget you?*

I starred at my phone for a few minutes, unsure of what to write back.

He isn't going to find you interesting now that you're sober. No one ever does.

'Can't you leave me alone just for my birthday, *please?'* I pleaded out loud.

I knew A wouldn't listen, especially now that Liam had messaged. My heart was beating twice as fast.

It was the first time I'd heard from him since the night we'd met, and I'd been asked to cover the earlier shifts at work over the past week, meaning I hadn't been receiving my nightly fix of staring at him from my office window either.

From: Brooke

05/02/2018

9:06am

Sorry, I think you have the wrong number.

I wouldn't dare go off with a random boy from the street.

I threw my phone to the end of the bed in sheer panic. *You're an idiot. that's not funny. He won't get the joke. Now he is just going to think you were too drunk to remember anything.*

'Brooke!' Jamie's voice interrupted my frantic state.

I ignored the ping of my phone as I ran down the stairs. I wasn't ready to receive rejection just yet.

I burst through the door, greeted by a room filled with bright yellow balloons and presents wrapped in matching sunshine colored paper.

'Happy birthday!' Jamie squeezed me and dragged me towards the mountain of presents like an excitable child on Christmas morning.

'Jamie…' I began, but she shot me a disproving look before I could even start my sentence.

'If you say I didn't have to do this I will be really annoyed, B.'

She knows me so well.

'Thank you.' I smiled instead as a plate of burnt bacon and thick pancakes were shoved in my face.

We devoured our breakfast before partaking in the usual tradition of opening presents while Jamie told me every detail of the meaning behind them, where she brought them from and how she will probably borrow all of it (especially the clothes).

As it drew closer to the afternoon, Jamie had reluctantly torn herself away from our dining table discussion and gone to work, leaving me once again alone with the burning desire to run upstairs and see what Liam had replied.

Instead, I cleared up the mess we had made from present opening and breakfast.

After that, I took a long and thoughtful shower until the hot water ran out.

Then, I blow dried my hair which I knew would take ages because it was so long and thick.

Still not happy with the thought of succumbing to the urge to check my phone, I decided to put on some makeup to pass some more time.

It was around 1:30 p.m. and I had nothing left to distract myself with.

I stood over the bed where my phone was silently sitting, starring up at me, burning a hole into my overactive brain.

I could see my reflection in the screen, still wrapped in a fluffy pink towel but my makeup and hair looked impeccable.

Wow, I should probably start making this amount of effort on my appearance every day.

Do you really want to draw more attention to yourself, Brooke? A chimed in.

Yes, you're right. The less attention the better.

But I do look good.

I felt silly for even thinking it, but Dr Daw had always told me that positive affirmations were the way forward.

Inhaling deeply, I *finally* picked up the phone.

From: Liam

05/02/2018

9:07 a.m.

Okay, because I seem to remember someone fitting your description agreeing to go on a date with me?

What about today?

Today!

An unbearable thirst to see the beautiful curly haired stranger ran from my throat to the pit of my stomach.

Okay, okay. You can do this.

From: Brooke

05/02/2018

13:39 p.m.

It's a date.

I threw my phone back on the bed and squealed.

This is so not your territory, this date is going to crash and burn...

'A, please, just leave me alone!' I screamed at the invisible annoyance inside of my head.

I made a mental note to book in another session with Dr Daw. She should probably know that A was back full time again.

I ran downstairs and threw on some of the new clothes Jamie had gifted me.

After an hour of rushing around the house, I stood awkwardly in the entrance hall and glanced at the mirror to the nervous shaky girl starring back at me.

I had chosen a white blouse, a short black pinafore dress, black tights and a pair of Jamie's black Chelsea boots. I knew that my scuffed and comfy work shoes wouldn't be appropriate to wear on a date.

A date. My stomach churned.

Although all of my natural instincts were yelling at me to cancel and hide under the covers all day — I pulled open the front door and off I went.

Off I went to go my date.

Ah!

Liam stood in the doorway of the bus that had just stopped next to me.

'Come on, I've paid for your ticket already,' he ushered.

I climbed inelegantly up the steps and followed him to the seats at the back. As I looked down at my shaky hands I was thankful he had asked me not to drive.

Maybe he wants to get you drunk again. You need to be careful.

I noticed he was dressed a bit smarter than the last time I had seen him, but he still wore the infamous green coat. 'Are you going somewhere nice?' I asked with a smirk, studying his ensemble of black skinny jeans and a tight white shirt.

His sweet smelling aftershave filled the air and my heart fluttered. He smiled knowingly but stayed silent.

I had never experienced meeting such a mysterious person before. I was so used to living in the generation that found it acceptable to plaster their whole life story over social media. It was exciting and very nerve wracking to meet someone of whom I knew nothing about.

I peered out of the bus window as we passed trees stripped bare of their leaves due to the harsh winter.

I felt empathy. I too felt like I have been stripped bare over the course of my life. I wanted to start fresh, bloom into something new.

'Are you okay girl?' he asked, touching my leg only for a second, but a second was long enough to send a surge of electricity through my body.

How does he do that?

I didn't realize I was making my emotional state so obvious; I needed to put a smile on my face and forget about my intolerable mother for good.

'Yeah of course, nothing out of the ordinary,' I lied.

He seemed to accept my answer for the moment as he didn't reply.

A few stops later, Liam jumped up and grabbed my hand, tilting his head for me to follow him.

'Where are we going?' I giggled as we exited the bus.

He weaved his way out of hurrying shoppers and I laughed nervously as I tried to stay with him.

After a few more minutes of being blindly led to another one of Liam's unknown destinations, he swiftly stopped and pulled me towards him.

My heart started beating faster and the hairs on the back of my neck stood up.

He paused for only a second; searching my face for a reaction, the tension between our close bodies filled the air like smoke souring off of a bonfire.

I looked into his big, brown eyes and I knew in that moment that I was well and truly fucked.

Locking his hand tighter around mine he led me into the pub that I hadn't even noticed we were standing next to. The warmth hit me as soon as we entered, along with the smell of delicious food and strong beer.

'Liam!' A petite, glossy, black haired woman emerged from behind the bar. She was wearing an apron over a short, ebony dress and effortlessly carrying a drinks tray.

'Hello stranger!' She smiled warmly.

'Katrina,' he nodded politely. 'This is Brooke.' He held me tightly around the waist. The current of the electricity tripled.

'Oh, you didn't tell me you had a girlfriend, Liam?' she winked at me.

'Oh no...' I began to correct her, but Liam interrupted.

'Yes, beautiful isn't she?'

He peered down at me with what I could only perceive as a loving look in his eyes.

Of course you would perceive it as that. You are bat shit crazy!

'Aw! Go sit in the corner and I will get you the menu babe.'

'What was that about?' I hissed.

He led me over to an intimate corner of the pub where a lone fawn table was already set for two people.

'They do a couple's discount on a weekend, hope I didn't weird you out?' He raised his eyebrows.

'Oh, Er... No of course not.' I chuckled, but felt slightly disappointed. Hearing him refer to me as his girlfriend was actually rather nice. No one had ever referred to me as their girlfriend before.

He waved at a group of aged bearded men who were cramped together on some burgundy leather seats in one of the many small booths that were scattered around the room. They were all drinking out of tall glasses of refreshing looking beers and had big, friendly grins on their weathered faces.

'My lady.' He grinned as he pulled my chair out and bowed.

Katrina wiggled towards us and laid some large menus on the table.

'Couples weekend discount, ten percent off of the main menu. How are you doing anyway babe?' She leant against the beamed wall casually.

'I'm good, how you been?' I noticed that as he spoke Liam kept darting his eyes back to mine. I fidgeted nervously in my chair as I listened to their conversation.

'*Very* good, which you'd know if you'd been to see me recently! I'm engaged!'

She held her hand out, gracefully folding her fingers into her palm so that she could present the large diamond ring.

'No way? Congratulations! Who is he? It's about time someone snapped you up.' Liam held her hand carefully and examined the sparkling rock.

The light seemed to bounce off of the diamond and into his eyes, causing them to glisten magically.

I swallowed my urge to gasp at his beautiful existence.

'Congratulations.' I smiled shyly at her. Liam glanced over to me with the same loving look as before.

Katrina beamed at me before continuing her conversation with Liam. I got the impression that they had known each other for a very long time.

'Oh, no one you know. You need to meet him.

George would have liked him.' She said somberly.

'Oh well, didn't you say she liked any man?'

'Yes, she did indeed.' Katrina giggled. 'I'll leave you two to it, call me over when you're ready to order!'

'Who's George?' I asked nosily as I read through the traditional pub menu.

'My mum,' he smiled at me. 'Her and Katrina were good friends, my mum used to work here actually, before I was born.'

'Oh right, where does she work now then?' I questioned again.

'She died.' He glanced up at me, still smiling as if to reassure me that he was fine.

'Oh, I'm so sorry.' I reached out and grabbed his hand without even thinking twice about it.

Was that too forward?

Oh no, he is holding my hand back.

Wow.

74

'Brooke, its fine.' He reassured me, squeezing my hand. 'It was a long time ago, I promise I will tell you everything, but not now, I'm meant to be cheering you up.'

'You don't have to tell me. And cheering me up? There's nothing wrong.'

He frowned. 'Brooke, I don't know you well, but I can tell when someone's got something on their mind.'

'Maybe you know me a lot better than you think then.' I sighed.

Who are you? Where did you come from?

He gazed into my eyes intensely for what seemed like quite a while, still clutching hold of my hand; 'Maybe…' he finally replied.

For the first time in what felt like forever I wasn't worried about my surroundings or the fact that I was in a place I'd never been before with people I didn't know.

I didn't worry about the fact that I didn't have my car to make a quick exit or that I didn't know where the toilets were in case I became nauseous.

I didn't worry that my phone wasn't in my hand in case I needed to call for help.

I wasn't worrying, and it was a feeling so alien to me that I didn't know how to take it.

I released my grip of his hand and began to study the menu again.

'You said you hadn't been asked on a date before, is that true?'

For goodness sake, do you not keep anything to yourself? I scolded drunken Brooke, she should have known better by now.

'Yeah… it's true' I blushed.

His eyes widened and his eyebrows rose.

'So you've never had a boyfriend?' His smile grew a little larger.

Oh no, the personal questions have started already.

I was beginning to regret the pancakes and bacon for breakfast as my stomach twisted up apprehensively.

'No, I've never had a boyfriend. I have a… I have a friend.' I laughed nervously.

Why am I telling him this? Why aren't you stopping me? I searched frantically for A.

My stomach twanged with pain, a feeling I was familiar with.

There you are!

One minute you're telling me to go, now you want me to stay? Make up your mind Brooke!

'A *friend?* But he hasn't asked you to be his boyfriend?' his eyebrows rose even further up his perfect face.

I grimaced. I really didn't want to be discussing my irrelevant relationship with Daniel. Yet again my verbal diarrhea had disclosed too much.

'Er, it's more like I don't want him to be my boyfriend,' I replied honestly.

I thought back to the many times Daniel had attempted to start the 'So where is this going?' conversation.

Liam chuckled. 'Right, that makes more sense.'

'He is the only person I've ever… he is the only friend I've ever had… I don't just go around making friends with everyone…'

Crash. And. Burn.

I told you so. '…sorry, I'm waffling aren't I?' I trailed off as I glanced down at the menu being held by my unsteady hands.

I could feel my cheeks burning.

Liam chuckled, which I noticed he did quite a lot. Why did he find everything amusing?

He's just laughing at your inability to hold a normal conversation, Brooke.

'I've never had a serious girlfriend either.'

He made the statement boldly, not batting an eyelid.

'*You've* never had a girlfriend?'

I looked at his perfect face and his luscious chocolate locks in a state of pure confusion.

'Why are you so shocked?'

Because you look like you was carved by angels. Because you look like you have quite literally fallen from heaven. Because every time I look at you I can't contain myself. Do I need to go on?

'Oh… just because you're older than me,' I lied.

'I guess I've never had the time.' He shrugged. 'Plus I've never met anyone that I would even remotely consider a relationship with.'

'Oh…' I looked down at my menu but I couldn't focus on any of the words. My head was spinning from the intense conversation.

'Until now that is.' He raised his eyebrows so that they almost disappeared behind the curls that had fallen effortlessly onto his forehead.

The clicks of Katrina's heels interrupted the moment and I breathed a huge sigh of relief that I didn't have to think of a reply.

Until now! He said until now!

'Have you decided what you want yet?' Katrina jolted her eyes between the two of us.

I wondered if she had picked up on the tension that was surrounding our tiny corner of the pub.

'I know what I want. Do you, Brooke?' Liam's eyes bore suggestively and intensely into mine; he didn't even look up to acknowledge Katrina.

Right, Brooke. I know I don't usually help you. But this guy is extremely hot and I'd hate for you to mess this up. Play along. You can do it.

My stomach filled with butterflies and their wings fluttered into my heart. It was as if my anxiety had somehow turned into excitement.

Thanks, A I acknowledged her kind gesture.

'If it's what you just said. Then I want the same as you.'

I stared back at him, trying to gauge his reaction to my sudden moment of confidence.

I smirked smugly as his face turned into a mixture of surprise and amusement.

I think I even saw a hint of lust in his eyes.

So you do have it in you! We are going to have some fun with this.

'Okay, well I want the Full Monty.' He mirrored my smug grin. 'Please,' he added as he handed Katrina the menu.

He leaned back in his chair and folded his arms.

The full monty? He just openly said that. Oh my god.

My cheeks flushed red and I looked up at Katrina, expecting her to feel as awkward as I did. She didn't seem phased.

'It's the full English Breakfast, Brooke. They call it the full monty here...' Liam added, obviously noticing my embarrassment.

'Oh, yeah. That too please.'

Crash. And. Burn.

'And we'll have a bottle of wine?' Liam directed his question to me.

'Red please… Whatever is best…' I asked timidly. I felt so flustered.

Katrina took my menu and graciously turned on her heels to the direction of the kitchen.

Liam leant forwards. His magnificent arms swallowed up the space on the table.

'So, you want the same as me?'

'I was hoping you'd skip over that hopeless attempt at flirting.'

Suddenly, my internal dialogue was spilling out of my mouth again before I could stop it.

Liam chortled, his eyes once again filled with a mixture of amusement and longing. 'How could I skip over that?'

'*Could* you skip over that for me please?' I could feel my cheeks turning to a new found shade of maroon.

'For you, anything.' He winked.

The date succeeded in cheering me up and I left the pub that night in a much greater mood than the one I had entered it in.

After devouring our food, we had stayed long into the evening. Liam joined in with conversations happening all throughout the pub. The group of weathered men told us about their time in the army and navy and how they loved to spend their retired days fishing. A lot of jokes about moaning wives waiting for them at home were made too.

Katrina's fiancé came by for dinner. He had just finished work and was wearing a gorgeous navy suit that fit his toned physique perfectly. He had his pale blue tie pulled down and the first few shirt buttons undone. His hair was the same glossy black as Katrina's.

I wondered if everyone in Liam's world was this good looking. It was like I had fallen into a vampire movie.

I mean, it made sense. I was a helpless, anxiety ridden girl who probably stank of vulnerability. Isn't that how those stories usually went?

We listened to the many romantic tales about how he and Katrina had met and how he proposed to her at a candlelit, private dinner in the mountains of Italy. Liam's eyes lit up at this point, I was surprised at how much he really did *love* romance.

As the night went on and everyone had probably consumed a lot more alcohol than they had first intended to, the karaoke machine was switched on.

I watched from the corner table and hysterically laughed as Liam took part in duets with the hairy older men.

He seemed to know the dance moves to a lot of the songs, which everyone found highly amusing.

When the infamous *Dirty Dancing* song began to play, Liam danced and shimmied his way over to our table.

He lifted me up and spun me around — the smell of his aftershave and hair was so intoxicating. I didn't need the wine to feel giddy around him.

Eventually Katrina rang the last bell and we reluctantly grabbed our coats and said our goodbyes.

'We'll be back soon!' Liam called as we left the pub, still laughing.

He wants to see me again!

Anxiety had seemingly forgotten her role in my head and was doing cartwheels and waving pom poms around like an adolescent cheerleader.

I didn't know what to do without her pulling me back to reality — I felt so out of control.

The cold wind of the winter's night hit me and I shuddered. Liam gently wrapped his large, green coat around my shoulders and led me back up the narrow street.

'This is my favourite thing about you,' I said under my icy breath.

'What, my tatty old coat?' he laughed in amusement. 'I don't have much going for me then do I?' he added.

I giggled. 'I just mean it's so you. You couldn't wear any other coat...'

He laughed at my drunken statement. 'I can't believe you didn't tell me it was your birthday!' he sighed. 'I would have got you something.'

'You don't need to get me anything, my own family hasn't even got me a card.' I glanced up at him as he put his arm around my shoulders sympathetically.

He took the bus with me and walked me to Jamie's front door.

Such a gentleman.

'Thank you,' I slurred. 'I've had such a good night.'

He chuckled, tucking a lose strand of my hair that was blowing in the wind behind my ear before leaning around me to knock gently on the door.

'Oh hey birthday girl, where have you been hiding?' Jamie laughed as she opened the door and pulled me inside.

'Wait, your coat,' I murmured, looking back over my shoulder to hand it back to Liam, but the mysterious brown eyed stranger had slipped away into the darkness, once again leaving me breathless.

'Who are you talking to?' Jamie frowned.

'Is that Daniel's coat? Were you with him? You look so nice in the outfit I got you! Why are you so dressed up? Come on you're drunk, I'll make you a cup of tea.' Jamie waffled as I followed her into the living room.

I threw myself down onto the comfy velvet sofa and kicked off Jamie's boots.

I couldn't wipe the smile off of my face.

'So how was Daniel?' Jamie shouted from the kitchen as she flicked on the kettle.

'I wasn't with Daniel...' I knew this was going to lead to a million questions — but I didn't mind — I wanted to talk about my night with Liam.

'Who were you with then? That Harriet girl?'

'No, I was on a date actually,' I stated proudly.

Jamie jumped back into the room. '*You* were on a date?'

'Don't sound so surprised!'

'I am surprised, you don't date!'

She disappeared into the kitchen and returned with two cups of tea and an assortment of biscuits on a plate.

'So who were you on a date with?'

I blushed, the butterflies in my stomach woke up, and my grin grew even larger.

Jamie's mouth opened in shock. *'Look at you!'* she laughed loudly.

'I know. It's ridiculous. I've only known him for like, a week.'

'Am I allowed to know his name?'

My phone pinged loudly from my bag. I retrieved it hastily.

From: Liam

06/02/2018

1:04AM

I forgot to say, you looked beautiful tonight.

Until next time…

X

I sipped my tea, picked up a Digestive biscuit and grinned. 'Liam. His name is Liam.'

The sound of my phone alarm the next morning rudely awoke me from my slumber; I squinted at the clock, 8:15 am was staring up at me very brightly. I pressed the snooze button and fell onto my back again; I wanted a few extra minutes in the cozy spare bedroom of Jamie's large home to prepare myself for the long day ahead.

As I left I was careful not to wake Jamie up on her only day off. My headache was almost unbearable.

I sighed as I recalled the events of the night before and how I longed to be back with Liam already.

His coat was draped tightly over my crossed arms.

The crisp morning air was blowing my long pony tail over my shoulder and stray strands of hair annoyingly flew into my mouth and eyes.

I jumped into the warmth of my car and scrolled through my extensive playlist.

The street was just waking up; birds chirped in the trees, a few curtains twitched as nosy neighbors looked out of their windows.

The old lady across the street was in her dressing gown, standing outside her chipped, red door, pursing a cigarette between her lips whilst searching for something in her deep pockets.

I decided on some old school Chris Brown to wake me up and crept out of the driveway reluctantly.

I unwillingly strolled through the steel rotating doors and into the bright blue reception that I was so familiar with. I walked across the hall to the front desk, deciding I wanted to find out if anyone knew where Harriet had disappeared to. Also, I was trying to waste as much time before having to endure another day in the office.

'Hey Carla.' I greeted the middle aged woman tapping away on her computer behind the front desk.

'You're Brooke, right?' Carla pushed her glasses up her nose and smiled. 'How can I help?'

'Harriet, she was doing training with me, she hasn't been here for weeks and I was just wondering if she got moved to another place or something?'

The whole time I spoke, Carla tapped a pen annoyingly against the desk. 'I know another one of the trainees quit just before Christmas, maybe that could be her?'

'She wouldn't just quit,' I answered as I placed my bag on the desk to pull out my phone.

'Well I don't know I've never met the girl, boss man just told me that another one had bit the dust the other day.

There will be none of you left soon, such a waste of resources and money, training people up for months just for them to quit and go and work in a corner shop…'

'…Mr. Daniels told you that?' I rudely interrupted, but Carla was known for holding people up at reception due to her mundane droning and I wasn't in the mood to be polite today.

I don't know, you go on one date and think you're the queen. Remember who you are, Brooke!

'Yes, gorgeous isn't he?' she grinned, her pink cheeks flushed.

Oh god, is that what I look like around Liam?

'I guess so,' I murmured. 'That's weird that she would just *quit*, she loved it here.' I rummaged around in my bag but couldn't feel my phone in there. 'Or not…' I sighed. Grudgingly, I signed in and made my way towards the rusty lift in the far corner of the room.

I repeated the same routine I always did daily, but this time instead of just noticing Liam walk to the bench, I found myself waiting for him to make his appearance. *You're pathetic.*

I swiveled around in my squeaky office chair; chewing on a pen and starring at the minutes go by on the loud wall clock above my head.

I decided to look into Liam's little TV appearance; I hadn't asked him about it as I didn't want to ruin the perfect picture I had created of him in my head. I knew that there had to be something wrong, nobody was that perfect in real life.

After a few Google searches, a YouTube clip of the news report popped up, I watched closely as Liam appeared, screaming and swearing at the body guard standing in the background.

He was an extremely scary looking man, his biceps were larger than my head and he had a horrendous scar running down the entire right side of his face.

Liam was shouting at the man, 'Guedo you coward, what did you do?'

'Guedo,' I whispered to myself. 'There can't be many people with that name.'

I typed the name 'Guedo' into Google, hoping for a full Wikipedia page on the man, but all that appeared was meanings and interpretations of the name.

It seemed to be a slang term for Italian American's who conduct themselves in the way a mobster in a film would. I wondered if it was an ironic nickname he'd given himself, maybe it was a middle finger to the historically demeaning nature of the word.

I sighed; I couldn't find anything about Liam anywhere, no Facebook, no Instagram, and no more news reports. Just the video on YouTube and an old Myspace account from when he was about eight years old.

I was glad when Mr. Daniels stormed through the door, asking us to type up some more reports because he had 'important business to tend to.'

'Always the same excuse.' Nyema rolled her eyes at me and smiled kindly as soon as Mr. D was out of ear shot.

'Important business, do you think he is getting a pedicure?' I replied half-heartedly as I studied the papers that had been thrown on my desk.

The office erupted with sniggers and a few comments about Mr. Daniels sitting in a beauty parlor getting ready for a 'back, crack and sack' were passed around before everyone became intently focused on the task at hand.

The papers I had been given were notes that Kate had jotted down in her latest interview with Andrew Spence. He had now been arrested and was awaiting his sentence. It would be a very long one.

At around 6:50 pm — not that I was watching the time — I noticed Liam take his place on the same spot on his bench, pull out one cigarette from his pocket and spark it up. He stretched his legs out and lounged back into the bench. Like every other day.

I glanced at his green coat I had hung on the back of the door, thankful that I had a conversation starter.

I quickly typed out the last part of Kate's lengthy report. "Although Mr. Spence has been compliant and helpful in all police conducted interviews, and has disclosed I believe, as much information as he possibly could to us.

Releasing Mr. Spence would not be an option.

Mr. Spence has — under section 25 (1) committed several offences as stated above.

He has assisted in the unlawful immigration of thousands of

young women and children from as far back as 1998–present and it would be a danger to society to grant him bail or a lesser sentence of any kind."

I grimaced at the thought of Andrew Spence and his skeletal face.

Kate and the team had produced a very water-tight case against him so I believed that it was enough.

I printed out the reports and placed them into the correct filing cabinet, breathing a huge sigh of relief that I had completed my work for the day and skipped happily out of the doors.

And there he was, waving at me from across the street, leaning against the bus stop with a cigarette held on top of his ear.

Wow.

'You aright, girl?' Liam beamed that dangerously dreamy grin at me as I threw his coat at him.

Of course he caught it with one hand, effortlessly.

I stood awkwardly in front of him for a second as our eyes lingered intently at each other.

'Do you fancy doing something tonight?' He asked wearily, probably wondering why I had lost the ability to speak.

'Yeah… I'd like that.' I tilted my head to the side and smiled. *I would really like that.*

I lead him across the street to my car. It felt strange that I was leading him somewhere for a change.

'All right miss BMW.' He raised his eyebrows at me as he relaxed into the passenger seat. 'You surprise me every day.'

'Why?' I laughed as I started the engine, the music I had been blaring through my speakers that morning boomed through the car making us both jump.

Chris Brown was midway through singing the chorus to

Back to Sleep. I blushed as I noticed Liam's eyebrows raise even more.

'Sorry, I was feeling a type of way this morning,' I muttered as I turned down the volume and switched to a different playlist. Liam burst out laughing as some classical music played through the speakers.

I tilted my head and smiled innocently. 'The real me is in fact, an angel.'

'Have you had a good day?' Liam smirked at me as I switched to a generic radio station.

'Same old.' I studied him closely, he was wearing what looked like navy blue overalls.

'I'm a mechanic,' he explained, as if I knew what I was thinking. 'Sorry, do I look a state?' He ran his hands through his curly hair and straightened out his stained clothes.

'No, no you don't...' I whispered as I watched him.
God you're beautiful.

Brooke, you're in the driver's seat idiot. Drive! 'Where do you want to go?' I tore my eyes away from him and to the car parked in front of us.

'I really don't mind.' He squeezed my leg softly and let his hand sit there for a moment. I could feel the electricity build up in my stomach and between my thighs.

Just don't crash, whatever you do.

Do not cause this beautiful specimen to become disembodied in a fatal car crash.

We drove around for a while, singing along to music and chatting as if we had known each other for years.

Eventually I pulled up at the cinema in Camden and we strolled in to see what films were currently being shown.

'It's our lucky day!' Liam beamed.

'Why's that?'

'There's a new love story, come on!'

He paid for two tickets to see the film *Irreplaceable You.*

The girl behind the counter flushed as Liam ordered our snacks. *Does he have this effect on everyone?*

We sat at the back of the cinema like two teenagers, sharing popcorn and slurping annoyingly loud on our drinks.

Liam yawned and placed his arm around my shoulder halfway through the film which made me giggle a little bit too loud.

'*Shh.*' A podgy looking lady shot us a look from a few rows in front. I cupped my hand over my mouth trying not to laugh even more as Liam pulled a funny face at her in reply.

The film turned out to be rather sad. I had to hold back the tears towards the end, although I'm sure I saw a glisten in Liam's eyes too.

'Any quotes worth remembering from that film?' I asked Liam as we strolled out of the ODEON and back into the cold of the night. I shivered as I rushed towards the car park. We flung ourselves into the car and quickly switched on the heater.

'You've loved and been loved. You're one of the lucky ones…' Liam quoted word for word.

Our eyes darted towards each other and lingered vigorously.

'I had fun tonight, Brooke.'

'So did I.' I smiled timidly.

You don't want the night to end now do you?

No, of course I don't!

Well ask him to come round then! Do it!

Okay, stop shouting at me!

I rubbed my achy head and frowned. 'So, do you want to go home or…' I paused and looked at him. I wasn't sure if I was brave enough to finish that sentence.

'Or…' he winked. '…Or sounds good.'

'Hello B,' Jamie answered her door cheerfully, before laying eyes on Liam. '*And* B's friend.'

'Nice to meet you, heard a lot about you. I'm Liam.' He smiled politely.

'*Liam.*' She grinned and nodded approvingly at me. 'You two love birds coming in or you just gonna stand there?' She grinned, pulling on Liam's arm so he fell through the front door.

'I haven't heard *anything* about you; she's so secretive when it comes to boyfriends.'

I shook my head and laughed as I followed them into the house that was basically my home now.

'Sorry J, I left my door keys here this morning, again.' I laughed.

'So what are you doing here?' Jamie asked as she wiggled over to the kitchen and retrieved three bottles of beer from the fridge.

I watched to see if Liam noticed how short Jamie's pajama bottoms were, but he kept his eyes firmly set to mine the whole time.

Wow.

'I had a long day at work, then we went to the cinema, Liam was just...' before I had a chance to finish Jamie butted in, like always.

'...Liam was just here to keep you company?' She smirked as she passed us the opened bottles before falling down on an armchair.

'Do you mind if I use your loo?' Liam asked confidently, finally tearing his eyes away from me. He placed the bottle on a coaster and stood up. I looked up at him in awe as he towered over Jamie and I.

Jamie pointed him in the right direction and as he left the

room she turned to face me. 'WOW!' she mouthed.

'Jamie, honestly, that's all I think when I look at him.'

We giggled quietly and she gave me a high five as if we were two children who had just played kiss chase on the playground.

'I mean, he is *hot!'* Jamie gawked again.

'Hands off.' I shot her a look, knowing how much she enjoyed a good looking man.

'Hey, I have Charlie…'

'Charlie? I thought it was Luke?' I frowned.

She took a sip of her beer and sat back down. '*Charlie* is the fitty from the Christmas fare, remember?'

I nodded.

'So we can double date now!' Jamie squealed. I shot her a *have-you-forgotten-who-you're-talking-to?* look. 'Oh Brooke, it won't be *that* bad. Besides, I want to get to know the man who has stolen your heart.' She mocked.

We both grinned as Liam entered the room again. He had pulled down his overalls and tied the sleeves around his waist, revealing a tight fitting white T-shirt.

I could tell he had attempted to clean his appearance up as some of his hair was damp and he smelt of minty mouthwash.

Is he trying to impress me? Job well done if he is. I almost drooled at the sight of him.

'I was four when mum died.' Liam sniffed, taking a long pull of another cigarette and then passing it to me.

Jamie had finally taken the hint that we wanted to be alone and had reluctantly stomped upstairs; I could hear the theme tune of *Keeping up with the Kardashians* from her open window.

Liam and I were perched on the back door step with a bottle of wine, a pack of cigarettes and the starry night sky as our only companions.

'She used to work where you work, when I was old enough to understand that mum was missing I used to walk there every day and sit outside hoping that I would see her, I suppose after a few years it just became habit.' *Finally,* I had an explanation to why he always sat on that bench.

'Then she got this boyfriend, I don't know how they met, I don't know anything really, I never really got a word she said about it, I was too young to understand.' He paused and smiled as if he was having a loving memory of her. Although he was smiling, you could clearly see the pain in his eyes.

'I remember her coming home one day, *Liam baby, mummy's gonna be a rich bitch after this promotion!* I remember I was eating dinner, beans on toast. She always called me that, Liam baby.'

'That's cute.' I smiled. 'She sounded lovely. What about your dad, was he not around to help you find her?' I realized I didn't really know much about Liam, for the number of things we had spoken about recently. I felt guilty for not knowing more.

'I never knew my dad, he left mum when he found out she was pregnant.' He replied matter-of-factly.

'Oh, I'm sorry.' I was running out of things that I could say in response to his heartbreak.

'Don't be, I'm not.' He managed a smile. 'Anyway, yeah, I

guess she was working overtime, through the nights, early mornings, never really slept, I remember her never really being home,'

'But you were only young,' I whispered, not wanting to say anything bad about his mum, but I couldn't believe a four-year-old was left alone to fend for himself.

He shrugged in response to my comment before carrying on. 'I started doing some digging when I was a bit older, found a few notes from work lying around the house, I just remember reading something about a Rebecca bird who worked with her, she was in a car crash or something and had been sent to jail. But apart from that it was all just cases they had been working on and it was all a bit depressing.'

'So that security guy on the news, that had something to do with your mum?' I asked carefully, not wanting to dig too deep and upset him, but I also really wanted to know who Guedo was.

'That was her boyfriend...' Anger filled his voice and poured out into his beautiful eyes.

'I wouldn't be alone all the time, he was always lingering around. I remember a lot of shouting, mainly him shouting at her, her coming downstairs with bruises and blood over her, why she was with him I'll never understand. Since she's been gone people always tell me about how many men were after her, like Katrina from the pub the other day. She said my mum could have had anyone she wanted... Fuck knows what she saw in Guedo.'

I shook my head, I couldn't believe what I was hearing, and I thought I had it hard with my spoilt little brat problems, at least I had a mum.

'Mum was never late home from work; I think maybe she hated leaving me alone, but didn't have a choice.

I had to walk with Chris from next door to and from school

because she couldn't take me. He is a few years older. One morning I woke up and mum was shouting up the stairs, *Liam baby,* see *you at normal time yeah? Mummy loves you.* And then that night, she never came home.'

'How did she die?' I wasn't sure if I was over stepping the mark with my many questions.

Liam didn't seem to care about my inquisitiveness as he answered without batting an eyelid. I wondered if he'd answered this question many times before.

'I don't know; no one has ever found her, no one even really knows I exist. I was only in the second year of school, funny thing is I carried on walking with Chris to school and back even after she'd gone, just because I thought that's what I had to do.'

'You were four and you used to get yourself ready and go to school?' I was shocked; I'd never heard anything like it.

'Yeah pretty much, Chris used to come in and help me from what I remember, like in the mornings he would make me a packed lunch and stuff. He was there quite a lot because his mum and dad were druggies. He didn't really like being at home. We're still mates now actually, but he doesn't live next door any more.

Then one of my mum's friends, Carlos, moved in with me once he had found me alone after a few weeks of her being gone. He just called school one day and told them I was moving, pretending he was my dad; I never went to another school again. I got a job when I was twelve, with him at his garage, where I work now, and that's it really.

I found out Guedo was gonna be working where that interview was happening on Christmas Day and went to confront him, didn't know there was gonna be so many cameras and the news there, but seeing him again after all these years made me so pissed off, I just went for him.'

'Oh,' I whispered, in shock at everything he had just disclosed. I'd never known anyone who had lived a life like him. 'And you've been trying to figure out what actually happened to her?'

'Yeah, I guess so. We always know what Guedo is up to; Carlos promised he'd never stop looking for her.

I think deep down he loved her. But Guedo has been quiet for years, pops up in a news report or something here and there because his security firm caters for the rich people and the politicians. But no, we have never stopped looking for answers.' Liam explained, looking down at his feet, he almost seemed ashamed.

I thought I was drawn to Liam because he was mysterious, but now that I knew more about him, I could feel myself falling even more.

I wrapped my hands around his muscular arm and lent on his shoulder, not knowing what in the world I could say to comfort him in that moment.

V

BEFORE WE FELL IN LOVE
I finally made the appointment to visit Dr Daw as A had been making many an appearance recently.

I'd been attending counselling since I was about nine years old and it had become part of my routine now.

I'd had periods of a year or so where I wouldn't need to go, but then the anxiety would creep up on me again, like it had recently, and my mum would insist on me re-visiting Dr Daw, probably because it was easier to pay for me to speak to a stranger than sit and listen to her own daughter herself. Of course, now it was different, I had to pay Dr Daw myself.

I had always suffered with incapacitating panic attacks, bought on by my anxiety disorder.

I had been diagnosed by many doctors, pediatricians and therapists at the age of seven as I would often end up in hospital as a result of not being able to breathe.

We ruled out asthma, lung cancer (which my mum was adamant I had, ever the drama queen) and all other physical illnesses until I had seen a child therapist who professionally diagnosed me as having anxiety with just a hint of depression, you know just something a little extra for some added flare.

I wasn't one to talk about it, or let people know that I had a weakness — so coming to counselling was a nice escape for me. I liked Dr Daw too, she said some stupid things sometimes that only someone with a degree would say, but she was nice enough. As I walked in I noticed dreamy Daniel leaning against the vending machine, his ripped jeans were rolled up around the ankles, and his loud shirt was tucked in on one side.

'The 1980's just called; they want their clothes back,' I shouted at him from across the room.

A few chuckles echoed through the waiting area, Daniel's face lit up with pure glee. He leapt over the chair in front and spun me around in his arms. I wondered why he had to leap over chairs and spin me around, why couldn't he just walk over to me and greet me like any normal human would.

Then I thought that if Liam leapt over a chair to greet me I probably would have fainted on the spot, so maybe it only irritated me because Daniel was the wrong person.

'Hello you.' He leant down to kiss me, but without even thinking I stepped backwards, avoiding the kiss so obviously that I can imagine he wanted to turn back time and retract that move.

'Well that's never happened before.' He laughed nervously. 'Are you all right?'

'Sorry, I'm fine. Just you know me and public displays of affection.' I laughed, playfully punching him on the arm.

Oh wow, I forgot how big those arms were.

No, Brooke, you cannot do your counselor's receptionist in the storage cupboard again, no matter how fit he is. I argued with my straying thoughts.

At that moment, Dr Daw appeared from the ladies' toilets.

'Oh hello there, Brooke.' She greeted me with a nod. 'Would you like to come through?'

Thank god for that.

I smiled. 'I'll see you soon, yeah?' I reassured him, giving him an awkward wave goodbye.

'So, you said it was urgent on the phone. Is everything okay?' Dr Daw took her place in her beige armchair as I bunglingly *threw myself onto the sofa that I was so well acquainted with. As usual I detected the strong smell of lavender dancing around the room.*

'A is back...' I declared grumpily.

'Ah, I see. What does she have to say for herself this time?'

'The same old really, I'm useless, I'm ugly, and I'm going to die alone...' I laughed half-heartedly as I picked up one of the decorative mirrored balls she had placed on the coffee table in front of us and crossed my legs.

I noticed Dr Daw's face screw up in slight disgust as my tattered Vans touched her lovely, clean sofa.

'And what did I say last time that A was around?'

I threw the ball from one hand to the other as I avoided eye contact with her.

'Brooke, you wanted to come here to talk. So let's talk.'

'You said that A was my coping mechanism. A is just a personification of my emotions as when something is human, I can handle it better.' I didn't want to piss Dr Daw off. I'd always imagined her to be a ruthless angry person.

'Yes, anthropomorphism is a tendency I have come across many times. And I suppose you've been telling yourself that you're crazy again.' Her eyebrows rose as I blushed. This woman knew me better than my own mother ever could.

'Has anything changed recently? Last time A was around you were taking the transition from primary school to secondary school.' I felt myself blush even more. A lot had changed since our last meeting.

'I've met someone...' I whispered. Dr Daw nodded at me to continue.

'He is really nice, he asked me on a date and I had a really good time. I kind of forgot about my anxiety for a while.

Obviously that's a good thing, but when A isn't in my head or I'm not on the verge of a panic attack I don't know what to do. It's a really alien feeling...'

I placed the decorative ball back in its rightful place and played with the frayed end of my knitted jumper instead.

'Well firstly, I'm glad you have met someone who is treating you nicely and you feel safe and comfortable around. Secondly, don't think too much into it for a change. If you are out on a date and you don't feel anxious then just go with it. Enjoy it. Do you think that when you're in a happy moment, you could just be in the happy moment?' She chuckled because she knew that this was a hard task for me. But it sounded like something I could manage. I nodded shyly, 'I think I can try that...'

'Brooke, like I have said many a time, social situations are not your trigger. Being around another person — even a new person — is not going to cause you any harm. Being alone for long periods of time is what triggers your attacks; we have observed this time and time again, have we not? So, get out there and meet as many people as possible. That's your homework!'

It was a normal Friday evening; I had finished another week at work and taken the same dreary road back to Jamie's — which was now my permanent residence.

I hadn't heard from my parents since my mum's delightful text message on my birthday.

I was quite content with not seeing my irritating family members for the time being.

I had collected all of my stuff whilst they were out and moved into the spare room of Jamie's house.

She was happy to have the company, and with my contribution towards the bills she didn't have to work so tirelessly to make ends meet.

I breathed an exasperated sigh of relief as I relaxed into the warm bubble bath with a glass of wine and Shania Twain singing to me through the speaker system.

I was just about to dose off when my phone buzzed loudly from the shelf above the bath. The screen showed no caller ID but I answered anyway.

'Hello?' I placed my phone on the toilet seat next to the bath and pressed the loud speaker button.

'Hey, Brooke…' a familiar voice greeted me from the other end of the phone.

'Oh, Liam, hi…' my heart was in my throat, I sat up so fast I almost caused a tidal wave.

Shania sang 'You're still the one I want…'

How very fitting.

'What are you doing right now?' he asked casually.

We had been speaking over text almost every day, but he hadn't been sitting outside work and I had been too afraid to ask him why. I'd come to the conclusion that he was trying to avoid me, of course.

'Er, you've actually interrupted a really relaxing bath,' I said bluntly.

'I'm sorry I didn't call sooner, I've been thinking about you a lot, Brooke.' I could almost hear his beautiful smile as he was talking to me.

What is wrong with you?

'You've missed me a little bit too haven't you?' he stated confidently.

I smiled to myself, rubbing the smooth body wash up and down my tanned legs.

'I've been thinking about you a little bit too I guess,' I admitted, ignoring his comment, he could pull the arrogance off.

'So why did you want me to come over again?' I asked, standing nervously at his front door.

I knew it looked so desperate of me to turn up as soon as he rang, but Dr Daw had given me homework and I was only following her orders.

Liam's face lit up. He looked at me as intensely as always. I couldn't help but melt a little every time his big brown eyes looked my way.

'I've missed you!' he proclaimed loudly, gesturing for me to enter his home.

I brushed up against him as I turned left into his living room, and the hairs all over my body stood on end. *Brooke, for goodness sake pull yourself together!*

I entered a dark, plain room. There were two chocolate colored sofas placed in an L shape in the middle, with a shabby wooden coffee table just in front of them.

A large television hung on a grey wall and there was a table with some mismatch chairs scattered around it in the far corner, placed next to a small kitchen.

There were photos of him and his mum everywhere.

'You okay?' he asked as he led me onto the largest of the sofas, his hand placed gently on the middle of my back.

'Yeah, fine…' I muttered as I attempted to get comfortable, ignoring the rush that had surged through me from his touch.

'You're not though are you?' he frowned, slumping himself down next to me and reaching for a new box of cigarettes.

'Why wouldn't I be?'

I tried to control the surging fire that was flowing through my veins as I looked at him.

'Because your mum has kicked you out and now you're spending your Friday night with a complete and utter idiot,' he stated bluntly as he blew the smoke away from my direction.

I raised my eyebrows. 'What makes you a complete and utter idiot?'

He frowned at me again, his eyes locked onto mine. 'You at least deserve someone to call you every morning and every night to ask how your day has been, and I haven't even been able to do that... I've been so wrapped up in my own stuff...'

I shrugged casually, attempting to act as though I hadn't checked my phone every single waking minute for the past week waiting for his messages, and that the eye contact he was giving me was making it very difficult not to act on how I was feeling.

'You don't have to text me, I'm not really anything to you am I?'

Liam's big, chocolate eyes continued to stare straight into mine. I looked down nervously. 'You always do that.'

'Do what?' he laughed, not breaking his eyes away from my face for one second.

'Stare into my soul, well I'm sorry but you'll find it's very black in there.' I kept the eye contact that time and realized why all those over times I looked away.

If I stayed lost in his eyes for too long, then I knew I wouldn't make it back out alive.

Liam chuckled and cautiously lowered his eye level.

Well now I feel even more on fire.

I straightened out my off the shoulder jumper and wiggled in my seat.

'When I thought about it all and how whatever was going on with my mum and Guedo led to her being killed, well I didn't want to involve you in something I thought you couldn't handle, but then I realized something...' he paused.

Whoa, where has all of this come from?

105

'And what was that?' I breathed.

'That who am I to decide what you can and cannot handle? I mean, I get the impression that you're pretty strong Brooke.'

'*Me?* Strong?' I chortled loudly at him without a second thought. *He has me so wrong!* 'I'm not strong Liam, if only you knew the half of it…'

Liam looked disappointed at my sudden outburst.

I wondered if he had been rehearsing his little apology and I had thrown a spanner in the works there.

'What do you mean?'

'Do you really want to know?' I breathed in. He had divulged so much about his mum that I thought maybe I should share a little bit with him too.

'Of course, I want to know all of you, Brooke. The good and the bad,'

Careful what you wish for buddy, she's the bad, the worse and the ugly!

Oh, here you are, I was wondering when you'd surface.

I'm always here, Brooke.

'…Brooke?' Liam's eyes were wide with worry.

'It's just my problems seem so *petty* compared to yours!'

His thick eyebrows narrowed once again and I didn't want to disappoint him any more so I told him almost everything.

I told him about my years of counselling. I told him about my god-awful mother.

I told him about my daily struggles, my mental and physical symptoms.

I told him of how I was just exhausted, exhausted with the anxiety and exhausted with life.

After I told him I thought he would run for the hills.

But he didn't. He simply held my hand and squeezed it tight.

That one small gesture seemed to make my insides feel just that little bit lighter, like I had passed some of the weight onto him.

He kept hold of my hand and I wanted to kiss him, I wanted to tell him how I felt, I wanted to rip his clothes off, but instead I dropped my gaze so he couldn't see my stupid smile.

After a few moments of silence, he finally spoke.

And it was as if he knew that I had said enough and wanted to change the subject completely. 'So yeah, I'm very sorry for not calling you every day, and I'm also sorry for underestimating you. Do you accept my apology?'

I nodded in reply and Liam squeezed my hand a little tighter. 'So for now, let me just say, without hope or agenda...'

'You are *not* about to quote Love Actually to me are you Liam?' I interrupted.

'Wouldn't dream of it,' he smirked. 'I'm just a boy, standing in front of girl, asking her to forgive him.'

'Okay Julia Roberts, give it a rest.' I rolled my eyes.

'Er, I'm defiantly Hugh Grant in that one,' he contended.

'So before I aired all my dirty laundry, you said you thought I was strong? What gave you that impression?' I prodded. I'd been called a lot of names in my life, often by my mother — but never strong.

He chuckled. 'Your dirty laundry really isn't that dirty. And I'm good at reading people...'

'Oh yeah?' I raised my eyebrows at him.

'Well even before you aired your dirty laundry...' an amused look swept across his beautiful face. '...I could tell that you were preoccupied with other stuff. Sometimes when we're talking you seem to go off to another place entirely.'

Courtesy of me!

Shut up, A, a hot boy is paying us a compliment!

Are you not going to introduce us?

I've told him a lot tonight, A. but I will never tell him about you. A pouted disapprovingly at me.

Well you never care about my feelings? Why should I care about yours!

'Right on queue!'

We both laughed.

'Sorry, I know, I do that a lot.'

'No need to apologize... do you know what else I've noticed about you?'

I tilted my head to the side. He was still holding onto my hand and had begun to stroke my knuckles with his thumb absentmindedly.

'You're smart, talented, funny and...' he stopped.

'...And?' I prompted.

'Beautiful.'

I blushed and gazed in adoration at him for a moment. I wondered what beauty this gorgeous stranger could see in me that I couldn't.

'Crazy isn't it?'

'What is?'

'What are the chances that you would work at the same place my mum did, that we would even meet?' he smiled, 'I mean you're a beautiful rich girl, and I'm... I'm just me.'

Just you? Just you, is just perfect.

'You said you've been thinking more about your mum. Do you want to talk about it?' I questioned timidly, not ready to express all of my inner thoughts to him just yet. I'd disclosed enough for one day.

He used his free hand to tuck my hair behind my ears and shook his head. 'Not tonight.'

He stood up and held out his hand so gracefully. Every movement he made was done so effortlessly, so beautifully, I had never known someone to be so perfect in every single way.

I took his hand and he gently pulled me upwards and guided me out of the room. We walked up the creaky staircase, my heart pounded as we approached his bedroom.

I'm not ready for that! I hardly know him! Oh god...

My mind went into overdrive and I stopped, frozen in the middle of his hallway, causing me to slightly tug on his hand. He turned to face me, and obviously saw the horror and panic in my eyes.

'We're not going in there, come on...' he tugged on my hand in retaliation, and I relaxed slightly. He chuckled.

We walked past the bedroom and into the room at the end of the hall. The walls were deep red and the carpeted floor was filled with beanbags and fluffy cushions. It smelt deliciously of popcorn and scented candles.

On the back wall a large projector screen hung magnificently and leant against the adjoining wall was an enormous bookshelf filled with countless DVD's.

Of course a few videos were scattered around the collection as well.

'This is amazing, Liam.' I wondered at the towering bookshelf filled with every genre imaginable. My heart rate lowered back down after my moment of sheer panic, although I didn't think it had ever beat normally around him to begin with. I ran my fingers along the shelves directly in front of me, studying each title closely.

Gone with the Wind,
An Affair to Remember,
Roman Holiday,

10 Things I Hate About You,
Casablanca,
Dirty Dancing and The Notebook were just a few of the many romantic films that lived in this stunning room.

I noticed how worn the cases were. 'I'm assuming this is your row of favorites?' I giggled.

'Of course,' he smiled, 'but this…' he pulled out a DVD from the very end and held it proudly towards me. '…This is my favorite at the moment.'

'Let's put it on then,' I suggested. 'I've never seen When Harry Met Sally before.'

Liam's eyes lit up in shock. 'You've *never seen* When Harry Met Sally? Oh you are so lucky I'm here to teach you about the world of cinema!' *I'm very lucky you are here Liam.*

We each curled up on our own beanbag and Liam wrapped a fluffy blanket over my shoulders. A chill ran down my spine as his fingers lingered against my neck.

He dimmed the lights and the film begun.

Liam spoke over the infamous quotes of the film as if he had written the script himself.

'Men and Women can't be friends because the sex part always gets in the way.' Harry and Liam spoke in unison, my heart rate tripled as he interlocked his fingers with mine.

We kept a hold of each other right up until the final sentence. Liam whispered, *'we were friends for a long time, and then we weren't, and then we fell in love…'*

There was a moment of silence as the credits began to roll. A mesmerizing song played loudly through the speakers.

Liam watched me for a moment before swiftly standing up and holding out his hand. 'Dance with me?' The flickering light of the projector gleamed around him like a halo as his eyes starred down hopefully at mine.

'Together we're going a long, long way...' the stunning voice sang.

I took Liam's hand and he pulled me up and into a ballroom-like hold in one swift movement. I gasped at the unexpected display of romance. I couldn't help but smile. 'Who sings this? It's beautiful.'

My long hair swayed to and fro as he danced me elegantly around the room, somehow avoiding the cushions and beanbags as he did so.

'Harry Connick Jr. This version.' He seemed to have an answer for everything, he knew so much about life.

Tension snaked through the air as the song stopped, but we carried on dancing to our own beat.

'So?'

'I loved it.' I smiled shyly up at him. I knew he was asking for my opinion on the film.

'Are you just saying that?'

I laughed. 'No, No, I promise, I loved it.' I truly did. I had loved the whole evening and I didn't want it to end.

'Good,' he whispered. His large hands made my fragile ones look as though they could break in his tight grip.

'So does that mean I'm still welcome here? We can still be friends?'

He was silent for a moment as the room fell into darkness. Only the light through the slightly ajar curtains allowed me to still see his perfect face.

He looked at me so intensely that I felt as though everything around us had disappeared. He tucked a loose strand of hair delicately behind my ear as we stood still, holding it there for a second as he leaned forwards.

111

My heart fluttered.

His hand slowly moved from my ear to my arm and then down to my waist. He forcefully pulled me in closer to him, our lips lingered millimeters away.

'What, no quote from Titanic? Ghost? Dirty Dancing?' I joked in almost a whisper. I could feel his breath on my lips. Liam smiled and shook his head.

I knew why. The moment was too perfect to disturb with any more words. The only appropriate thing to do, was to kiss.

And so that's what we did.

Wow.

'What are these?' I glanced down at the coffee table to a pile of papers and picked them up. I hadn't noticed them previously.

We had returned to the large sofa and ordered some pizza, both not wanting the night to end. He took them from me and rustled them up in his hands.

'I found some bits I kept of my mum's, I've never really looked through all of her work stuff properly before. Suppose I've just been so focused on Guedo having all of the answers.' He eyed me warily, I wondered why he always looked for my reaction. Surely he didn't need *my* approval. 'I mean these people seem proper dangerous Brooke, the last few days it's all I've been reading, you don't have to get involved, I just wanted to show you what I found...' he rambled, carefully searching through them until he came to what he was looking for, he handed it back to me.

'I'm in.' I reassured him as I studied the paper he had handed to me. It looked like a witness statement; I had seen a fair few of those at work.

Friday 2nd December, 1994.

15:32 p.m.

"I entered my office this morning, I clocked in at 8:17 a.m. Thirteen minutes before I was due to start. The door was ajar which I found strange as I always close it when I leave. As I opened the door my co-worker, Britney was laying on the floor in a pool of blood. I noticed a bullet wound to her head and some bruising to her face, there were clear signs of a struggle in my office."

'Then there's this.' Liam passed me a page which looked as though it had been ripped out of a diary, the page was dated the 2nd of December just like the witness statement.

There was some scribbled writing that I could just about

113

make out, it read:

Just a reminder of how much I love you.

Meet me tomorrow at our favourite place.

G xx

'Was that meeting the day she went missing, the Saturday?' I asked him, placing the papers back down onto the coffee table, he replied with a slow nod. 'Oh... I don't know what to say, I'm so sorry.'

'I think that was aimed at my mum, reminding her that she couldn't get away from him?' I turned to him; his eyes were filled with tears.

'In some weird twisted way, maybe it was. Is this all you know?' Liam nodded again.

'Well it's a lot of what if's, Liam. We need real evidence if we're going to find out what happened to your mum.' He managed a smile.

'We will find out what happened to her.' I held his hand again. 'I promise you.' He squeezed my hand tightly in return.

I frowned as I thought about work and how Harriet still hadn't returned. I had left countless voicemails and text messages, but still nothing.

'What is it?' Liam asked as he released my hand and lit up a cigarette. It was nearing on 11:30pm, his long eyelashes seemed to be weighing his beautiful, tired eyes down.

'It's probably nothing, it's just my friend has been MIA... and she works with me... I guess there are just some similarities... her boyfriend didn't seem too kind either.' I grimaced as I thought back to our run-in with Matt.

'Similarities with my mum's disappearance you mean?'

'Well, yeah I guess so. I'm just worried about her that's all.'

'I have a friend who could possibly track her down, no

questions asked.' *Of course you do.*

'Okay, thank you.'

Liam pursed the cigarette between his lips as he scrolled through his phone, eventually finding who he was looking for and pressing the loud speaker button.

Oh, we're doing it now. 'Hello?' A timid voice came from the phone after only a couple of rings.

'Bill, listen I know it's late mate. But you couldn't do me a favor next time you're in work could you?'

'Another favor Liam…' he sounded exasperated.

'I know, I know, but it's not about mum this time.'

Liam stubbed the cigarette out in the expensive looking astray resting on the arm of the chair and turned to me. 'What's your friend's name?'

'Harriet Clancy…' I croaked, not sure whether to direct my answer to Liam or the posh voice on the other end of the phone.

'Yeah, Bill, did you hear that?'

'I did indeed, hello Liam's lady friend,'

I giggled. 'Hi.'

'*Lady friend?*' Liam repeated, amused.

'Well I'm sorry I had to point it out, this is the first girl you've been around since preschool isn't it?'

I like this Bill, he is funny.

And he is giving us good dirt on our guy, take notes!

He is not our guy, A. He is my guy.

Don't be so pedantic Brooke. Anyway, there's enough of him to share.

'Preschool.' Liam scoffed. 'Just let me know what you find, yeah? Thanks Bill.'

'Of course, bye Liam. Liam's lady friend…'

'Bye.' I blushed as Liam hung up the phone.

'He'll call tomorrow probably. He usually gets the job done quite quick.'

'Thank you, Liam.'

'Anytime.' He grinned, leant forwards and planted a kiss on the middle of my forehead.

My heart skipped a beat.

'I'm having a bit of a gathering here tomorrow, do you and Jamie want to come?'

'Er...' *Oh god, this is such a small room, there will be no way out. Sounds like hell.*

Brooke, think of your homework!

I thought back to my last counselling session and how Dr Daw had insisted on me getting out there and meeting new people. The pit of my stomach churned.

'I'd really like you to meet all of my friends...' Liam studied my face hopefully. How could I say no?

'Sounds good.' I smiled through the panic.

'Do you want me to do your hair?'

I had made it home at around two am the previous night and had very little sleep.

My mind was buzzing about the party, what to wear, what to say, do I kiss Liam in front of people? Do I act aloof and hard to get?

I still didn't know the answer.

He'd insisted that Jamie and I bought an overnight bag and crashed at his as apparently that's what most people usually ended up doing.

I began to brush through Jamie's long, soft hair as we sat cross legged on the bed in the compact spare room of Liam's house. We were surrounded by cardboard boxes which I assumed were where Liam kept all of his mum's belongings.

'I miss being little Brooke, my mum used to brush my hair for me every morning like this, why did all of that change?'

'I thought you liked being alone?' I asked as I wrapped her hair around some curling tongs.

'No, I mean it's all right, but it gets boring,' she replied, 'don't you miss your parents and the twins?'

I was silent. I had spoken to the twins on the phone when they were with Auntie Ron, but I hadn't heard a word from either of my parents since I'd moved in with Jamie. I felt a twinge of sadness towards the memory of my doting dad, but soon shrugged it off, that dad no longer existed. 'I miss Riley and Ruby, but they seem like they are okay without me,' I replied after a while. I'd made sure Auntie Veronica was keeping an eye on them, knowing full well that my useless parents would forget to feed them dinner every night without me being there.

'Do you think our parents even miss us?' her voice cracked a little.

It wasn't like her to become emotional over her parents, I wondered if they'd recently had a falling out. 'Probably not, they've always been selfish. That's why I'm glad I have had you all these years. We would be so lonely otherwise.' I attempted to cheer her up.

'Hmm...' she sighed. 'I got a text earlier saying that mum and dad will be back for a day and then they are going up to visit my mum's cousins in Devon, but no invite for me.'

'It's messed up; you work so hard to look after yourself. I'm sorry babe...'

'It's fine, you know what though B, I think we should find a place of our own, together, we're adults now, we should probably stop pining after our childhood and I really don't want to stay in that house any longer.'

'Sounds good to me!'

'We'll start looking as soon as possible, but what about Liam?' she wondered, as she touched up her makeup in a small compact mirror.

'What about him?' I frowned.

'Won't you be spending more time with him now that you're all loved up.'

She glanced at me in the reflection as I blushed at the thought of him. 'We're defiantly not loved up, we're not even together, and even if we were, you'll always come first,'

'I like him for you,' she said coolly.

'Yeah, he'll do.' I laughed, finishing off her hair and sitting on the floor next to her.

'Just don't ditch me for him; boys aren't everything you know,' she added.

'Coming from *you*!'

It's always just been me and you.' She ignored my joke,

obviously not up for any arguments.

I thought I'd best appreciate the rare occasion. 'And it always will be, nothing is going to change now that we're getting older.' I assured her. I felt a tear creep into my eyes, I was so lucky that I had such a close friend.

After about an hour and a half of Jamie and I getting ready and chatting about anything and everything, there was a loud knock at Liam's door. I listened as the door creaked open; there were some faint mutters from the other side.

I heard a deep voice say, 'How you been man?' We sat in the room silently, listening into their conversation.

'How's your girlfriend, Bill?' I heard Liam's angelic voice ask. *I wonder if that's the Bill who was looking into Harriet.*

'Probably sexually frustrated.' The one with the deeper voice answered for him. There were roars of laughter from this apparently funny comment.

The boy that I assumed was Bill butted in, the only one not laughing. 'Leave it out,' he said, his wimpy voice could hardly be heard over the booming laughter.

'Just a joke, bruv,' said the boy who had made the comment. 'Chill,'

'Girls!' Liam shouted up the stairs. 'You ready?'

'Girls?' all of the boys said in unison as their voices trailed off into the living room. We looked at each other and laughed at their typical male behavior.

We slowly walked downstairs, careful not to fall over in our ridiculously high heels.

'Who wears heels like this to a house party Jamie, I feel like an idiot,' I hissed at her.

'Brooke, take it from me, the expert, we defiantly do not look like idiots.' She reassured me, flicking her hair over her shoulder for the millionth time in five minutes.

As we entered the front room, everyone stopped what they were doing and stared, the room was filled with silence for a few seconds. I smiled at everyone and held Jamie's arm.

'Hi,' I greeted them politely.

'Why is everyone so gormless?' Jamie whispered into my ear.

'Aren't you used to things with dicks staring at you?'

I peered over at Liam; he was sitting on the sofa next to a skinny, blonde boy who seemed to be suffering with severe acne problems. His teeth stuck out so he couldn't even close his mouth and he was dressed differently from the rest of the boys. The others were all clad head to toe in designer gear whereas he was wearing a *CSI* jumper and some old, warn out jeans.

They seemed to be lost in a deep conversation. Liam was frowning, as always. I noticed how stunningly drop-dead gorgeous he looked.

He wore a pale blue polo top paired with grey chinos and some bright white trainers. His hair was extra curly and he was clean shaven.

Wow-ee!

I tugged Jamie towards the sofa so that we were standing inches away from them. I smiled at CSI boy as he peered up at us warily. Liam glanced up at us and did a double take. His eyes filled with the same desire I noticed the night we had met.

'Hi' he mouthed.

'Hi…' I blushed back.

'This is Brooke and her friend Jamie.' Liam gestured towards us, he didn't break our eye contact for one second.

'Hello, I'm Billy. It's very nice to meet you both!'

So you're Billy. CSI jumper. Able to access information on missing people. Go figure.

A big, bulky boy walked over and stood in front of us. 'All right,' he nodded. I remembered his face from the first night I'd met Liam.

'Nice to see ya again, Brooke,'

'Hi, it's Dale, right?' I smiled at him as he nodded. 'This is my friend Jamie.'

'Beautiful name,' he winked as he said this. 'My dog was called Jamie, she died.'

'Oh, I'm sorry.' I bit my lip to hold back the laughter.

I felt Jamie dig her nails into my arm as she let out a squeak. He grinned obliviously as he slid past us and into the kitchen where he started an annoyingly loud conversation with a large group of boys who were all in deep discussions over bottles of beer and cigarettes.

When did they all get here?

'When did *they* get here?' Jamie repeated my thoughts, but in a completely different tone. Her perfectly plucked eyebrows raised at me and she was off. She strutted into the kitchen to flirt outrageously with everyone in the room as usual. Clearly Christmas fair boy was a distant memory. I couldn't for the life of me remember his name.

Another one bites the dust.

I laughed and sat down next to Liam, he smelt divine.

'Bill's worried that you're going to dob him in...'

'Liam!' Billy exclaimed. 'Brooke, I apologize on behalf of this buffoon. Just, aren't you a police officer?'

'National crime agency, just an apprentice,' I replied timidly.

'Sorry, I don't mean to make you uncomfortable.' He smiled apologetically.

'No, you're not, it's fine. I'm not police, and if it's for Liam

121

you could murder someone in front of me and I wouldn't care.' Liam looked amused and slightly shocked at my response.

'Well I won't be murdering anyone in front of you *or* behind your back Brooke, not really my style.' He grinned. 'But I can help in any way I can. I work as a criminal profiler, I have a degree in computing, I'm perfect for the job.'

'Hang on, why do you need a criminal profiler? No offence...' I blushed.

'He can get hold of information, like I said. He has found your friend's address already...'

'You've found Harriet?' I interrupted. 'Thank you so much!'

He nodded proudly. 'If you'll excuse me, I need to get another drink.' Billy slipped off of the sofa and towards the kitchen.

'Did I offend him?'

'No, that's just Billy, he's... he's socially awkward.' Liam chuckled.

'So, what is he going to help you with?' I prodded.

'He has been doing me favors for years, like finding out where Guedo is working and where he is going to be... but I just asked him if he could look more into the death of Britney Johnson, and mum's work...' Liam shrugged. 'I guess after talking to you I realized I shouldn't be focusing on being angry at Guedo, I should be using my resources for good and not evil.' He winked.

'Oh right, that's good!'

'Anyway, let's enjoy tonight and not worry about all that now. I have Harriet's address and we can go whenever you like.'

He leant over and placed a delicate kiss on my forehead. 'Let's get you a drink.'

After a while, more and more people began to pile into Liam's small home.

It made me happy knowing that although Liam hadn't experienced the best start to life he clearly had so many people around him that cared about him.

I had met his childhood friend and neighbor, Chris.

He was a muscular blonde guy, his smile was kind and his voice so soothing that whilst Jamie mingled with everyone, I gravitated towards him the most.

'It's nice to see Liam so happy.' Chris observed as my beautiful stranger span my equally beautiful best friend around as they danced drunkenly together to the loud music.

'Who wouldn't be happy when they're dancing with Jamie?'

'I meant with you Brooke.' He chuckled deeply. 'But yeah, she is pretty amazing.' He gawked.

'Oh, I'm not anything… but I'm glad he is happy.'

It was around one am, and I had made my way outside, allowing myself a break from the growing crowd of people and deafening music. I wondered if his neighbors were at the party and that's why there hadn't been an angry knock at the door.

I slumped myself down on the step that led into the garden room and shivered as I chugged on a cigarette and sipped what must have been my tenth glass of wine.

The skimpy dress I was wearing was not fit for being outside in the winter, but I had swapped my uncomfortable heels for a pair of slippers I had packed so at least I'd still have my toes in the morning.

I held my head up to the sky and smiled as the stars sparkled brightly into my eyes. The door creaked open and I looked down to see Liam walking towards me.

'Beautiful aren't they, the stars?' I slurred.

He laughed as he perched on the step next to me, nudging me playfully with his elbow.

'Thank you for being there for me, Liam. With my mum kicking me out and everything, you have been such a good friend, I'm so glad I met you.' Drunk Brooke was suffering from the effects of the truth serum again, but I failed to care. He looked down to the floor as I said this. His infamous frown had reappeared.

'What's wrong?' I held his hand and squeezed it. 'Billy is going to help you, everything is going to be fine. We'll find out what happened to her.'

'I know I know…' he said as he looked into my eyes once again.

'Well, what then?' I frowned back.

'Jamie was asking me how I felt about you earlier…'

I flushed crimson. 'Sorry, I don't know why she was asking you that. I haven't really told her anything about us, I promise. Not that there is much to tell…'

Crash and burn. You're bringing new meaning to that term, Brooke.

NOT NOW! GO AWAY!

He pulled the hand that I was holding up to my cold, windswept face and cupped my cheek. 'She's your best friend, why would I care whether you've told her anything about us?' he studied my face closely.

I shrugged and tilted my face into his warm hand a little bit more. 'I don't know, maybe you'd want to keep me a secret?'

'I'd want the world to know.' He smiled adoringly. My heart skipped a beat as he continued to speak. 'I don't just see you as a friend, Brooke…' he whispered.

'Oh… Really? Me too… I thought…'

He looked amused now. The worry from his face had disappeared. 'You think too much,' he laughed.

'Yes, I guess I do.'

'What would you want to do right now? Without thinking?'

'Kiss you.'

A raised her eyebrows. *Wow, you're confident when you don't think.*

Because I don't have you badgering me!

Liam pulled me close and replied with a kiss. I'd been yearning for our lips to meet again. I couldn't stop thinking about how one kiss from him could send my mind, body and soul into complete oblivion.

I'm not sure if it was from the bleak temperature or the electricity surging through my body once again but I shivered.

'Let's go in here, you're cold.' He pulled me to an upright position and waited in amusement as I steadied my spinning head.

He pushed open the door that we were sitting by and we fell into the darkness; Liam fumbled around for the light switch which dimly lit up the conservatory style room, he turned the key to lock the door and looked fiercely at me. 'Can I just say you look out of this world tonight girl.' He complimented, placing his big hands around my waist which was perfectly outlined in my tight mini dress.

'Yes, you can just say.' I giggled and tumbled forwards, causing us both to fall onto the velvet tub chair that was placed in the corner of the room. We lay on the chair laughing, our bodies tangled and my hair flailing off in all directions.

'How much have you had to drink?' He chuckled as we found our way to a seated position, he pulled me onto his lap. I shook my head in embarrassment as the last few giggles spurted out of my mouth.

Liam smiled dotingly up at me. 'I haven't stopped thinking about you, not for one second.' He confessed. His big, brown eyes seemed to light up as he spoke.

'Me neither,' I swished my hair so it fell behind my shoulders.

'You should be kissed and often, and by someone who knows how,' he breathed.

'Gone with the Wind?'

'You're getting good at this, girl,' he replied in a whisper before kissing me again, sending me to a whole other universe.

I sat up suddenly and looked around me; I was sprawled on the garden room floor wrapped in one of the blankets from the cinema room. There was a cup of orange juice with a note stuck to it placed next to me.

Morning sunshine x

I peered through the glass into the main house as I gulped down the orange juice. Most people had left, but Dale and Chris were still there, lying on the kitchen floor, hugging bottles of beer.

Wow you all look so classy. A sneered.

I heard some voices in the garden, and out of the large window on the other side of the room I could see Liam and Jamie sitting on a chipped wooden bench, having a cigarette and a cup of tea.

I wrapped myself tightly in the blanket and made my way outside to join them. The brisk morning air made my head spin.

'How do you two manage to drink so much, but look fine in the morning?' Liam questioned us as I sat on Jamie's lap, squinting in the morning sun.

'Oh why thank you Liam,' Jamie replied. 'Are you okay, B?'

'I don't know,' I said, but the voice that came out sounded like I had been possessed by a demon, and they both burst out laughing.

'All right Bob.' Jamie snorted. 'Where did you two disappear to last night anyway, did you sleep in there?' she nodded towards the garden room.

Liam was gazing at me fondly.

'Yeah, Brooke was very drunk so I thought I'd best take her somewhere quieter.'

'*Oh* take her somewhere quieter, can't you keep it in your pants for one night, fancy the host of the party leaving everyone!'

Liam laughed. 'Get your head out of the gutter, nothing like that happened!'

'Good. If you were taking advantage of my best friend I'd have to kill you.'

'Anyway you weren't complaining, you loved being left alone with all those guys eating out of the palm of your hand.' Liam rolled his eyes.

I smiled as I listened to my best friend, and my glorious stranger joking around with each other. Why couldn't life always have been this good?

'Are you feeling well enough to go to Harriet's?' Liam smiled at me. 'Bill said he would come with us.'

'I'm going to need some pain killers and a shower first.' I croaked.

'Sure thing.' He smirked.

VI

Billy, Liam and I piled into Billy's car, leaving Jamie back at the house to tidy up with Chris and Dale. She and Chris seemed to be getting on very well so she was happy for me to go.

Liam constantly leaned back from the passenger's seat to squeeze my leg or ask if I was OK. We drove past the address slowly, there didn't seem to be anyone there. Billy circled around the area again and parked a few houses up. I immediately ran to the chipped front door and knocked a few times.

'Brooke!' I heard Billy hiss from behind me. 'What are you doing?'

I frowned in confusion. 'She's my friend? I'm knocking on her door?'

'Ah, just don't say how you got his address, okay?'

'*His* address?'

'Yeah, it's her boyfriend's address. But she is registered here as well,' he explained. I starred at the tattered front door of the bungalow nervously awaiting someone to appear, hoping that it wasn't Matt.

'She's all right, she's got this.' Liam smirked at me, his eyes filled with desire.

I knocked again. 'No one is answering!'

'Well I guess we try again another day then.' Billy began to wonder back to his car.

'We're here now... let's try another way.' I demanded.

Liam cocked his head at Billy. 'She's got a point. What if her friend is in there hurt or something?'

129

Billy rolled his eyes and sighed as he walked back over to us.

Stepping back, I noticed there was a side entrance. The alley way was narrow; there was a rusty gate at the other end which looked as though it was leading into a garden. There was a window that was slightly open and I knew that was the only way of getting in.

Are you really going to break into someone's home, Brooke? You're not this person. Go home.

No, you go home, A!

This is my home; I live in your head. Surely you know that by now.

'Oh shut up,' I hissed under my breath. She was really beginning to do my head in — no pun intended.

'Liam, go look into the garden. I'm going try get in here,' I said as I gently pushed open the window.

'Are you mad?' Billy panicked.

'Yeah, she is.' Liam smirked earnestly at me again before sneaking over to the fence.

I stood on my tip-toes and looked into the open window; there was a small, somber room on the other side. I could faintly make out a bed and a chest of drawers. 'Billy,' I hissed. 'Help me up.'

The window wasn't high, but me being five foot nothing meant I couldn't quite reach with my legs without some assistance.

'I really don't think this…' he stammered.

'…You only have to help me up, you don't have to do anything else.'

'Okay, okay…' he held his hands up in surrender.

'Sorry Billy, I'm just worried about her.'

He nodded and assisted me as I hoisted myself in to the window.

'You want me to just stand out here on my own?' he complained.

I managed to get one of my legs into the room, I looked back at him. 'Come in with me then?'

He respired, his eyes darting around the road before following me in swiftly before anyone noticed us.

I swung my other leg over the window and jumped down into the room. Billy followed shortly after me, 'What about Liam?'

'Liam can look after himself,' I replied half-heartedly as I began to look around the room. I opened the drawers and rifled through them, but there was nothing — just men's underwear, socks and packs of cigarettes.

'What are you looking for?'

I shrugged. 'Just being nosy I guess; I don't know anything about Harriet's life any more. I didn't even know she had a serious boyfriend.' I wondered if I had been so wrapped up in my own stuff that I hadn't noticed the warning signs. Was Harriet in an abusive relationship and I had been to self-absorbed to see? I really hoped that wasn't the case. 'Guess we're gonna have to go out there.' I leant my ear against the bedroom door, but I couldn't hear any movement. I gestured for Billy to come with me. We crept around the half open door, I was eager to get inside.

The room was sparse, there was a worn leather sofa under a cracked window, and a table placed in the middle of the room.

Empty beer bottles, stubbed out cigarette butts and food wrappers were discarded carelessly on the bare wooden floor. I noticed that there were a few baseball bats and shovels leant against the wall. I swallowed nervously.

You're in way too deep here Brooke. I can feel it.

For once, I agreed with A.

Our attention was drawn to the back of the room where there was a notice board screwed to the wall, much like the one Mr. Daniels used to display evidence. 'This doesn't look like somewhere Harriet would live.'

'This doesn't look like somewhere *anyone* should live,' Billy replied in disgust. 'Why do I know that name?' He murmured, pointing to a photograph at the very bottom of the notice board.

I studied the man and woman in the photo. They were dressed smartly and both smiling from ear to ear.

The lady had a red circle around her and was labelled:

Rebecca Stevens-Prison

Rebecca's photo was part of a row of photographs all labelled with the same bright red marker pen.

'Britney Johnson.' I gasped, starring at the familiar name scribbled above a beautiful dark haired woman with piercing blue eyes. She had a red cross covering her face.

'What… Why…' I was gob smacked. Why in the world would Matt and Harriet have information like this pinned up in their living room? And where the hell were they?

Billy pulled out his phone and took a few photos of the board, before turning his attention elsewhere around the room. 'It really smells like weed in here,' he stated as he inspected the cramped living room some more.

I nodded as I rustled through some books and notepads that were sprawled across the sofa.

I recognized Harriet's neat handwriting.

'Billy, listen to this.' I called out to him as he began

132

investigating the kitchen area. 'Matt was told by some work mates today that seven, the person in charge, was moving abroad in July. That's what Harriet has written in this diary. Seven is the person we've been investigating at work!'

'Has she dated it?' Billy called back.

'This is the last entry; it was written almost two weeks ago.' I flicked through the other pages of the notepad, trying to make some sense of the situation in my head.

Why was Harriet talking about work matters with Matt? How did she even know about Seven, she hadn't been at work since that was announced! And Matt talking to people at *work?* Surely he didn't work in a human trafficking organization? My stomach churned at the possibility of Harriet being caught up in all of that.

I passed Billy through the kitchen area and into the back garden to see what Liam was doing, I needed some air. He was walking towards the house. 'Is she in there?'

I shook my head. 'But there's a lot of fucked up stuff in there...'

'What do you mean?'

'Stuff about Britney Johnson, and loads of other women.' His face dropped. 'Oh, god, no! There's nothing I can see with your mum's picture or name. Sorry.' I was so caught up in the confusion I had completely forgotten that I only knew Britney's name from Liam's mum's reports.

What does this all mean?

I didn't have time to ponder the answer to that question as the sound of a car pulling up on the driveway stopped me.

Without thinking I ran towards the fence, but a tall figure began to speed up the alley way towards me, as he drew closer I could see it was a very angry looking Matt. A dog barked loudly from the back of the car, I could see the silhouette of another person.

'Who the *fuck* are you?' Matt shouted.

Liam and Billy were standing by the back door, frantically waving for me to follow them, they ran back into the kitchen and I followed straight away.

Just as we reached the living room, the front door opened, and Matt strolled confidently through it.

Liam and Billy jumped behind the sofa before he could see them, but I wasn't as quick.

'I ain't gonna ask you again, who the fuck are you?'

I froze on the spot. 'Matt?' I questioned apprehensively, *you can turn this around Brooke.*

'How do you know my name?' he demanded as he walked towards me. I took a few steps backwards every time he drew closer.

'You're Harriet's boyfriend right? We met at the Christmas fair remember?' I reminded him. He looked even worse than I remembered. His eyes were sunken and tired and his skin looked grey and weathered.

'And what the fuck are you doing in my house?' he asked, pulling something from the back of his frayed jeans.

'Brooke?' Harriet's voice followed through the front door. She was holding onto the snarling German Shepherd's lead tightly, her eyes were filled with exhaustion and confusion. 'What are you doing here?'

Despite everything, I was so happy to see her.

'Oh, you're okay! Thank god!'

'Why wouldn't she be okay? What have you told her?' Matt turned angrily to Harriet.

'No, No. She hasn't told me anything! We haven't spoken,

134

that's why I'm here, I was worried about her…'

I glanced apprehensively at Harriet who was retreating backwards to the bedroom door. She stayed silent as she gripped tightly onto the metal dog lead.

Matt looked down at me sinisterly. 'Silly little bitch. Don't lie to me, Harriet would never have told you where she lived, it's too risky. You didn't tell her did you, babe?' He turned his head to face her once again. She shook her head timidly in reply.

I heard a click from behind his back.

'Matt, please don't!' Harriet pleaded as tears began to fall down her gaunt face.

Oh, god. What the hell is he going to do to me?

A was cowering sheepishly in the depths of my stomach, causing it to tie up in knots. I attempted to move as far away from the sofa as possible, not wanting Liam or Billy to get caught up in whatever was about to happen. 'Look, honestly Harriet is my friend and I found out where she lived that's all, I haven't seen her in a while so I thought I would visit her and just make sure she was okay. I'm sorry for intruding, I'll just leave. She clearly doesn't want to see me today do you?' I rambled.

'I'm sorry Brooke,' she whispered as she disappeared with the dog into the bedroom and slammed the door behind her. Even through the closed door, I could hear her loud sobs.

'Na, you can't know this address without being sorted out,' Matt threatened.

'My memory is really bad.' I laughed nervously. 'I won't even remember this address once I leave.'

'You're not going to leave,' he replied as he revealed what he had been hiding behind his back.

He has a gun!

'No!' Liam cried as he jumped out from behind the sofa,

grabbing Matt's hand and pointing the gun away from me. 'Brooke, run!'

'I'm not leaving you!' I argued as I looked around the room for anything I could use to fight Matt off. The baseball bats and shovels were too far away.

'Oh, how sweet.' Matt had struggled out of Liam's grip and before I knew it Liam was being forcefully hit on the head with the handle of the gun. He fell backwards and his head ricocheted off of the edge of the table and onto the hard floor. He let out an awfully loud cry of pain that made my heart sink.

'Brooke, run!' Liam hollered desperately as he clutched his bloody head.

Oh shit, I'm next. I tried to retreat, but before I could get anywhere Matt was pulling my hair viciously and throwing me face first up against the wall. 'Maybe I'll have some fun with you while your boyfriend watches,' he sneered.

I closed my eyes as I felt his fingers curl tightly around my hair, his fingernails scratching my scalp as he did so. My head was thrust forwards repeatedly, painfully meeting the wall each time. My vision blurred as my eyes filled with something liquid, I couldn't tell if it was blood or tears. Matt's hand moved from my hair down to my top as his rough hands slid underneath it.

'Please no,' I begged; I thought I was going to be sick.

'Get off of her!' Liam's voice roared from behind me, I felt Matt being pulled off of me and before I knew it Liam was in front of me with his arms spread wide. 'Don't shoot her, if you're gonna shoot anyone shoot me!' Liam shouted with blood now gushing down his face at a rapid rate.

'Liam…' I wept as I attempted to push him out of the way, my vision still blurred.

'You don't understand; I ain't got a choice!' Matt's voice

rumbled around the room.

I thought that was it, there was nothing I could do, Liam and I were both going to die in this crack den and that's how our tragic love story would end, before it had even started. For a split second time seemed to slow down to a halt. One last time I attempted with all of my remaining strength to push Liam away from me.

He toppled and fell sideways, just as Matt shot the gun. I felt a sharp pain in my leg and screamed as I fell to the floor, everything returned to normal speed as my mind registered what had just happened.

I had just been shot, and I was about to be killed.

The pain was unbearable, Liam — with blood still pouring out from the wound in his head — was helplessly trying to pull me into the kitchen, attempting to get me as far away from Matt as he could, tears were flooding down his bloody face.

Matt walked towards us, aiming the gun at my head.

Harriet had now emerged from the bedroom and was screaming something at Matt that I couldn't make out, everything was muffled and blurry to me.

I could just about see when Harriet flung herself across the room with some force, there was a muffled bang as she landed against the table, her body lay still on the floor.

Liam was still trying to drag me out of the house as Matt pointed the gun back towards my head, but before he could shoot there was a terrible cracking sound that even I couldn't have missed, and he fell to the floor like a rag doll.

I looked up helplessly, clearing my eyes with my hands. Billy was towering over us holding a baseball bat above his head, a crazed look filled his once kind eyes as he hit him again, and again and again.

'Stop! Billy, stop!' I tried to scream as Matt's blood splattered against my face.

Liam jumped up and grabbed the bat from Billy's hand. 'Fuck man, leave him, he's dead,' he panted.

Billy looked at the bloody bat in Liam's hand and the battered body lying on the floor by his feet and fell to his knees.

Liam dropped the bat and ran back to me, pulling his jumper off and wrapping it around my leg. 'Come on, we need to get out of here.' He wheezed as he picked me up and left the house. I was in and out of consciousness, but I could feel Liam's arms wrapped tightly around me as he carried me back to Billy's car.

I felt the cold leather of the seat on my warm body as he carefully placed me down, I faintly heard him say, 'I'll be back; I need to go get Billy.'

The next thing I remember was being driven away by Liam, his beautiful face was filled with blood and tears and his clothes soaked in what I assumed was my blood, Billy was sitting in the front and they were shouting at each other.

'What are we going to do?' Billy was crying into his hands, 'I killed a man, his dead.'

'You were saving us!' Liam was reassuring him.

I closed my eyes and drained them out.

As I opened my eyes again I was being carried into a room.

I could hear panicked voices and screams. I didn't like the noise so I closed my eyes and sang Auntie Veronica's bedtime song to calm everyone down.

The last thing I heard was Liam's desperate voice screaming for someone to help me.

48 HOURS LATER

'You scared me so much B,' Jamie said as she sat down on the bed with a tray of food for me. 'How does your leg feel?'

'My leg?' I looked at her frowning.

'You were shot...' She said slowly. I carried on looking at her with a blank expression. 'You were shot in the leg.'

I laughed at her worried expression. 'Do you think I could forget this? It hurts so much.'

'Well Neil had a friend over who knew how to treat gun shots...'

'...Who's Neil?' I interrupted.

'Oh shit, you don't know them do you?' she chuckled, 'Neil and Carlos are the most amazing men I've ever met, they seem like characters out of a film or something.'

'Someone's got a crush.' I mocked her through a mouthful of porridge. I felt famished.

'Probably married.' she shrugged, 'Anyway, I have my sights firmly set on Chris.' She blushed.

'Jamie? Are you *blushing*?'

'Should I get Liam and tell him you're awake? He's been worried sick about you B.' She ignored me.

'Does he really want to see me?'

'What do you mean?'

'I bet I look like a ghost, my hair hasn't been brushed in god knows how long *and* I stink...' I grimaced as I sniffed under my arms. 'Really badly.'

'It's better than the alternative isn't it?' she said as she took the empty bowl from me. 'Anyway, Liam worships the ground you walk on, B. Your moisturizing routine could involve smothering pigs shit on your face and he'd still think you were the most beautiful thing on this planet.'

'Can't I get up?' I asked, ignoring her slightly jealous sounding tone. I noticed some crutches and a wheel chair on the other side of the room.

'It's only been like forty-eight hours since someone *shot* you, don't you think you should wait?' she protested.

'I've been in bed for two *days*?' I exclaimed. 'I'm getting up.'

Jamie shook her head in disagreement as I attempted to pull myself to the side of the bed. I felt so weak, but I was determined to carry on as if my leg didn't feel like it was constantly on fire. 'I told Liam I would help him.' I sighed, trying one last time to swing my legs out of bed.

'I'm sure he'll understand,' she scoffed. 'Being shot is a pretty good excuse.'

After arguing back and forth Jamie finally caved in and helped me out of bed and into the wheelchair, she wheeled me to the top of the stairs and we looked down them for a second, clueless.

'We didn't think this through did we Jam?' I laughed, trying to hide how much the laugh had made me wince.

'It was your idea to get out of bed, don't blame me. Shall I just throw you down there?' She rocked the chair backwards and forwards jokingly.

'I could shuffle down on my bum, you know like we used to do as kids,' I suggested.

Jamie laughed as she slid past me and waltzed down the stairs, leaving me stranded in the hallway.

'Oh, I see how it is, just leave me I'll be fine on my own!' I called after her as she disappeared into the front room. When she reappeared again she was joined by a bewildered looking man.

'How the fuck are you even awake? Let alone trying to get

downstairs?' he laughed as he carefully pulled me out of the wheelchair and into his large, muscular arms.

'It's boring up there.' I moaned. Flinching as the movement sent a shooting pain through my leg. 'I'm Brooke, who are you?'

'No, you're a fucking hooligan,' he muttered as he carried me into the room, placing me carefully onto the sofa. 'I'm Neil, Liam's friend.'

Everyone stared at me with a mixture of disbelief and adoration as I lay back on the sofa, breathing out a huge sigh of relief.

'How are you feeling'?' Dale questioned, handing me a cigarette and lighter.

'Thanks,' I breathed as I took them from him. 'I've felt better, not going to lie.'

'I bet, there was so much blood, Chris nearly fainted when we had to clean it off the floor.' Dale laughed, rustling Chris' hair. I glanced down and noticed one part of the carpet was a lot darker than the rest, I shuddered. Chris peered up at me, clearly embarrassed. 'Sorry,' I mouthed.

At that moment the back door burst open and Liam sped through the room to kneel by my head.

'Brooke, you okay?' he gasped, but before I could answer he carried on hysterically blurting out words.

'I was so worried... why didn't anyone tell me she was awake? I've been in that room every day, I left for one fag and you wake up... I'm sorry... I didn't leave... I promise... I'm gonna look after you... I'm sorry... are you okay?'

I placed my index finger on his lips and smiled. 'I'm fine...' I pulled my finger away and replaced it with my lips, kissing him like I'd never kissed him before.

There was urgency in the kiss, like we were both silently

saying 'Thank god we didn't die!'

Everyone in the room awkwardly looked in another direction, and there were a few heaving sounds coming from Jamie, but I didn't care.

'I'm fine.' I reassured him again as I lay back down, attempting to cover the breathlessness the kiss had caused me.

'Are you sure?' he frowned as I blew smoke towards his direction. 'You shouldn't be smoking, give me that,' he ordered, trying to pull the cigarette from my fingers.

'Stop worrying,' I pleaded. 'Obviously it hurts, but at least we all got out alive...' I stopped as I said this. Studying the room, I realized Billy wasn't there. 'Where's Billy?' I whispered, not sure if I even wanted to know the answer. I closed my eyes as a memory of the fight flashed through my mind. Billy was hitting Matt again and again. I felt the blood splatter on my face and I put my hands up to wipe it off.

Liam narrowed his eyes as I done this, so I pretended that I was scratching my forehead and tried to push the memory from my mind.

'Billy's fine babe,' Liam stated as he tucked a strand of my matted, greasy hair behind my ear.

'Is Matt still there?' I hissed, glaring up at Dale as I noticed him watching us talk.

Liam turned his back to Dale and the others and shook his head. 'His been dealt with. You've missed a lot while you've been out. I'll fill you in I promise, but when you're better.'

'Tell me now. I'm going to worry otherwise,' I ordered. There was a knock at the door, Liam jumped up and hurried over to it.

'Liam bought in the big guns,' Dale muttered.

I was briefly confused by this comment, but when the man

walked in I could see exactly what he meant. He was huge, his muscles bulged through his tight, black top and he towered over everyone in the room.

Neil stood up and greeted him straight away. He was only slightly smaller than him in height, but was still immensely huge compared to the rest of us who had all evolved like normal human beings.

Liam knelt on the floor next to me once again and Neil and The Hulk sat down next to each other at the dining table. 'So, basically after the whole thing at Matt's, I called Neil and Carlos.' Liam began his explanation, nodding in their direction as if he was thanking them. 'I explained everything, they sorted you out with a doctor first of all, that's all I cared about, and then they went back to the house to clean up. Er, Matt's body is at the bottom of the Thames, and yeah I think that's it on that whole situation?' He turned to Dale and Chris as they nervously glanced towards each other, seemingly shocked by this information.

'Where have you two been?' I glared at them inquisitively. Chris tilted his head towards me as I spoke like a dog listening to the word treat.

'We were here when you all came back from Harriet's, and you were bleeding out everywhere, we left when the doctor came, which was quite quickly so we didn't really know what the hell had happened. We went to get some supplies for everyone to make ourselves useful. I guess we were gone a few hours. When we came back we cleaned up the blood, but we didn't know someone had been *killed?*' Jamie was sitting next to him cross legged, she stroked his shoulder gently as he placed his head in his hands.

Dale's face was turning redder by the second, but he didn't say a word.

Liam looked at them both warily. 'I guess we missed a few minor details out.'

'You think?' Chris groaned as he clutched on to the hand that Jamie had placed on his large shoulder. I guessed that Chris had been Jamie's shoulder to cry on whilst I had been recovering, it was nice to see her spending time with someone so kind and sweet for a change. I shot her an approving smile as she gazed at me worryingly. Her eyes were sunken and tired.

'Liam, the amount of shit I have done for you over the years and you couldn't even trust me with this?' He added quietly.

'You prick! A few minor details? We're part of a fucking murder cover up! Why didn't you tell us?'

Dale finally broke his silence. His voice bellowed through my pounding head and I winced.

'I wasn't thinking straight, I just wanted to make sure Brooke was okay…' Liam frowned. His bruised head looked as though it had been stitched back together again. Chris nodded as if Liam's explanation was enough, pulling Jamie closer to him and placing a gentle kiss on her forehead.

'Are *you* okay?' I eyed Liam, ignoring Dale's outburst completely.

'I'm fine, Brooke. Don't worry about me. It's just a few stitches.' He looked exhausted.

'Harriet?' I whispered as I remembered her body flying across the room. 'Do I even want to know what happened to Harriet?'

'Fuck this!' Dale stormed out of the room.

Neil and Carlos shared a bemused look, but stayed silent. They didn't need to speak; their presence alone was enough.

Liam stroked my arm softly. 'Harriet wasn't there when they went back, the dog was still in the bedroom but she wasn't there.

144

We took the dog to an animal shelter yesterday, said we found him on the street.'

I smiled lovingly at him. Even with all of this going on he had found the time to make sure Harriet's dog was okay. 'So hopefully that means she is as far away from all of this as possible. We have tried calling her, but no luck so far.' Liam continued filling me in, I felt too exhausted to even grunt out an answer. 'Billy's fine, he just wanted to be alone for a few days. Carlos is my mum's old friend, the one who found me at home when I was younger, we work together now at his garage.'

I nodded, remembering when Liam had first told me the story about his mum.

'Neil is Rebecca's brother; it turns out that mum and Rebecca were quite good friends, they worked together around the same time…'

I held up my hand to stop Liam talking. 'Who is Rebecca? Or am I suffering from memory loss too?'

'Rebecca's name was pinned up on a board in Matt's house, Billy had photos of it on his phone. And I remembered that I'd read about her before, I think I told you that? She was in a car crash and arrested.

Neil never mentioned that they were related because she's in prison and they don't speak.'

I closed my eyes as Liam mentioned Matt and Billy; I couldn't shake the memory of it from my mind.

'I didn't know what good bringing up Georgina would do for Liam either,' Neil added in his profound voice.

'What does your sister have to do with Liam's mum disappearing?' I was trying so hard to piece together all of the information I was being given, but all I could think about was closing my heavy eyes and falling asleep in the safety of Liam's arms.

'Rebecca was put in prison for life for the attempted murder of Guedo. She was friends with Georgina, Georgina was dating Guedo, there was some sort of argument in a car, I don't know, I'm a bad brother and I didn't go to the trials, I thought she'd done it...' He coughed and shuffled in his chair. Carlos shot him a reassuring look, but still didn't speak.

'I didn't know this until yesterday, my mum keeping reports on the crash makes more sense now. That was in 1994, the year mum died again,' Liam whispered.

Then I remembered, the notebook I had found in Harriet and Matt's house mentioned something about Seven moving abroad.

'Where is the notebook I found in the house?' I ordered.

Liam shrugged. 'Billy probably has it, why?'

'I found Harriet's notes, it looked like Matt had been telling her stuff... stuff that is classified information... or should be. We have been investigating an organization at work, I shouldn't be saying any of this but... well the person in charge, we think, is called Seven. In Harriet's notes it said that Seven was due to move abroad soon... what if we have the answers to this whole organization just sitting in that notebook? What if Matt worked for them? What if Harriet and Matt knew what was going on? What if Guedo is involved somehow? What if *your mum* is involved somehow?'

Everyone remained silent for a while after that. I could see the concerned expressions painted on their faces and I wondered if they too felt like we had suddenly bitten off a lot more than we could chew.

That night Liam and I lay silently on our backs in his capacious king-sized bed.

The last I had checked, Chris and Jamie were snuggled up in the cinema room watching a film. Carlos and Neil had walked down to the local pub to 'discuss things'. Whatever that was supposed to mean. And Dale was MIA. We had all dispersed into our different corners of life to deal with the revelation of our earlier conversation.

My mind was buzzing with possibilities, surely it wasn't all one big coincidence?

I felt as though I was Alice falling down the rabbit hole, and I was about to fall flat on my arse with a ton of problems waiting for me. But in that moment all of it seemed irrelevant because I was alive, and so was Liam.

'I'm so glad you're okay Brooke.' He felt for my hand in the darkness and our fingers interlocked. 'I don't know what I would have done if you'd been killed and I hadn't got to tell you how I feel...'

I'll leave you two to it. A saluted as she disappeared into the depths of my mind. She was too exhausted to stay.

'I want you.' He said in a whisper. But I heard him loud and clear. I gasped at those three small words. Those three small words which held so much meaning.

'You do?' I tilted my head to face him, it was the only part of my body that had any energy left in it to be able to move.

'You're perfect. Of course I do.'

I looked back up to the ceiling and exhaled deeply.

'You're tired.'

'Very observant.'

He chuckled. 'Not too tired for sarcasm I see?'

'Never.' I yawned.

'Sleep in here tonight?'

'I couldn't move even if I wanted to, Liam.' I replied as my eyelids grew heavier and I gave in to the exhaustion.

147

VII

Jamie had called into work explaining that I'd 'undergone emergency surgery' and wouldn't be in work for a while, all whilst I was unconscious after the incident at Matt's. It was now the Thursday after, eleven days had been and gone since the traumatizing ordeal and none of us were coping any better.

Chris and Jamie had resorted to having annoyingly loud sex every night in Liam's spare bedroom. I wasn't sure why she didn't go home, but I guessed she wanted to stay wherever I was to keep an eye on me.

It meant I could spend more alone time with my beautiful, curly haired... well I hadn't figured out what he was at that point, but he certainly wasn't a stranger any more.

Dale was still ignoring everyone, and Billy was staying well away. I can't say I blamed them.

I'd received a call from Mr. Daniels asking if I was well enough to attend a meeting with him to discuss my sick leave. After receiving a thorough once over from the dodgy doc, who seemed to think I was recovering well-despite what my throbbing leg and my gut instinct were telling me — I'd agreed to go into work.

I thought it was the perfect opportunity to do some fishing and see if any more progress had made on the 'Seven' situation.

'So I guess that just about covers it...' I said as I shifted in my chair, unnerved by Mr. Daniels' intense gaze.

I'd explained my made-up illness to him, the one I had rehearsed a million times with Liam and Jamie the night before.

'Appendicitis? And you collapsed at the top of the stairs from the pain?' He raised his eyebrows, studying the crutches I had placed next to me. I held my breath in anticipation. 'Sounds like you were very unlucky; I trust you are on the mend?'

I breathed a huge sigh of relief that he seemed satisfied with my lie. 'Yes, I feel much better than I was thank you. The scar where they removed my appendix is very sore, and my leg is still swollen and painful from the fall. But better.'

I knew the lie was slightly extensive. But I also knew that taking as much sick leave as I was hoping for because of a broken leg wouldn't be accepted.

My appendix had been removed, and I did have a scar, it just didn't happen quite as recently as I'd let on.

There's medical records he can check. This is a stupid idea.

My stomach clenched. A was probably right.

We'll cross that bridge when we come to it.

Maybe you should just jump off that bridge when you come to it.

Maybe you're right.

'Take as much time as you need, I can email over any work I need you to do and you can complete it at home. Nyema and the others will just have to take on more of a work load here. She is trustworthy enough for now.' Mr. Daniels said matter-of-factly as he swiftly began signing the relevant paperwork.

Sliding it towards me and handing me the pen, I noticed he seemed slightly distracted. I gulped as I signed the paper and handed it back to him.

Now or never, Brooke. 'Sir, do you have a minute before I

go?' I asked timidly.

'Of course, what can I help you with Brooke?' He sounded polite, but the expression on his face was anything but.

I looked shyly down at my hands so that I didn't have to see his will-somebody-get-this-girl-out-of-my-office look. 'I have a friend; he knows someone who used to work here. Her name was Georgina...'

I looked up at him through my eyelashes, his expression changed immediately. *He remembers her.* I was shocked. 'You knew her?'

'Yes, I know who Georgina is,' he replied sternly, leaning back in his towering chair. 'Who's your friend?'

I was confused by his questioning; why did it matter who I was friends with? 'Er, it's her son, Sir. I was just wondering what happened the day Britney Johnson was shot because that weekend his mum, Georgina, went missing. It just all seems really coincidental doesn't it?' I winced as I let my words run away from me.

Coincidental? You sound like you're accusing him of something.

Maybe I am!

He looked at me for a few seconds before replying, as if he was contemplating the correct thing to say.

'I wasn't head of the department then; I hadn't been here for very long, this was what? twenty years ago?

'Yes, twenty-five years ago sir, it happened when my friend was four.' I answered in the same matter-of-fact tone he had been addressing me with throughout the whole meeting.

He shook his head. 'Well how am I supposed to remember something that happened twenty-five years ago Brooke?' he looked bewildered, like a deer in headlights.

'Sorry, Sir, I just wanted to know, I'm sure you can understand he just wants to find out about his mum?'

'Aren't you a little young to be hanging around with a twenty-eight-year-old anyway Brooke?'

I was becoming angered with his rude questioning, I'd never been around him alone for long enough to realize what an unpleasant man he was.

'I'm twenty-four Sir, not really,' I replied bluntly.

He stood up and walked towards the window.

'That bench over there, night after night you sit there with that rugged boy.'

I was thrown by this comment. 'Yeah, that's my friend?'

'I don't want my employees to be seen having friends like *that*,' he remarked. His comment reminded me of how snobby my mother could be, and this instantly put me in defense mode. 'I'm guessing you speak to him about topics from work then, if he is asking about his mum and Britney?'

I folded my arms and glared at him crossly. 'Well no actually, because most of what I know is about an ongoing investigation so I couldn't talk about them even if I wanted to.'

Whoa Brooke, remember your place!

No, you remember your place A.

I watched her smugly as she retreated back into the pit of my stomach where she would stay most of the time now.

See sometimes I can shut you down!

He sneered at me and walked back to his desk, standing over me as if he was attempting to be intimidating. 'Don't give me that bull, Brooke.'

'It's not sir, it's the truth.' I looked up at him, making eye contact to show him that he doesn't scare me in the slightest, even though he really did.

'I really want to pass my apprenticeship and do this job, and If I was walking around talking about classified information to random people then I wouldn't have much of a chance would I?'

'He's probably just using you for information, you're young and vulnerable, he will drop you as soon as he realizes you don't know anything.' He sneered at me.

I was astounded at how this conversation had panned out, I couldn't believe I had been working for such an arrogant man and not even realized it.

'Don't know anything about what, Sir?' I grabbed my crutches and slowly stood up, attempting to act as confident as I possibly could in that moment.

He leaned in close to me, his breath reeked of coffee and tobacco. 'Sometimes, Brooke, people are too clever for their own good and they dig a little too deeply, and these people need to learn that they are playing a very dangerous game.' I could see that he was attempting to sound menacing, but it came across as more of a panic.

What is he scared of? 'Are you threatening me, sir?' I glared at him.

'Of course not, Brooke.'

'Sir, do you know who Guedo Altair is?'

I studied his face looking for a reaction — and I definitely got one. His eyes grew large and his face turned crimson.

'I suggest you take this leave of absence as of today and when you return to work these questions and silly accusations will have stopped.'

Oh good, I still have a job.

'And maybe rethink who you are befriending before somebody ends up getting hurt.' He added. His eyes jolted to his mobile buzzing on the desk. I noticed it was an unknown number.

Seizing my chance to make a swift exit, I retrieved my bag and left, as fast as my crutches and excruciatingly painful leg would take me. 'Hello? Yes... I'm dealing with it...' I heard him say as I hurried down the corridor. I kept hobbling as fast as I could until I was in the safety of Neil's car.

'How did it go?' Neil eyed me as he took my crutches and placed them on the back seat.

I turned to face him slowly and tears started uncontrollably rolling down my cheeks.

'Shit, that bad?'

'Brooke!' Liam greeted me as Neil opened the door, but his expression soon changed as he saw mine. 'What's wrong?' Neil shook his head as a warning to not pry, but he ignored him. 'Brooke? What happened?'

'I don't think we should do this anymore.' I sighed as he held onto my shoulders.

'Do what?' he questioned, a wave of disappointment crashed across his face.

'I want to help you find out what happened to your mum, but he knows who you are. I can't let you get hurt,' I spluttered out. He led me into the living room and helped me sit down. I was getting sick of not being able to get around on my own. I really wanted to put my headphones in, go for a run and block the whole world out.

'Who is gonna hurt me?' he asked, his eyes scanning my face frantically.

'Mr. Daniels, I think he knows something,' I whispered.

Liam didn't say anything, he just pulled me towards his warm body and wrapped his arms around me.

'B, are you okay?' Jamie frowned as she barged through the door wrapped in just a blanket.

'Does everyone just live here now?' I laughed half-heartedly.

Liam shrugged. 'I don't mind, it's nice having everyone here. Although I wish you two would stop using my spare room as a sex dungeon.'

Jamie flushed as Chris followed her into the room wearing a pair of low hanging jogging bottoms and nothing on top. His blonde hair was extremely messy and hung over his baby blue eyes, I could see what Jamie was attracted to, especially as I lowered my gaze to his toned stomach.

He kissed her on the cheek and slapped her behind cheekily.

Jamie giggled, I had never seen her like this around a boy before. It was so nice.

'Yeah. I guess I should probably go home. Are you going to return home anytime soon?' she frowned at me again.

'Not while she's still suffering with her leg, I need to look after her.' Liam insisted as he sat down next to me.

'*She* can answer.'

'I'm fine. And I'm fine staying here.' I was more than fine when I was with Liam.

'Don't lie to me, what's going on?' she insisted as she pulled the blanket tighter around her petite physique. I knew she would gather that something was wrong soon or later — she could read me like a book.

'She's fine she just needs to rest don't you?' Liam tried to save me from the third degree, but Jamie wasn't having it.

'...I wasn't asking you, Liam. I was asking *her*,' Jamie snapped loudly.

Chris widened his eyes at me and slid past Jamie towards the kitchen, not before planting another kiss on her now scrunched up face. 'That's my cue to leave,' I heard him mutter as he strolled away.

'It's just my boss, he said some things to me today and it upset me that's all. All I'm saying is the name Daniel is bad luck.' I joked in an attempt to lessen her worry.

Jamie smiled. 'I hear you there sister.' Liam looked at both of us with a confused expression on his face. 'Long story,' Jamie nodded at him. 'Your middle name isn't Daniel is it?'

My surroundings were dark and misty; the owl's calls echoed through the gaps between the trees and the stars glistened brightly. The light of the moon was reflecting magically as if the trees were made from pure glass.

My heart was drumming loudly against my chest. A rush of cold wind blew past me, blowing my long, hair with it. A chill travelled down my spine as if someone had just walked over my grave.

Then I realized someone did, I did.

I looked down and there I was, my name carved into a grey, marble slab. A twig cracked behind me and I turned around to see Mr. Daniels towering over me.

I tried to run, but I fell backwards onto the grave, mud started to seep over my legs. I noticed that there were figures slowly walking towards me as I sank lower.

The figures had blurred faces, but I could see that it was my mum, dad and the twins, Jamie, Liam and Mr. Daniels all looking down at me. A voice in my head was saying *hold out you hand.* I reached out and Liam grabbed me, as he pulled me up, everyone else disappeared. It was just Liam and I; standing in the middle of the moonlit forest.

'Brooke...' Liam started to speak in the most magical voice. But slowly his face begun to melt away, his voice became deep and gruff and drowned out by my bloodcurdling screams.

I sat up in a cold sweat; it had been a long time since I'd had a nightmare that bad — but it didn't compare in the slightest to the sleep paralysis and night terrors I'd suffered with as a child. Thankful that I could sit up, I looked around the room. Liam was sprawled out next to me, fast asleep. His brown curly hair was veering off in all directions, his nose flared slightly as he breathed in and out.

I sat there for several minutes, thinking about nothing but my confusing conversation with Mr. Daniels. 'Brooke?' I looked down at Liam's sleepy eyes gazing up at me. 'You okay?'

'Yes, I just had a bad dream.'

'I've been thinking.' He yawned.

'Did it hurt?' I giggled childishly, thinking back to all of the times my dad had aimed that joke at my mum and how it never received a laugh, not once.

Miserable bitch.

'Hey!' He nudged me playfully. Look I don't want this affecting your job…'

But before he could finish I snapped at him. 'Whatever you're about to say just save it. I'm sick of people thinking that I'm not capable.'

Because you're not, Brooke. You're useless. 'Oh, go away!' I shouted. I glanced down at Liam's confused expression as I realized I'd said that out loud.

Well it was only a matter of time before he found out you have a screw lose.

'Brooke?'

'I'm sorry. It's just the dream, I think I'm still half asleep…' I lied, hoping that his sleepiness would ensure he accepted whatever I told him.

'Come here.'

He nuzzled into my neck and wrapped his arms loosely over me.

Thank god for that.

The anxiety inside of me had been bubbling away in my stomach since Mr. Daniels and I had our run in.

I knew it was only a matter of time before the emotions came falling out of me, it always happened one way or another.

157

I really need to go back to counseling again.
I made a mental note; I couldn't keep avoiding it forever.
Liam sighed and kissed the back of my neck through my
hair. 'Get some sleep girl.'

I woke up the next morning with Liam's arm still wrapped
around me. The bright light from the window lit up the room. I
looked at Liam, still sleeping. His warm breath was blowing
against my face. I giggled as it tickled me, he stirred and woke
up.

    'Sorry.' I laughed. 'I didn't mean to wake you up.'

    'What's so funny?' he asked grumpily, rubbing his eyes with
his free hand and squinting in the light. I grinned at him.

    'What?' he smiled back at me.

    'Nothing.'

    Oh, everything.

VIII

We walked into the square, grey room. I clung onto my crutches tightly.

'It's fine,' Liam reassured me. 'Don't be scared.'

'Of course she's going to be bloody scared, idiot,' Jamie argued.

'Now, now children.' Neil rolled his eyes.

The truth is I wasn't scared at all; I was just in so much pain that I thought if I let go of Liam or the crutch I would never be able to get back up again. But if they thought I was scared, I'd rather them believe that than worry about me even more than they already did.

Liam hadn't left my side for the past few days and they were adamant that I should have just stayed in bed.

We followed Neil's lead as he sat down at a large metal table in the corner of the brightly lit room, squeezing onto a bench on one side of the table.

Thank god I can be close to Liam.

I studied the room cautiously as we waited, there were ten other benches placed around the room and each one was filled with people waiting just like us. I could sense the despairing mood of every single person, waiting longingly for their loved ones to come out from behind the door just to see them for a short period of time.

After what seemed like an age, the heavy, grey door clunked open and the guard started to let the prisoners into the room. They were all wearing grey tracksuits with yellow bibs placed over the top.

Right at the back of the line was a skinny, fatigued looking lady. She had brown, wiry hair and her skin was wrinkled and pale.

Rebecca.

She looked up as the guard pointed to our table. Her eyes seemed to light up when she spotted Neil. She slowly made her way towards us. I tensed up with nerves, but Jamie and Liam seemed fine.

'Rebecca,' Liam said confidently as she sat down, he held out his hand that I wasn't clinging onto for her to shake. She didn't acknowledge his reached out hand so he put it back under the table.

'Who are you?' she asked in a croaky voice, leaning back in her chair and crossing her arms. 'And Neil, it's been a while, what do *you* want?'

The moment of joy caused by seeing people seemed to have passed just as quickly as it had come.

'The truth.' Liam remained calm and collected, clearly not put off by her rudeness. 'The truth about Guedo.'

Rebecca rolled her eyes. 'Like telling a few kids the truth is going to help me, Neil, who are these kids?'

'Well these *kids* know a lot more about Guedo than most people, he killed my mum so you start talking.' Liam lowered his voice.

Neil nodded at her. 'They are fine, Rebecca, just help us yeah?'

Rebecca stared suspiciously at us, looking Liam up and down before sitting forwards and putting her frail arms on the table. 'Okay, what do you want to know?' Her eyes jolted around the room, looking for anyone who might have been listening.

'How do you know Guedo?' Jamie piped up.

'How do I know Guedo?' she sniggered sarcastically. 'I wish I'd never met the bastard'

Neil exhaled heavily. 'I knew this would be a waste of time. You've never told me anything so why would you tell them.'

Rebecca's sunken eyes grew wide as Neil spoke. 'I never told you anything because you never come to see me Neil,' she murmured. Neil shot her an apologetic look; I wondered why they had grown so far apart. 'I'll tell you, you've come all of this way,' she continued. 'I worked as an NCA officer with my friend Georgina, who I'm guessing is your mum?' She glanced at Liam as she said this; he nodded in reply. 'Okay this little visit makes sense now.'

I could feel Liam's body tensing up with every word she spoke.

'We worked there for a few years, we were really good friends, then she started dating Guedo. I told her right from the start he was bad news, she kept skipping work, would go missing for days at a time…'

I glanced sideways and watched helplessly as Liam's face dropped in despair. All of this time he had thought that his mum was working nights and overtime to provide a better life for them, when really she was leaving him alone to go off with her abusive boyfriend.

Rebecca and Georgina's situation seemed to resemble my current one with Harriet. Apart from we'd taken care of her abusive boyfriend for her. My mind wondered to where Harriet could be, but I knew this wasn't the time or place. I needed to be there for Liam. I squeezed his hand as I didn't know what I could say to him in that moment to make anything better. He didn't say a word as he carried on listening to Rebecca's story, holding back the tears.

'…We were all really worried about her. We were working a big child trafficking case at work, it was traumatizing and I don't know if that got to her, with you being so young and all. I popped round a few times, when you were really little actually, tried to talk her out of seeing Guedo. I told her she wasn't acting like herself, leaving her little one home alone and not showing up for work. It was like she was brainwashed.

Anyway, one day Guedo overheard me telling her to leave him; he pleaded with me that if I got to know him I would realize that he wasn't all that bad.'

Neil shuffled in his seat. 'Rebecca, why didn't you tell me any of this? I knew George, I could have helped.'

'What good were you going to do? You were drugged up and in your little gang at that time Neil, if it wasn't for Carlos you'd be dead in a ditch somewhere,' she snapped. Neil didn't reply, he just looked down at the table shamefully. I felt sorry for him, it must have been terrible visiting his sister when she'd been behind bars for so many years. She looked so different to when she had first been put away, even I could tell the difference in her and I'd only seen old photographs.

'*Anyway,*' Rebecca continued. 'I agreed to go to lunch with them. I drove us to the local pub and we had some food there, he was pleasant enough and I thought maybe I'd overreacted a bit; maybe she was just acting like a woman madly in love. After a few hours I got back into the car to drive us home, I started to feel really weird half way and insisted I needed to pull over. I was dizzy, felt sick and my vision was blurry. I couldn't find anywhere to pull over and was begging for Georgina to help me, when I turned around to the back seat she wasn't there.'

Liam frowned. 'She wasn't in the car the whole time? How

could you not know, I don't get it?'

Rebecca sighed. 'I don't know what happened, I don't know where she went, I could have sworn she was in the car with us when we left. Guedo told me he'd spiked my drink so obviously the effects had already began taking place in the pub. The next thing I remember he was grabbing hold of the steering wheel and we were veering off of the road into a tree.

I was arrested for driving under the influence and he later made a statement that I'd driven into the tree on purpose because we were arguing. His statement was some bullshit about how he had told me he was going to leave me for another woman and I said that we would both die before that happened.' A tear filled her tired eyes, but she wiped it away before it could even fall. 'People believed the story, that we were a *couple*. Of course there was CCTV of us leaving together.'

'And mum wasn't in the CCTV footage?' Liam queried.

Rebecca shook her head. 'They only showed the footage of us leaving in the trial, and it was just Guedo and I, she was nowhere to be seen.'

'Do you remember what date this was?' I piped in.

'Of course, it was Thursday 1st December, 1994,' Rebecca stated matter-of-factly.

'The day before…' I began.

'The day before Britney was murdered?' Rebecca finished my sentence. 'I know, I thought that was weird as well. It was like Guedo was tying up any lose ends before…'

The guard walked past our table and Rebecca's face changed to a friendly smile right on queue. 'Oh that's so lovely darling, I'm so happy your exams went well, I'm so proud…' The smile dropped as soon as he walked away. She paused, studying our shocked expressions intensely.

'Before what?' Liam breathed, his hand was shaking uncontrollably in my grasp. I think mine was too.

Rebecca shrugged. 'I really don't know what he was up to. I don't know what he was planning for George either...' There was a long moment of silence as we all took in what she had just said. 'He is sick' Rebecca added bluntly. 'All he cares about is getting what he wants, and he will do anything to get it.'

Liam fidgeted in his seat and pulled my hand closer onto his lap.

'Five minutes left of visiting time,' the guard boomed from across the room. He was looking at our table suspiciously so I began to smile at Rebecca attempting to look as though I had known her for more than twenty minutes.

'Do you have any idea what happened to my mum, any idea at all?' Liam pleaded.

Rebecca shook her head. 'I'm sorry, I know you thought I'd have all the answers but I really don't. If she stayed with him, then she's more than likely dead honey.' My state of constant shock was only getting worse as I listened to Rebecca's story.

What are you doing, Brooke? You need to forget about this boy and go home.

I was sitting in a prison speaking to a woman who had been convicted for attempted murder, my leg still had a very painful *bullet wound* in it, and somehow my friend was linked to a human trafficking organization. But none of those things came close to how bad the thought of leaving Liam and going home made me feel. I was in too deep, not even A could talk me out of this one.

The guard began to walk over to us. 'We will do everything we can prove your innocence Miss Stevens.' I smiled at her, realizing Liam was too choked up to say anything else.

'Well I won't hold my breath, but thank you. Just please be

careful.' She nodded to Neil, who nodded back slowly, before standing up and making her way back out of the room to her cell.

I felt an overwhelming sense of sadness for her.

'You're quiet…' I turned to Jamie.

'This is all fucked up, we are not having anything more to do with this. End of.' She jolted up in her seat and made her way towards the exit, swiftly followed by Neil.

'Liam? We need to go.' I glanced at the guard who was impatiently tapping his foot as people left the room.

'She's right, Brooke. You're having nothing more to do with this, or me.'

'What?' I glared at him as he helped me back onto my crutches.

'End of.'

'No, not end of!' I hobbled after him as he followed Jamie and Neil out of the prison.

No, No, No. He doesn't mean this. I can't stay away!

'Yes Brooke, end of!'

'NO!' I shouted as we fell out into the car park.

I received some disproving looks from people getting into their cars, but for once I didn't care.

'I don't appreciate both of you speaking to me like I'm a child. I can make my own decisions and if I want to be with Liam and all of his baggage then I will!'

Jamie starred at me, stunned. Neil slumped down into the driver's seat of his Range Rover with an amused look on his face.

Liam walked towards me, eyes as wide and intense as ever.

'You want to be with me?'

'And all of your baggage.' I repeated, my breath fastening as my leg throbbed along with my heart. My arms were shaking as I attempted to balance on the crutches.

'You want to be with me?' Liam repeated again.

'Yes Liam I want to bloody be with you!' I replied angrily.

This was not how I imagined this moment going down.

Liam stepped towards me some more and scooped me into his arms, kissing me so passionately that I nearly fainted there and then.

'Oh for god sake.' Jamie remarked as she climbed into the back seat.

Of course the most romantic moment of your life would be in a prison car park. A sniggered. But the nerves in my stomach had diminished, so I knew she was happy for me really.

Liam pulled his face away and looked down at me dotingly. His breath was fast and so was mine.

'You sure?'

'Don't make me say it again.' I breathed.

'As you wish.' Liam grinned.

I knew that was probably a romantic quote from a love story that I should have recognized, but I didn't have time to think about it as I blinked and he was kissing me once again.

IX

THE LAST TIME MY LIFE WAS NORMAL

'I think you should acknowledge your accomplishments a bit more, don't you?'

'My accomplishments?' I queried. 'None spring to mind.'

'If you had to name one accomplishment from your whole life, what would it be?'

Dr Daw leant forwards in her chair. Today she was wearing a very expensive looking Chanel necklace and matching earring set. Her hair, as always, was scooped up to a perfectly placed diamante clip on top of her head.

I'd always wondered if Dr Daw ever let loose, I knew her name was Roxanne and ever since watching the film Moulin Rouge when I was younger, I couldn't get it out of my head that Dr Daw was actually a prostitute in the red-light district, and you know, she'd just got a degree in counselling as something on the side.

But there I was again, making unreal scenarios up in my head so that I didn't have to face reality — this is something she had told me I had a habit of doing.

It was fast approaching Easter time, the weather was warmer and the sun was shining for longer, but I felt as though I couldn't escape from the darkness.

It had been nearly three weeks since the incident at Matt's house and I was still suffering severely from the trauma of it all, both mentally and physically.

As I sat across from Dr Daw I wanted to blurt out everything that had happened. I wanted to tell her how scared I was and how much pain I was in. I wanted to explain the nightmares I'd been having every night and how I couldn't close my eyes without experiencing flashbacks of Billy repeatedly smashing Matt's skull.

Above all, I wanted to explain how it was all worth it because I was deeply, dangerously and unconditionally in love. But instead, I just answered her routine questions and lied through my teeth about everything.

I had worn the baggiest jogging bottoms I could find so that the swollen wound on my leg would be hidden well. I was still limping and my leg was severely scarred from where the dodgy doc had cut out the bullet.

This meant that I had to invent a story about falling over in a pair of heels and being impaled by a broken metal fence. It was easy to spin that story to my family, with whom I had been speaking to on the odd occasion. As soon as I told them it had happened whilst I was drunk my mum saw that as a perfect opportunity to lecture me on my life choices and the dangers of alcohol. I had practiced my 'I'm okay' smile in the mirror a million times before meeting with Dr Daw that day.

'Probably my job,' I replied after a while of mulling over possible accomplishments I could think of. There weren't many at all.

'Okay, yes your job is a huge accomplishment, all those years of university with your anxiety, you got through it and now you're training in a field you love.'

Love is a strong word. I thought, but I nodded and smiled in agreement.

'What about your relationships? You've managed to keep the same best friend for your whole life, that's admirable. And you waited to get a boyfriend that truly values who you are, you didn't settle for anything less than you deserve.' She complimented, which made me quite uncomfortable.

I wondered if anyone had the answer to what you were supposed to do and where you were supposed to look when someone paid you a compliment.

'My friends convinced me that I should talk to my mum again, said life is too short and all that.' I stated, changing the subject.

In reality there had been many arguments with Jamie and Liam, they had both drilled into me that I needed to be on speaking terms with my family.

'B, you were shot for fuck sake!' Jamie had shouted at me, 'if that doesn't make you want to see your family then what will?' So that's really what happened, my friends had convinced me.

'My mum took my apologizing and wanting to be in contact again, as a sign of 'change' and as much as I hated seeing her again, it's really nice to see the twins and my dad.'

'You said the word change with some disgust then, I'm just wondering, do you not see change as a good thing?' Dr Daw questioned insightfully as always.

'I don't think change is a bad thing, I just don't think I've changed,' I retorted bluntly.

'It's been a few weeks since our last session, has anything changed since then?' She inquired in her soft, reassuring voice. She had this great skill of making it sound like she really truly wanted to know the answer to every question she asked. I wondered as I examined her face, if she was mentally making a shopping list for later, or if she was wondering what to have for *dinner and that like most people, she really wasn't interested in the answer to her question at all.*

Obviously, an immense amount had changed, but I couldn't express it all to her. So I told her the parts that I was allowed to speak about.

'We spend a lot of time together all of us. Jamie, Chris, Liam and I. So that's changed, I have a better group of friends now,' I replied.

I wasn't lying there; I liked my new social life. Liam and I spent a lot of time at his house with the usual gang.

'But I think my mum thinks I've changed as a person, when really I've just toned myself down around her, to be the version of me she can tolerate, because quite frankly I've had enough arguments with her to last a lifetime and I cannot be bothered to deal with any more now.'

Dr Daw nodded, and wrote some notes in her book, before closing it and leaning back into her armchair. 'But what I'm worried about is the fact that you have to tone yourself down for others, you should be authentically you and nothing else. Is there anyone you can be the real Brooke with?'

I thought about it for a second and sighed, it was a good question.

'I mean who is the real Brooke really though? For my mum, no, I could never be myself, whatever that is. Around my best friend I'm the quiet one, the one that agrees with what she says and does what she wants to do, around my auntie I'm still the little vulnerable girl who needs looking after...'

I stopped as I thought about who I really was. I wasn't expecting to get so deep and meaningful in this session.

'And your boyfriend, you haven't mentioned who you can be when you're around your boyfriend?' She inquired.

I thought back to all of the times that Liam and I had spent alone, and how confident and alive I felt, I couldn't stop myself from smiling.

'Ah,' Dr Daw grinned. 'I like him for you, it's not often we see our Brooke crack a smile.' She winked.

'I suppose he brings the best out in me, as cliché as that sounds.

I mean, I don't have better manners, or a better sense of maturity, or make better life decisions or whatever else it is that my mother and this world expect of me.' I paused as Dr Daw picked up her glass of water and took an annoyingly loud slurp.

'But he doesn't seem to care about all of that stuff, that's not important to him.' I continued. 'He makes me want to dance on tables, hug strangers, take risks...' I smiled. 'He makes me want to live and not just survive, which as you know, I've never done. I've spent my whole life on auto pilot, just surviving and getting through every shitty thing that comes my way and acting exactly how I was always expected to act. I've never truly lived.'

It was only then that I realized how many years of my life I had wasted.

And in that second I wanted to run out of that room and straight into Liam's arms.

As I walked out of the waiting room, feeling like I could hold my head a little higher, I heard Daniel's voice call out after me. 'Sorry, can't stop, I have a thing.' I shouted as I rushed out of the door as fast as my newly patented hobble would take me. Maybe I shouldn't hold my head too high, I thought. I was still treating Daniel like he didn't exist anymore.

As I brushed my teeth in Liam's dimly lit bathroom, I reflected on everything that had transpired over the last couple of months. I glanced at my reflection in the cracked mirror above the sink. It's almost as though you could see it in my eyes, I defiantly wasn't the same girl I used to be, and that was a fact I was glad of.

I noticed that Liam was leaning against the doorframe observing me as I carried out my bedtime routine, his alluring smile radiated across his exquisite face, a face I knew I would never be tired of looking at.

'What are you smiling at?' I asked through the mirror as I bent over suggestively to splash my face with the cold running water.

'What do you think?' he whispered, wrapping his muscular arms around my waist and pulling me towards him, his soft lips caressed my neck and, like always, the hairs all over my body stood on end.

'You are amazing Brooke,' he whispered.

I turned to face him, but before I could say anything he picked me up, my legs wrapped around his waist so naturally as if that was where they had always belonged. I flinched slightly as my bad leg had its regular spasm of pain, but I ignored it as I didn't want his spell to break. Liam holding me was exactly what I needed in that moment.

We entered his bedroom and he laid me down so tenderly onto the bed — we didn't even acknowledge the wide open door and the muffled voices of our friend's downstairs. He stared intensely into my eyes like he always did, and I gazed back longingly because I could never look away. I wanted to stay in that moment forever, the feeling of passion, tension and danger that had built up over the past few weeks surged between our bodies.

Our eyes locked together, our hearts were beating perfectly in sync.

'Brooke...' Liam breathed almost silently as he gazed once again into my eyes. He left a trail of kisses from my forehead down to my neck and caressed my face with the hand that wasn't resting under my lower back. 'I love you.'

I breathed sharply, although we both knew it deep down, neither of us had said those words out loud up until then.

'I love you too...' I whispered as I twisted his soft, curly locks around my fingers.

He released his hand from my lower back and slowly began to undo the buttons of my satin pyjama top before continuing the trail of kisses from my neck down to my stomach and then back up again.

It felt as though he was kissing away every tear I had ever cried, every time my heart had ached uncontrollably and every morning I'd not wanted to open my eyes.

'I can't resist you any longer.' He breathed.

Then at last our lips touched, our bodies intertwined, and our clothes fell to the floor one by one.

How *could* we resist any longer?

How I felt about him in that moment, how the electricity surged through my body, how his touch made me melt, it had become well and truly irresistible.

'Me neither,' I replied through his kisses. The heat that had built up between our bodies could have started a fire, and nobody could stand in a fire without being completely and utterly consumed by it.

X

MAY

'More wine?' Auntie Veronica asked as she floated out into her vibrant garden.

'Always.' I grinned, holding up my glass for her to fill. I could see my mother shaking her head in the distance. Liam was perched casually on the edge of the raised flower bed next to me. His long legs stretched out as always. The bright sun shone down on his glossy and freshly cut hair. Thankfully he hadn't cut it too short, his beautiful curls were one of the thousands of reasons I loved him so.

'So whose birthday party is this again?' he asked for the hundredth time.

I laughed and rolled my eyes. 'Sally, our family friend, Auntie Ron loves to a throw a party at your house, don't you?'

She nodded as she took a gulp of her wine. 'Oh yes darling I do, especially in the garden with the birds and the bees.'

'Let's not start talking about the birds and the bees,' I joked.

'You have a lovely home, Veronica,' Liam complimented politely as his eyes jolted admiringly around the garden. I was very impressed at the effort he was making to get on with my family members. He hadn't yet met my parents, but they were now in such close proximity that I couldn't avoid it for much longer.

'Thank you darling, it's very nice to meet you. We didn't know that Brooke had a secret boyfriend.'

I scowled at her as she placed herself next to him on the edge of the flower bed, but couldn't help my grin as she caught my eye.

'I don't think she's even referred to me as her boyfriend yet so don't worry.' he chuckled.

'Boyfriend?' My mother's voice bellowed from above me.

'Oh hi. Liam, this is my mum,' I pointed towards her in a careless fashion. 'Mum this is my *boyfriend* Liam.' I smirked at him.

His eyes lit up adorably as he grinned at me before turning to greet my intolerable mother. 'Hi, nice to meet you.' He nodded.

'So you've been together for a long time?' my mum continued, ignoring Liam completely. She'd cut her perfectly bleached hair even shorter, which made her look almost pixie-like as she always had it tucked behind her ears.

Were you expecting her to greet him like a normal civilized being?

Of course not.

'Er, it's still quite new.' I stood up and pulled at the bottom of my summer dress as I noticed the scar on my leg had been slightly on show.

I hope Auntie Veronica didn't notice that. I'll have to stay standing.

'Right…' mum glared at me. 'So not serious then?'

Why does she care?

'I'd say it is…' I narrowed my eyes at her.

'I'm very serious about her,' Liam added confidently. 'It's been the best few months of my life.'

'Oh, how lovely!' Auntie Veronica cooed from next to him as she stroked his arm. I knew that they would get along well.

My mum looked down her nose at him which angered me

immensely. At that moment Ruby and Riley ran towards us. I scooped them up, one snotty, out of breath twin on each hip, and planted a sloppy kiss on their sticky foreheads.

Oh, how I've missed them.

'Brookie!' Riley wiped my kiss away, giggling as he did so. Ruby kissed my cheek and giggled too. Their giggles were probably one of my favourite sounds in the whole world. Liam's coming in at a close second.

I placed them down on the floor as my leg was beginning to pulsate. I wondered if the pain would be a constant thing now — it was becoming very irritating.

'There's someone I'd like you to meet!' I held each of their hands and turned them around to face Liam.

Auntie Veronica was sipping on her wine absentmindedly, I noticed she hadn't acknowledged her sister at all.

'Hi guys!' Liam beamed as he knelt down to meet them at eye level. 'I'm Liam.'

'Hi!' they replied in unison.

'I'm Riley, it's a pleasure.' He held out his hand formally for Liam to shake, making him laugh.

'When did you get so grown up?' I ruffled his hair.

'And you must be Ruby?' Liam smiled gently at my shy little sister.

'Are you having sex with my sister?' Riley asked loudly and abruptly.

'Riley!' my mum squeaked and flushed the same color as my dad's new red sports car, the mid-life crisis on wheels. Auntie Veronica couldn't hold back her chuckle.

'This isn't funny, Ron!' my mum barked. 'You see what Brooke has taught them? She's disgusting!'

Liam swiftly stood up and shot her a disgusted look.

Jamie strolled over from the wooden tikki bar with Chris held proudly on her arm, she shot me a do-you-want-my-help look and I nodded. 'Hey you two. Shall we go and get some ice cream?' The twins squealed with excitement and ran into the house without a second thought, Chris and Jamie smiled awkwardly at my mum as they followed them.

'Those kids, the things they've witnessed you do, look how they've turned out...' my mum hissed, not wanting to cause a scene and ruin her pristine reputation no doubt.

'Come on Claire, don't be ridic...'

'Shut up for once, Veronica!' Auntie Veronica stood up and walked away, gesturing with her head for Liam to follow — but he stayed put, which impressed me even more.

'Here you come waltzing back in like we haven't *disowned* you, with an older man on your arm like some sort of...' she waved her hands towards me and screwed her nose up in disgust.

'Some sort of what?' I stepped forwards.

You will not get away with this anymore 'mother.'

'I just think this is something you should tell your family about before turning up unannounced, don't you Brooke?'

'Not particularly, not if my family's opinion of who I associate myself with doesn't really matter to me. And also we didn't come unannounced, Auntie Ron invited us.' I stated proudly. I wasn't going to back down this time.

My mum ignored my reply as she tucked her hair firmly behind her ears. 'So what do you do?' she looked down her nose once again at Liam, who I thought looked extra sexy in his all grey attire.

'I'm a mechanic,' Liam replied bluntly. His eyes bored into hers angrily. He wasn't one to hide his emotions very well. Another reason I loved him so.

'A mechanic.' she snorted, 'Is there much money in that?'

'Mum!' I gasped, but Liam didn't seem phased by the question. He towered over her eye level as he stepped forwards slightly. 'I understand that you don't know anything about me, because you and Brooke don't speak. But I can assure you that I am defiantly *not* good enough for your daughter.'

I frowned at his statement in both confusion and awe.

As if I couldn't adore him any more, he also seemed to despise my mum just as much as I did. *He's a keeper!*

'You're *not?*' my dad interjected as he had been standing nearby, clearly listening to our every word.

'No, not at all.'

'What do you mean?' My dad's eyes jolted at me with a concerned look painted across his face. I wanted so badly to reach out and hug him, I couldn't remember the last time I had. I smiled at him shyly and he mirrored my gesture. My loving father was still in there somewhere deep down, it was good to know.

'I earn very good money.' Liam raised his eyebrows at my mum as he said this. 'I have my own house, I work hard, I have good people around me. I treat Brooke well, I worship the ground she walks on, I *adore* her...'

'Sorry son, I'm not following? It sounds like you are more than enough for Brooke?' My dad's eyebrows narrowed in thought. My mum was scolding at me with pure hatred in her eyes as Liam spoke.

What have I ever done to this woman to make her hate me so much?

'Despite all of those things,' Liam continued. 'No, I'm not good enough for your daughter because no one will *ever* be good enough for this girl. Not me, definitely not you...' His eyes darted towards my mum intently as he said this. '...And not any future boy she may fall in love with.' I was in shock, I'd never seen anyone be so forthcoming to my mother before, she usually made people cower and shy away.

'You don't think I'm good enough for my own daughter?' My mum raised her eyebrows.

'No, I don't as it happens,' he replied sharply. 'If you're not calling her every single day to find out what your amazing daughter has done, or how she is, then no you're not good enough. She's incredible and she deserves people around her who make her feel like that. Do you know how successful she is in her job? Do you know how much she does for her friends? How much she does for *me?* How much it's killing her that you've disowned her and she can't see her brother and sister whenever she wants?'

My parents shook their heads like school children being told off by the head teacher. A few people close by were listening in to the conversation, their jaws dropping at Liam's lecture. No one had spoken to my mum like this. Ever. I didn't know what to say, I knew I should have pulled him away the minute my mum had started. But my legs were frozen to the ground.

I was just so *impressed.*

So turned on more like. A scoffed from the depths of my stomach.

'She's perfect, and it baffles me that you would willingly chose to not have her in your life.' Liam added. His eyes darted down at me apprehensively.

I smiled and stood up next to him, holding tightly onto his arm. He relaxed.

'Thank you, but you don't need to stick up for me with *her.*' I smiled reassuringly. 'Your opinion doesn't matter to me in the slightest any more, *Claire.*' My face involuntarily scrunched up

179

in disgust as I said her name.

There was silence for a moment before my dad shockingly held out his hand for Liam to shake. 'Son, that's all a father wants for his daughter, someone who loves her like that.' Liam shook his hand and thanked him as my mum stormed off. 'Better go make sure the old ball and chain is all right,' he joked awkwardly before scurrying off to her side.

Auntie Veronica clapped her hands in glee from a group of people gawking nearby, squealing about how much she loved Liam. They all seemed to agree.

'Was that a bit much?' Liam laughed anxiously.

'I love you.' I giggled throwing my hands around his neck and reaching up on my tip-toes so I could meet his lips with mine.

He groaned reluctantly for more as I pulled away. 'And *future boys I may fall in love with*?' My eyebrows raised. I couldn't imagine ever feeling like that about anyone else. 'There are no future boys, I have only ever loved you and will only ever love you.'

His smile grew wide across his perfect face and he wrapped his hands around my waist tightly, pulling me in closer to his delicious smelling body.

'Oh *really*?'

'Really.'

'So I'm the best?' he teased.

I rolled my eyes and chuckled. 'You're the best Liam.'

He kissed me again so passionately that I almost forgot that we were at a party with all of my family and their friends. My knees turned weak and my stomach flipped a full 360 degrees. I wondered if he would ever stop having that effect on me.

I ran my hands through his curls as he traced the outline of my spine through my dress. I wanted him there and then. He grinned against my lips as he picked me up and span me around.

'We should probably stop.' He gazed past me to the many onlookers we had gained.

'Until later...' he added in a whisper.

I lay breathless next to Liam in his large bed. His body had an indescribable hold over mine, one I would never tire of.

'Where have you been all of my life?' he sighed as he leant on his elbow to look at me. He used his free hand to brush my bed hair with his fingers, tucking each strand delicately behind my ear as he did so.

'Do you think Harriet is okay?'

Liam frowned. 'Honestly Brooke, I really don't know. Are *you* okay?'

'Yes and no…' I admitted.

'Go on?'

'On one hand I'm the happiest I've been in forever, I'm so happy with you. It's quite overwhelming how happy I am…' I rolled onto my side and gazed up at him.

'But on the other hand?'

'I just can't stop thinking about the last few months. My leg feels as though it's constantly on fire, and what Mr. Daniels said, and the notebook, and Harriet is still MIA. Dale and Billy hardly talk to you anymore, and Matt…' I closed my eyes as I remembered the horrific feel of Matt's hand running over my body. 'I can't stop thinking about Matt.'

'Brooke, I'd be worried if you *had* stopped thinking about Matt. That isn't something to be ashamed of, you're only human. *None* of us can stop thinking about Matt. Someone is dead because of our actions.' He planted a kiss on my forehead before rolling onto his back and starring thoughtfully up at the ceiling. 'You don't have to worry about your boss until you go back to work. And there's not much more we can do with Harriet's notebook until you're back at work and have more information on the whole thing.'

'I guess you're right. I only have to wait a few more weeks.'

I shivered at the thought of working alongside Mr. Daniels again.

'You should have told me about your leg, I did think it looked swollen still. I'll call Carlos and he will get the doctor back... And Billy talks to me, he messages, he is okay. Just doesn't want to come here... see you... it's a reminder.'

'Do you want me to go back to Jamie's?'

Jamie and I hadn't spent a night away from Liam's since the Matt and Harriet ordeal. I could only imagine the pile of letters and dust we'd return home to.

'No, no. I wasn't saying that. I love having you here. And Chris seems happy.'

'Jamie is really happy with him...' I smiled.

'I think we all need each other right now.'

'Hmm...' I agreed sleepily. 'I think you're right.'

'I need you, Brooke.' His voice cracked as he said my name.

I sat up and straddled my legs either side of his naked body in one swift movement. 'I'm not going anywhere.' I reached down and caressed his hair with both of my hands.

He pulled me into him and kissed me desperately. I melted. He really did need me.

At that moment the door burst open, filling the room with light. I screeched and rolled off of Liam, pulling the covers over myself.

'Fuck, Chris!' Liam squinted as his eyes adjusted to the light.

'I'm sorry, but something's happened. Something's happened to Jamie!' he blurted out frantically.

XI

I stumbled into Liam's living room adjusting his T-shirt that I had just thrown on over my knickers. He followed just as clumsily, pulling the waistband of his jogging bottoms up. Everyone stared at us. I noticed the room was busier than usual.

'Billy!' I cried as I noticed him sitting on the sofa. 'It's so good to see you! Are you okay? What's wrong? What's happened to her?' I panted.

Dale and Liam nodded at each other. 'Dale, it's good to see you mate. And you Billy. What's going on?'

Chris was pacing anxiously up and down the room, running his hands through his floppy hair. 'She went to get some cigarettes and snacks from the shop round the corner about an hour ago. I text her because she was taking forever and then someone sent me THAT back!' Tears began rolling down his face.

Billy handed the phone to Liam, eyeing me warily.

'Shit…' Liam exclaimed as he passed me the phone.

Do I even want to know what this says?

My heart was in my mouth and my leg was throbbing from bounding down the stairs too fast.

From: Jamie
06/04/2018
23:44 p.m.

We have her now. This is for snooping. You were warned.

I read and re-read the message, not being able to accept what I was reading. My best friend had been kidnapped. Because of me.

'This is Mr. Daniels isn't it?' I said after a while, handing the phone back to Billy. Everyone looked at me in a state of confusion and shock.

'He warned me. He said I needed to stop asking questions. He was angry when I asked about Guedo...' I trailed off, I couldn't hold back the tears any longer.

'When did you two get here?' Liam directed his question to Billy and Dale as he held my shoulders and guided me to the sofa. I perched on the arm and wiped away my tears as I listened.

'We were at mine, Chris called me. I thought it would be easier if I brought my laptop here so we could try and trace the text... so far no luck though.'

'We didn't want to interrupt you two...' Dale added sarcastically. My cheeks flushed red as I knew they had probably all heard me, the house wasn't sound proof at all.

Chris was still pacing. 'What do we do?'

'Chris mate...' Liam began.

'Liam! No! All this shit that keeps happening is because you can't accept that your mum is dead!'

He bounded towards Liam so their faces were centimeters away from each other. 'Get it in your thick skull Liam!' he pushed his index finger forcefully into Liam's forehead. 'She's dead!'

I starred at them in anticipation. I had never seen these gentle giants lose their tempers, not once. But I was about to. Liam's eyes filled with tears and anger. 'I know she's dead!' he hollered, pushing Chris so that he tumbled backwards.

'Do you? Fucking act like it then! People die all of the time Liam. Why have you carried on with this ridiculous hunt for her all these years if you know she's dead?'

'I need to know what happened!'

185

Chris marched forwards so that they were face to face once again.

Dale was staring at them in disbelief. 'This is why I've stayed away from you lot, you're all losing your minds!'

'Fuck off then Dale!' Chris shouted at him.

Dale turned on his heels and stormed out of the front door without another word.

'Well that's my lift home gone...' Billy muttered as he tapped away at his laptop, ignoring the petulant fight that was happening in front of him. Tears were still rolling down my cheeks and pain was shooting from the scar on my leg down to the tips of my toes.

'I'll tell you what happened, Liam!' Chris snarled nastily. 'Your mum was a waste of space drunk. I saw it. She was round my house drinking and doing drugs with my parents. She left you alone so she could go and get high with Guedo. She didn't love you. You've wasted your life trying to look for a druggie whore!'

In one swift movement, Liam had clenched his fists and swung a perfect punch, hitting Chris precisely on his nose.

'Ah!' Chris cried, clutching his bloody face. 'What the fuck Liam!'

Liam shook his hand and rubbed his bleeding knuckles. Glancing over at me guiltily. I stared at him in shock. My eyes were blurry through the tears and I couldn't concentrate through the pain in my leg.

Slowly, I stood up and hobbled towards them. 'Is this going to get Jamie back to us?' I croaked. They shook their heads in reply.

I was angry, but not at them. I was angry at myself for getting Jamie caught up in whatever this was. I turned and walked into the kitchen, leaning over the counter in pain as the weight on my leg from walking caused another excruciating ripple.

'Brooke?' I felt Liam's arms around my shoulders.

'I'm fine.' I winced.

Billy's voice called from behind us. 'The text came from a road twenty minutes away from here.'

'Brooke, I'm taking your car!' Chris shouted as he ran to the hallway. I heard my keys jangle from the side cabinet and the door slam shut. I was in too much pain to argue.

'Brooke, what's wrong?' Liam let go of me as he walked to the cupboard to get me a drink, it was only then that I realized he was the only thing holding me up. My leg buckled, I slid off of the counter and fell onto the cold, tiled floor with a loud thump.

'Brooke!' Liam called, panic stricken, as he dropped to the floor next to me. He held my trembling body as tight as he could. 'Bill, call Carlos. Now!'

I clutched onto my burning leg, Liam pulled me into his chest as I sobbed uncontrollably through the pain. 'She's my best friend, Liam. What have we done?'

My vision began to blur and my ears started to ring, it was like being back in Matt and Harriet's front room all over again. I could faintly hear Liam telling me to stay awake, but it was too late.

'JAMIE!' I screamed as I shot up. I was on Liam's sofa with a blanket slung over me, my forehead was dripping with sweat and my leg still felt as though it was on fire.

Liam jumped up from the floor, his curls were a mess and his eyes were tired. 'It's okay, I'm here, I'm here.'

I glanced at the clock on the TV — it was approaching seven pm — meaning she had now been missing for about eight hours. The contents of my stomach lurched into my dry throat.

'Is she still missing?' I asked softly as tears fell from my tired eyes. Liam looked at me apologetically as he switched the lamp on.

I'd received a visit from the dodgy doctor not long after I'd fainted.

'You must look after yourself,' he'd insisted in his graveled voice. He was an elderly man with scars covering most of his face and arms. Every time he'd visited I wanted to ask him what happened to him, but of course I never did.

'Your scar is infected, where I haven't got the correct tools to fix a *bullet wound* this was bound to happen. I tried my best…' he'd glanced at Liam unhappily. Another person dragged into this mess. How many was that now? I'd lost count.

'I know, thanks…' I'd managed a smile.

'Your heart rate and blood pressure are extremely high too, I think you had some sort of panic attack.'

I'd sighed. It was very likely that I'd fainted through sheer panic. It wasn't the first time it had happened.

Carlos had seen him out, thanking him for his time and handing him a hefty looking wedge of cash.

I still hadn't spoken to Carlos properly, apart from the occasional nod in my direction he stayed very quiet. Neil was the chatty one out of the two.

People had been in and out of the house throughout the whole day while I tried my best to sleep.

Billy was seemingly back on his full time shifts of sorting Liam's problems out. I wondered why he done it, he didn't have to be caught up in the mess that was Liam's life.

Your life now, Brooke! A reminded me smugly. She had worked her way back up to playing the role of center stage in my brain.

Chris had returned, deflated and emotional, from where Billy had traced Jamie's phone not long after Dr Dodgy had left. 'Her phone was just lying in the road…' he'd sobbed as he threw it, along with my car keys on the coffee table. 'Shit Brooke, you look awful.'

'She fainted,' Liam snapped defensively. I'm not sure as to why, I probably *did* look pretty awful. 'Where have you been? It's been hours!'

Chris had shrugged. 'Looking for her. I lost track of time.'

'The boys haven't stopped looking…' Liam said after a while. 'We'll find her. But you need to focus on getting better.'

'I can't believe I fell asleep…' I whispered guiltily.

'It was only for a few hours. You need it. Let me make you some food, you haven't eaten since your auntie's party…' Liam rambled.

'There's nothing wrong with me,' I snapped.

'You have to let me look after you, please.' His eyes were wide with worry.

'How can I sleep and eat and be *normal*, Liam? Would you?' I protested.

'If you asked me to, yes I would.' He caressed my hand. 'This is serious; you need to get better for me okay? Don't ignore it again. If it's hurting, tell me. You're no use to Jamie if you're weak.'

I nodded stubbornly and fell back onto the cushions.

I couldn't believe what had become of my life.

I noticed the house was eerily quiet.

'Has everyone gone home?'

Liam nodded. 'I told everyone to get some rest, we all need it. Now let me make you some food.'

He returned from the kitchen with a ham sandwich cut into perfect triangles, a packet of crisps, a huge bottle of water and a banana.

'Sorry, it's all I had.'

I took the plate from him and smiled. 'Thank you.'

My stomach rumbled in anticipation as I took a bite of the sandwich. I hadn't noticed how famished I really was.

Once I had devoured the contents of the plate and gulped down the water I felt much more awake and aware of how disgusting I was.

'I think I need a wash...' I managed a half-hearted smile.

'Your wish is my command.'

He swooped me up into his strong arms as if he was carrying me over the alter.

'One day, my darling, I'll be carrying you like this over the alter.' He smiled as if he had read my mind. I blushed happily at the thought of being his wife.

He carried me effortlessly up the stairs and stood me up carefully in his bathroom, lifting my T-shirt dress over my head so I was standing awkwardly in front of him in my mismatch underwear and a bandaged leg.

Oh wow, you look attractive. NOT! A sniggered at me.

He leant past me and flicked on the tap for the bath. It was a large stand-alone tub with an assortment of lush smelling bubble baths lined up on the shelf.

That must be why he smells so nice.

I hadn't noticed them before; I had always used his shower as it meant I could get back to him quicker.

You are so pathetic Brooke!

Liam ran his fingers along the straps of my bra, we both breathed heavily. I felt guilty for thinking of anything other than Jamie, but suddenly I wanted him so badly it made my stomach flip.

He walked around me and poured some delicious smelling vanilla bubble bath into the half-filled tub.

He pulled his top over his head, revealing his chiseled, god-like physique. *Oh, wow.*

He turned the tap off when the bath was filled to the top — bubbles overflowed onto the marble floor. It looked so inviting — before making his way back to me.

I could see the hurt and the exhaustion in his eyes, I knew

that mine probably looked the same. I reached out and stroked his cheek with the back of my hand.

'How are you?'

He smiled sadly. 'Who knows any more...'

'I'm here.'

'I know. I'm glad you are.' He caressed the straps of my bra once again before slowly pulling them down, he unhooked the back letting it drop to the floor.

I looked down at my bandaged leg and then back up at him. 'How's this going to work?'

'I'll help you.' He whispered as he pulled my knickers down my legs. The gentle touch made me shiver.

He helped me into the bath, I stood on one leg, concentrating with all of my strength to keep my balance before lowering myself slowly and draping my leg over the edge of the bath. Somehow I managed to sit down without getting the bandage too wet.

'There you go girl...' he smiled at me. I splashed him as he knelt on the floor next to me, covering his face with bubbles and water. I giggled uncontrollably.

You're such a bitch. Your best friend is missing and you're laughing! A scolded me.

'I could listen to you laugh all night...' Liam grinned as he wiped the water from his face.

I splashed him again.

'That's it!' he shouted, splashing me once more before standing up and pulling his trousers and underwear down in one swift movement.

I gasped as he climbed into the bath with me.

'Hi...' I smiled shyly.

'Hi you.' He grabbed the shampoo bottle from the shelf and

lathered it up in his hands.

I leant backwards so that my hair was immersed in the water.

I closed my eyes and attempted to find my way back to 'Brooke Land.' My best friend wasn't missing there, my leg felt perfectly fine there, we hadn't killed someone there.

I slowly succumbed to the depths of the bath, covering my forehead, my eyes, my nose and then my mouth with the warm water. The only noise was my fast beating heart.

This is where you belong. A's voice echoed through my body.

I just want to sleep.

XII

I was quickly brought back to reality as Liam pulled me from the darkness. 'Brooke! What are you doing?' His eyes were wide with fright as he clutched desperately onto my arms with his soapy hands.

I gasped heavily as air began circulating through my body once again. His nails dug deeply into my arms as he continued to stare at me, dumbfounded.

'Ouch.' I whispered. My bandaged leg was now completely absorbed in the water.

He pulled his arms down quickly and rinsed the shampoo off of his hands before scooting himself forwards so that he was sitting so close to me I could feel his breath on my forehead. I looked up at him under my eyelashes and sighed.

'What were you doing?' he repeated.

'I just want to sleep.' My voice cracked and I looked down timidly.

He tilted my chin back up to face him. 'Everything is going to be okay,' he whispered.

'Is it?'

'I love you.'

'I love you too Liam, but—' before I could finish he was kissing my lips, running his hands across my wet body and holding me in place with his legs locked firmly around me.

This is one thing you can't get in Brooke Land.

I was awoken by a knock at Liam's door.

He climbed off of the sofa and gently opened the door, hushing whoever was on the other side so that they wouldn't wake me up.

There were some faint deep sounding mutters before the boy's tip toed into the front room.

I sat up and gave them a half-hearted smile.

'Sorry if we woke you.' Chris managed a smile back at me as Liam opened the curtains. He looked as though he hadn't slept for a year.

'And sorry about the other day, you didn't have to see that after you'd just found out about Jamie,' Dale added.

'Yeah, Sorry…' Chris mimicked shamefully.

I sighed as I shuffled in my seat. 'Emotions are all over the place at the moment, but we all need each other, we can't be fighting right now.'

They nodded in agreement. Dale smiled at me. 'We will find her, we love Jamie to bits, just like we love you.' I wondered why he had come back, he seemed so done with all of us lately.

Billy joined us in the room, he had massive black bags under his eyes. 'Have you not been sleeping either?' I asked him sympathetically.

He shook his head. 'I have been looking into every way possible to help you find Jamie,' he yawned.

My heart dropped. I missed her so much. I looked around the room and a wave of emotion soured over me.

'Thank you everyone, I know everything that has happened lately has been mainly because of me. We were trying to find Harriet and now Jamie… but I'm so glad I met you all. You really are the best friends I've ever had.'

No one answered, they all just smiled at me with the same

emotional look I knew I had on my face.

Liam fixed his eyes to mine lovingly and I knew everything would eventually be okay. It had to be.

You're deluded if you think that. A sneered. I tried to ignore her, but somehow I knew that she was right.

After another hopeless day of attempting to find out where Jamie was, Liam and I had reluctantly taken ourselves to bed. Everyone had left feeling just as deflated as us. The antibiotics had finally kicked in and I could hobble upstairs and sleep in a comfortable bed for the first time in a few days.

'Maybe we should just call the police Liam,' I suggested nervously. 'I don't know what else we can do, we're out of our depth here.'

Liam pulled me onto his chest and kissed my head. 'I know; I was thinking the same thing. This is all because of me and it turns out my mum just didn't care about me. All of this was for nothing.'

'You don't know that,' I answered reassuringly as I wrapped my arm around his stomach. 'Everyone makes mistakes.' I jumped as that moment my phone rang very loudly, my heart was in my mouth, could this be Jamie?

'It's one in the morning, who's calling you?' Liam frowned as the light from my phone shone in his tired eyes.

'Unknown caller,' I whispered, jolting upwards. 'Hello?' I answered anxiously.

A deep voice bellowed down the other end of the phone. 'It was supposed to be you, Brooke.'

My heart flew into my throat, 'Mr. Daniels?'

Liam jumped out of bed quickly, chucking some clothes he had thrown on the floor on, he gestured for me to give him the phone but I shook my head.

'I just want to know where Jamie is, that's all, then we'll leave this alone. We don't know anything!'

'No, you won't,' he argued. 'You can come and get her if you want, I can tell you where she is, but I doubt you'll leave alive.'

Liam was fumbling around in the wardrobe for a pair of shoes. *'Where are you going?'* I mouthed to him. 'Just tell me where she is, please. We haven't gone to the police. We just want her back. Can I speak to her? My voice cracked.

'They are transporting to Italy soon; she'll be long gone…' he began.

'I know that,' I snapped. 'I've known about your trip abroad for months. So did Matt.' I tried to sound confident. *Italy! The trip abroad is to Italy!*

'Well then I guess you know that you're too late,' Mr. Daniels replied smugly. 'It was supposed to be you. We knew Georgina's old address and guessed the boy still lived there. My incompetent colleagues thought it was you walking to the shops that night. But anyway, they've been dealt with.'

My heart sank, it was supposed to be *me.*

'I don't understand. I haven't asked any more questions. I haven't even been at work to know any more!'

'Well, that was beyond my control. My boss made the decision to stop all of you snooping around. I'm just following orders.'

'Who *do* you work for?' I frowned at Liam as he paced up and down the room frantically. My anger was building the more I heard how confident Mr. Daniel's was about winning this sick little game.

'Isn't it obvious?'

'Seven…' I gasped. It was all beginning to fall into place. 'So you are involved in it all? Guedo, Britney, Rebecca, Georgina, the trafficking, Harriet, Matt…' my voice trailed off at the severity of the situation. I'd had my suspicions that Mr. Daniels was involved, but working directly for Seven, that was beyond my comprehension. The phone line went dead and I dropped the phone.

'Liam, where are you going?' I shouted as he continued to walk widths of the room.

'I don't know, I panicked, I thought he was gonna tell us where she was, did he? And what did he say?'

'I think I've just made it worse.'

'Brooke, how could it get any worse?'

Famous last words. Tears filled my eyes.

'I think his going to kill us all.'

Liam dropped down next to me in the bed. 'Like fuck is he going to kill you!' His phone began to buzz on the bedside table, making me jump once again.

'Bill?' Liam answered hysterically. 'Yeah... yeah she just got a phone call... yeah it was that prick... you've done that to all of our phones? Shit Bill you're a genius, yeah... yeah we're coming now.'

Liam hung up and his crazed eyes starred at me. 'So Billy has all our phones tapped, his traced that call you just got, we're gonna find her B!'

'I'm coming, don't even try and talk me out of it...' I shouted.

'I couldn't even if I wanted to.' Liam reassured me as he pulled me out of bed and helped me get dressed.

He brushed my knotted hair, gently wrapping it in a scrunchie before sweeping me up in his arms.

'We will find her, okay?'

It was about two am by the time everyone had arrived at Billy's house. 'The phone call came from an industrial estate in Brixton, so not too far from us at all. Whether he is still there now I don't know, but it's worth a try,' he briefed us all. 'We ready?'

'Let's get these fuckers,' Carlos hollered powerfully. That probably being the first sentence I'd ever heard him say. Liam jumped off of the sofa and I followed him as quickly as I could as he rushed out into the hallway.

As I caught up with him, I noticed he was rummaging through a big, black rucksack to check he had everything he needed one last time. I peered in and noticed a small laptop, his phone and a knife. I knew it was necessary, but the thought of Liam fighting anyone with a knife scared me to the core.

Billy followed us out. 'The plan's a solid one Brooke, we will be fine. Everyone remember to have their phones and lights ready on my signal, yes?' he addressed the crowded hallway.

'Remind me what your signal is again, Billy?' Neil laughed. 'A bird noise?'

'No it's not a *bird noise*, It's a text message, please don't be listening out for the call of an African Fish Eagle because you will *not* hear one.' Billy barked in response to Neil's tomfoolery.

Neil held his hands in the air jokingly, 'No pigeon mating calls, got it.'

'What do we do now?' I asked Liam.

I was uncomfortably squeezed between the huge units that were Carlos and Neil in the back of Billy's not so big *Ford Fiesta*. We thought taking Carlo's huge range rover would draw too much attention.

We had left Chris stewing at Billy's house. We had all agreed that he was too much of a liability — even he thought so too.

'Call me as soon as you find her!' He'd begged me as we'd

left.

'Chris. You'll be the first to know. I promise.'

My phone clock flashed to 2:47 am. It was still extremely dark outside, but we could make out the figures of a few men parked in the desolate industrial estate. 'Well they are still here, something must be going down tonight,' Liam speculated.

'Are there lots of them?' I breathed, trying to make out as many figures as I could.

'There's probably a fucking army of them,' Carlos grunted.

Billy turned around to face us all from the driver's seat. 'So we are all clear on what we are doing yes? Neil you're off on that direction...' he pointed left towards what looked like some old scaffolding surrounding a derelict building. 'Carlos, you're the opposite direction to Neil. Liam and I are going to try get as close as we can to them, just cover us, please...'

Billy paused, raising his eyebrows at Carlos and Neil. Carlos pulled a gun out from his back pocket and Neil followed lead.

They have guns! Why do they have guns?

What did you expect them to have Brooke? Bananas?

Oh shut up, A. Now is not the time!

A made my stomach hurl in response.

Bitch.

'Don't worry Bill,' Neil reassured. 'We have you covered.'

'Take these.' Billy handed them some round bulbs that looked like they belonged to a police car.

I wondered how many things Billy had actually stolen from his work in the years of helping Liam, and how he hadn't been fired or arrested yet.

He must be good.

They both took the lights before creeping out of the car to their assigned spots. Liam looked at me with a concerned expression on his face. 'You're gonna hate me for saying this, but Brooke you need to stay in here.'

I scoffed and glared at him. 'Like hell am I staying here.'

'Brooke —' he began to argue, but this wasn't up for discussion at all. Jamie was there because of me and I would be there to get her back again.

'Liam, I love you, but I am coming with you and Billy, I need to see this through to the end.' I insisted. He stayed silent, seemingly defeated.

We snuck as close as we could possibly get to where the men were standing. I noticed there were several large cars and one very long loading lorry. The headlights from the cars lit up a few of the figures faces as they stood in a circle; they seemed to be waiting for something.

There was a man leaning up against a shiny, black Range Rover. He was big, bigger than Carlos, bigger than anyone I had ever seen before. He took a pull of his cigarette before discarding it carelessly on the floor, still lit. He turned around so that the light from the headlights revealed the scar that I had seen in so many photographs, the scar that covered the length of his face and travelled over his eye.

'Guedo.' I gasped.

There is no way in hell you are getting out of here alive, Brooke!

After about ten minutes, Guedo's attention turned to a smaller car arriving. It stopped next to where the others were parked. I watched as a man appeared from the driver's seat, he was dragging someone towards the big group of men. I closed my eyes as I realized who it was.

'Oh god…' I felt Liam's hand squeeze mine, I was so scared for Jamie. I wanted to run over there and take her place.

Billy's whisper came from the other side of me. 'Brooke, open your eyes, we need all eyes on Jamie while this goes down.'

I noticed that he was tapping away at the small laptop Liam had packed and knew that the time had come.

The man who had Jamie threw her to the floor where Guedo was standing; her head was right by his feet. I felt sick. Then, he pulled out a gun and held it to her head. She screamed. I went to jump up, but Liam pulled me back down again. 'I'm sorry, you can't. We have it under control,' he insisted.

'They are going to *shoot* her!' I hissed. I looked next to me and watched Billy as he was still quickly tapping the keyboard. 'Billy! Hurry up!'

A few seconds after Billy had stopped typing there were the sound of police sirens from where Neil and Carlos had situated themselves. The blue lights lit up the area and I ducked lower against the storage container we were hiding behind and squeezed my eyes shut. I heard some car doors slam shut, engines roar loudly and tires skidding against the concrete. Then, there was silence.

I opened my eyes and peered over the container, all that was left was Jamie, still on the floor, I could hear her sobs. Guedo had given the gun to another man who was holding it to her head, he was looking around frantically.

I noticed Carlos and Neil run towards the man, pulling out their guns from their back pockets as they did so.

Carlos was shouting, 'Police, drop your weapon and hold your hands above your head. NOW!'

Liam breathed a sigh of relief and hugged me tightly. 'It worked, and you're okay.'

'Trust me, I am not okay. None of this is okay!' I hissed, longing to run to Jamie.

The man dropped his gun as instructed and Neil grabbed him before leading him back over to where we had parked. I wondered what they were going to do with him, holding someone captive hadn't been part of the original plan.

As soon as the coast was clear I was off, I hobbled over to Jamie as quickly as I could. She was kneeling on the floor crying — the sound of her awful cry echoed throughout the abandoned area.

I knelt down opposite her and she fell into my arms.

'I'm so sorry,' I whispered repeatedly. We sat on the floor sobbing uncontrollably as the boys searched the area. The lorry was still parked in the same place, there was no driver. Billy was attempting to pry open the doors and failing. Liam climbed in the driver's seat and returned with a set of keys — calmly walking to the back and unlocking the padlock that Billy was tugging on.

'Oh my god,' Billy shrieked.

I closed my eyes once more, not wanting to see what they had discovered.

'It's okay, it's okay, we're not going to hurt you,' I could hear Neil saying over and over again.

I didn't need to look. I knew straight away what they had found.

Billy drove us back to Liam's house while Neil stayed to sort out the new situation we had found ourselves in.

I looked at Jamie, she was still trembling. I had my arm around her tightly as she was leaning her head on my chest. My heart broke as I looked at her black eye and cut face, I didn't know how she could go anywhere near me. I turned the other way and gazed up at Liam. His curly hair was blowing in the wind from the open window. My heart fluttered.

The man we had somehow managed to kidnap was squirming around in the boot. I could hear his muffled cries for help from behind me.

What the hell have I got myself into now?

'All right,' Carlos and Neil nodded at me as I walked in the room.

I nodded back at them, picking up a cigarette box. 'You okay?'

'Yep, we're just talking about what to do with Ricky boy in there,' Neil snickered.

They had taken him out of the boot and into the garden room, tying him up on a chair. I wondered how they could be so calm and still manage to laugh with everything that had transpired that night.

It was now eleven am, and I hadn't slept a wink.

Chris was waiting on the doorstep when we'd arrived back at Liam's and hadn't left Jamie's side since. She had passed out as soon as her head hit the pillow and was still asleep now.

I wanted to see her, to sit in bed with her and brush her hair like the old days, but I knew if the roles were reversed Liam would want me all to himself. So reluctantly, I left them alone.

'What are we gonna do about him?' Liam asked as he walked over to me and placed a reassuring kiss on my forehead.

I sparked a cigarette and stretched my legs out in front of me, realizing I'd taken on a lot of Liam's traits without even noticing.

'I don't know.' Neil shrugged. 'Isn't that what you are for Billy? You know, the thinking and shit.'

Billy rolled his eyes before shooting me a fainted hearted smile from across the room. We still hadn't mentioned the Matt situation. I wasn't sure if we ever would.

'Neil, what happened to those people in the back of the van?' I asked, not sure if I even wanted to know the answer.

Neil looked at me apologetically. 'Not everyone was alive. We called the police, anonymously of course...' He glanced towards Billy as he said this, reassuring him that he had thought of everything. 'So I'm guessing you'll hear about that at work?'

'Probably, if Mr. Daniels even lets me through the door, what am I going to do?' I wondered.

'Are you okay Brooke?' Liam scanned my face.

A tear fell down my cheek, but I brushed it away. I wasn't going to continue being the girl who cried and let everybody else come to the rescue any more. I didn't want to continue feeling scared and letting my anxiety rule my life.

You wouldn't survive a day without me. Don't kid yourself. Argh! LEAVE ME ALONE.

'I'm fine.' I lied. He studied my knowingly. There was no way he believed that. Thankfully my phone buzzed and saved me from any more unwelcome questions.

'Hello?'

'Don't react.' A familiar voice hissed from the other end of the phone. 'Pretend it's a family member and leave the room.'

'Hi Auntie Ron, Yeah...' I did as I was told and walked out of the room, closing the door behind me. 'What do you want?' I spat in disgust at my monster of a boss.

'I'm calling to inform you that I'm stepping down effective immediately.'

I froze. '*What?*'

'Despite what you may think, Brooke. I never wanted any of this. I was being blackmailed, I had to protect my family somehow. But my wife hates me and my children won't speak to me. Apparently I've been a tad absent...'

'Do you expect me to feel *sorry* for you?'

'No. Not at all. But I bet you've done some things you thought you'd never be capable of, and you've justified them in the name of love.'

He was only too right. My thoughts entered the dark place in my mind where the memory of Matt was stored. I shuddered. 'So why are you telling me this?'

'I'm warning you. These people are dangerous. Andrew Spence has been released and the NCA will be back to square one again.'

'How has he been released? We had so much evidence on him!'

'You don't believe I'm the only person in a high up position that's being blackmailed do you? They are everywhere...'

They are everywhere. Those words reverberated horrifically throughout my mind.

'You still have a job. I have extended your leave of absence over the summer as I know you are probably very scared and stressed right now. You are not due back to work until September.'

'Why have you done that?' I breathed a mini sigh of relief— I had been dreading the return to work.

'You need to keep a low profile, you being at work right now with access to so much information isn't ideal for them.'

'So you've done it to benefit them.' I snapped.

'No. I know I can't make up for all of the horrendous things I've done, but I can at least do some good now.'

'Where was this attitude when you kidnapped Jamie?' I retorted.

'Don't push it, Brooke.' His voice turned dark again. *There's the real Mr. Daniels.*

'Just keep a low profile, they are moving out to Italy soon and hopefully this will all blow over...'

'I doubt it. So where are you going then?'

The phone line beeped as he hung up on me. I stood in the hallway for a moment, processing the conversation I'd just had.

'Brooke, you okay?' Liam opened the door softly.

I turned to face him, attempting my best fake smile.

'Yeah, sure. I'm fine.' I lied again.

XIV

'Right, I'm gonna take this tape off of your mouth mate, make a sound and trust me, you will never be able to make one again, okay?' Carlos threatened.

The man named Ric was sitting on a garden chair in the middle of the room, he had his legs tied to the chair and was clinging on to a half drunken bottle of water. He nodded in reply to Carlos.

Carlos patrolled around him and ripped off the tape, he breathed in and out deeply, gasping for air.

Liam, Jamie and I were sitting on turned-over boxes near the door. He stared at Jamie with a disgusted look on his face. Anger boiled inside of me. 'Don't even look at her,' I demanded. 'Why are we letting him have bottles of water? We don't care if he dies of dehydration do we?'

Pipe down, he would kill you if he wasn't tied up!

I don't care. I'm so angry!

'Come 'ere den and say that to ma face, ugly bitch.' He sneered; he had a strong Italian accent. His voice was horrible and rough — the sort of voice that went straight through you like nails to a chalk board. His dirty brown hair was stuck to his face from the amount he was sweating, and as he opened his mouth to speak I noticed he hardly had any teeth, the teeth he did have were as black as coal.

Carlos strolled back towards him. 'Didn't I just say, do not speak?' He bent down before quickly jolting up and punching him hard. Ric lent back in the chair and spat out blood.

'I told you not to Talk, Ric. And you're talking. Only talk when we ask you a question, yeah?' Carlos hit him again.

How did it come to this?

You asked them to find Harriet, that's how. It's your fault.

After Ric had recovered from the second blow, he nodded and didn't say another word, his eyes filled with fear and his head bowed submissively to the floor. Carlos paced around the chair and stopped behind him. Ric attempted to turn around, but failed as the chair nearly toppled over.

'He has a gun to your head!' I smiled mockingly at him. Liam and Jamie starred at me in astonishment.

'B!' Jamie whispered. 'What's gotten into you?'

Yeah, what has gotten into you?

Not you for once! I scowled at A.

An anger like I had never experienced before had been

boiling inside of me since I saw Guedo point that gun at Jamie's head. It crashed around my body like red waves of lava.

Carlos smirked at me. 'Brooke, come here.' He gestured with his head, I stood up and limped over to where Ric was sitting. 'Tell him why we have him, I think this dumb little shit needs everything spelled out to him.'

I looked down at Ric cowering in the chair, cowering because of *me*, a twenty-four-year-old girl who up until recently couldn't say boo to a goose. A girl who had spent her whole life hiding in the shadows of other people, too scared to cast her own.

Suddenly, I felt a rush of adrenaline. The red waves crashed high inside of me. A was attempting to stay afloat, but failed miserably as she was repeatedly swallowed up in the sea of rage, gasping for air.

Ironic isn't it? That's how you make me feel every day.

As the anger grew I thought of my mother turning her nose

up in disgust at me, my father cowering behind her, Matt rubbing his hands over *my* body as if I had consented him to do anything of the sort. I thought of Rebecca's anguished face as she explained what Guedo had done to her, Brittney's face with the X through it, Chris screaming at Liam about his mum leaving him to do drugs. The image of a four-year-old Liam home alone while his mum got high next door was too much to bear.

I leaned over Ric, one hand on each arm of the chair. The waves crashed higher in my body until they reached my head. My eyes were filled with the thick, burning lava as it spilled out of my mouth uncontrollably.

'You are *disgusting*. Scum of the earth. You have killed hundreds, fuck, *thousands* of innocent people. Those poor women, those *children!* Being tortured and sold like they don't matter. And then you kidnap my best friend. You had a gun to her head…'

'Brooke!' Liam was attempting to pull me away without being too forceful. I shrugged him off dismissively.

'It was supposed to be me, well here I am! What are you going to do? Cut me open for organs, sell me to men, how much would I cost?' I'd lost all control. My vision was as red as the fire inside of me. 'If you kill, is it okay for me to kill you?'

'Look what you've done to her…' I heard Jamie shout from behind me. 'You and all your shit, you've turned her into a monster.'

'Jamie…' Liam began, but the door slammed before he could answer her.

'Brooke!' Liam shouted again.

'*What* Liam?' I shrieked, turning to face him.

He looked angry, really angry. But as soon as our eyes met his expression changed from anger to hunger. As my eyes locked with his, the tidal waves of lava began to calm.

'What's the plan after this, Ric?' Carlos interrupted the tension in the air.

'The er-plan-er-I don't know. All I know is he transport money to Italy in Summer every year.'

Liam and I finally dropped our gazes, turning our attention back to the matter at hand. My cheeks were flushed red and my heart was in my throat, courtesy of my outburst. *Where did that all come from?* I sighed as I tried to breathe normally again.

'It goes to Italy because he is from there?' Liam asked as he eyed me warily.

'Er. I think so. Seven has been living there lately too. Maybe that-er-reason. Guedo in charge over here for time being.'

My body was still reeling with anger; I couldn't calm it down. *This has never happened before.*

I waited for a sarcastic comment from A, but she too had been left breathless and confused from the tidal wave that had consumed her.

'So Guedo isn't Seven?' Neil questioned. 'Have you met Seven before?'

Ric shook his head. I knew it wouldn't be that easy, if Guedo wasn't Seven then who was? It didn't surprise me to hear that he was now hiding out in Italy, whoever he was.

I thought back to mine and Mr. Daniel's earlier conversation, could *he* be Seven? It seemed convenient that he quit his job when Seven had suddenly moved abroad. He wasn't in any of Harriet's notes either, could that be because he had hidden his identity so well? If that was the case, he had been right under our noses the whole time. I huffed in frustration at the thought of it.

'What did Matt have to do with all of this?' I still couldn't quite get my head around how Harriet and Matt were linked to this

whole
organization.

'Matt was recent, like hit man, he just took orders from Guedo to kill, he is someone police not expect, just normal boy. Guedo told him, get involved with new girls Mr. D employs, so that he can be on the inside too. Think he got a bit deep with latest one though, talking about love, said he was going to quit and blow the whole thing up in anger once… probably good he dead.'

My heart sank, even though Matt would have killed us all and done unspeakable things to me, I couldn't help but feel sad for him. He was probably so on edge after threatening to talk to the police when we had arrived unannounced at his house.

If he'd only let us speak to him instead of pulling out a gun, then maybe we could have helped each other.

Liam was looking at me with an expression that probably matched mine. We wouldn't be telling Billy about this revelation.

'This all very-er-dangerous for you,' Ric cautioned as his eyes jolted around the room. 'I'd give up or you will all die.'

'Oh don't worry, Ric.' Carlos pretended to reassure him, walking around to the front of him and standing next to me.

'You've been a big help today mate, we won't hurt you. *That much.*' he ruffled his hair and walked out of room.

I turned on my heel and left the room, leaving the disgusting creature with Neil.

I heard Liam's voice behind me. 'Brooke…'

'*Don't* ask me if I am okay!' I turned around angrily.

An amused look covered his face, 'Are you—?'

'Don't do it!' I tried to keep a straight face, but how could I when he was giving me that deliciously dreamy smile? He pulled me towards him with my wrists and wrapped me lovingly in his arms. I nestled my head into his chest, how could I stay angry when he was around?

'That was intense in there.' He commented.

'You seemed annoyed.'

'Me? What about you?' he laughed.

'Touché.'

'I wasn't annoyed anyway; I was… watching you… you were just so…'

'Spit it out.' I giggled.

'You were so *hot.*'

I pulled away from him so I could see in his eyes if he was joking — nope — all I could see was that hungry I-want-you-now look.

Wow.

Our eyes locked together once more, the longing between us was almost unbearable.

'You're so fucked up.' I breathed.

'Yet you stick around.' His lips lingered millimeters away from mine.

There we were in each other's arms, standing outside a room where we were holding someone hostage, and all I could think about was being consumed by Liam again. His smell, his curls, his glorious brown eyes, his taste. That was all I cared about.

'Because I'm fucked up too.' I gazed up at him.

'Get a room you two,' Neil muttered as he strolled past us and into the house.

Liam raised his eyebrows. 'Good idea.'

We lay at the end of the bed, clothes and pillows scattered below us on the ground, gazing into each other's eyes. Liam stroked my face and I smiled. The lava had disappeared completely, A was sleeping off her near death experience somewhere in the back of my mind, and all that was left was pure happiness.

'What are you smiling at?'

'Just funny how one person has such an effect on your whole being isn't it...' I thought out loud.

'Hmm, don't I know it.' he leant over and kissed me sweetly on the tip of my nose.

'I've been meaning to ask you,' I said idly as he rested upon his elbows. 'What's the deal with Neil and Carlos?'

'The deal?'

'Yeah, where did you find them?'

Liam laughed. 'I told you, Carlos was mum's friend and Neil just came with the package I guess.' He shrugged.

'I know, but they're so...' I couldn't find the words to describe them.

'Carlos is ex-army, if that's what you mean?'

I ran my fingers absentmindedly across Liam's back. 'That explains a lot I guess. And Neil?'

'I don't really know much about Neil, I think he had a bit of a dodgy upbringing and ended up getting caught up with the wrong people. But Carlos helped put him on the straight and narrow.'

'Owning guns, keeping people hostage and covering murders is the straight and narrow?' I raised my eyebrows. We couldn't help but laugh at the ridiculousness of what I had just said.

'Are we terrible people?' I asked Liam, even know I felt as though I already knew the answer.

He shook his head sadly. 'You, Brooke. *You* are not a terrible person. You were looking out for the people you love.'

My mind reverted back to Mr. Daniel's comments.

I bet you've done some things you thought you'd never be capable of, and you've justified them in the name of love.

I sighed. 'That was Mr. D on the phone earlier.' I admitted.

Liam shot me a disproving look, but continued caressing my hair. 'Why didn't you say anything?'

'A lot happened today. He was just saying that he was quitting work, and that I don't need to go back until September.'

'Well I know you're playing it down, but I'm too in love with you to argue.' Liam stated matter-of-factly.

My heart fluttered.

'You are?' I grinned.

He pulled me on top of him and leaned up to tuck my hair behind my ears. I grinned down at my beautiful curly haired boyfriend, all wide eyed and sleepy and knew that this was where I had always belonged.

'Do you think I have changed you, Brooke?' Liam frowned up at me.

'No!'

'Jamie seems to think so. She said I'd turned you into a monster…' his eyes studied my face wistfully.

'Do you think I'm a monster?' he shook his head. 'Well then, don't listen to her.'

'You have bewitched me, body and soul and I…' Liam started.

'And I love you, I love you.' I finished. 'Pride and Prejudice right?'

'Right.'

'Right…' I repeated as he pulled me down to kiss him once more.

I knocked on the door of Liam's spare bedroom; Jamie's quiet voice invited me in. She was lying on the small, single bed, her hair dripping wet from her shower.

The bright alarm clock on the nightstand let us know that it was approaching eleven pm.

Wow, we've been in bed for a long time! I blushed.

She turned around and smiled at me, sitting up.

'How are you feeling now?' I whispered, placing myself down next to her.

'I'm just really shaken up B. I thought I was going to die. I don't know when I'll feel better. *If* I'll feel better.'

I didn't know what to say, I still couldn't help but blame myself even after the countless times Liam and Jamie had said it really wasn't anyone's fault. I felt entirely responsible for Jamie being taken. After all, she was my best friend — I had got her involved with it all.

'I'm so sorry,' I murmured.

'B it's not your fault, I told you.'

'It is, I'm just glad you're okay.'

'It's not over though, it's just the beginning.' She sighed sadly.

I knew she was right, there was a long road ahead before we had any type of peace and safety. 'Where's Chris?' I changed the subject.

'His gone home to pack his things.'

'Pack his things?' I eyed her cautiously.

'He lives with his brother, I told him I wanted to go home. I need to get away from all of this.' She waved her arms around the room. 'His going to stay with me for a while.'

'You're leaving?' My heart dropped. I didn't want anything to change.

'B, I only stayed in this shit hole to make sure you were okay after you were shot.' She grimaced as she said this.

'I know, I just thought...'

'What? You thought we'd all live here together forever. This little fucked up family?'

'No of course not...' I slumped my shoulders.

'I'm leaving, Chris is leaving, Dale is never around us any more, Billy either. You should leave too. That boy is bad news.' She glared at me.

'You can leave. But I'm staying.' I stood up.

How dare she speak about Liam that way?

She scoffed. 'Of course you are. Have you been counselling recently?'

'I went the other week. Why?' I snapped.

'You need to look after yourself.'

'I'm fine.' I said through gritted teeth.

'I'm tired. Goodnight.' She sniffed as she slid back down onto the plumped up pillow.

'Night J,' I whispered as I turned off her light and creaked the door shut.

I leaned against the closed door and slid down to a seated position, hugging my knees to my chest and allowing myself a silent cry.

Everyone leaves you eventually, Brooke. Liam will too.

Oh, you're back. I snarled.

Can't get rid of me that easily.

XV

JUNE

We sat in the very familiar afterglow of another passionate evening, breathless and more in love than ever.

Jamie and Chris had moved out that weekend, Dale had seemingly cut ties with all of us, Billy popped in every now and then, and Neil and Carlos were too busy tending to the hostage situation.

Every time I thought of them dragging Ric out of the house and throwing him back into Carlos' Range Rover I shuddered.

What had they done with him? Did they kill him?

I decided to keep my fears about Ric to myself, I wasn't sure if I wanted any answers. If I knew anything it would mean I was an accomplice to a kidnapping and quite possibly a murder. *Another one.*

With the absence of everyone, Liam and I had been left in our own little bubble. Despite everything, it was strangely perfect.

I knew I was being selfish, but consuming myself in Liam's world helped distract me from the world that was crumbling apart around me. And *my god* was he a good distraction.

Liam pulled on his boxer shorts and switched off the projector that had been left with the credits of 'The Notebook' rolling.

I smiled adoringly up at him and his chiseled body as he placed the DVD back on his favorites row of the shelf. *Wow-ee.*

'How many times do you think we've watched that one now?' I laughed.

'You think *you've* watched it a lot, think of me before I met you!' he exclaimed as he took his place next to me again.

'You don't watch as many films now?' I frowned.

'No I guess I don't...' he pondered the thought as if it was the first time he'd considered it.

'Oh...' I sighed. Had I made him lose sight of himself? That was one of the first things he'd ever said to me, how much he *loved* films.

I smiled as I remembered the night all those months ago that we'd met on the ugly little bench outside my work.

'Only because I'm living my own love story now...' he added in a whisper as he studied me intensely.

Oh, wow.

At that moment Liam's phone buzzed from inside his trouser pockets. He picked them up from the floor and retrieved it.

I stretched out onto the beanbag and watched as he threw on his T-shirt. He said *living our own love story!* I tried to contain my obvious glee, fighting the urge to snatch his phone out of his hands and put myself there instead. I wanted to savor every last second with him before he started working again. He'd had a lot of time off recently, not that Carlos seemed to care.

My thoughts strayed to how attractive Liam looked in his navy overalls and tight white T-shirt. I traced the outline of my lips as I watched him read his phone.

He examined the screen for a few seconds, before letting out a painful yelp, as if all of the oxygen had left his body and he was fighting for air.

'What? What's happened?' I gasped.

The expression of fear and sadness and pain was painted all

over the face that was smiling from ear to ear not five seconds ago.

'It's my mum,' he croaked.

'Your *mum*?' the words left a strange taste in my mouth. The woman who he'd thought was dead. The woman that he had dedicated most of his life to. The woman I had heard so much about. And she chooses to *text* him after all of this time. Surely not?

Liam passed me the phone, his hands were trembling and his eyes filled to the brim with tears just waiting to fall down his gorgeous face. 'It's my mum texting me.' I looked down at the screen; sure enough there was a text message from an unsaved number:

This all needs to stop one way or another, before more people are killed. I'm fine. I am moving to Italy with G. Just get on with your own life and don't worry about me anymore. Please.

Mum x

'Do you really think that's your mum?' I whispered.

We sat in silence for what seemed like forever, I could almost hear Liam's heart thudding against his chest. 'I'm going to Italy.' He said boldly.

I opened my mouth to disagree with him, but closed it again. How could I disagree? This was his *mum* we were talking about. Finding out what happened to her had been his whole life, if there was even a one percent chance it was really her on the other end of the phone, I knew he would take it.

He glanced at me apologetically, studying my face for a reaction.

I smiled at him reassuringly and sighed. 'We can't just enjoy our twenties, being young and in love, can we? There's always something.'

'Seems that way...' he mumbled. 'This is something I have to do though Brooke, please understand?'

I nodded, 'Of course I understand. I'm coming with you... and don't even try to argue with me.' I raised my eyebrows as he opened his mouth to disagree. 'I will go with you to the ends of the earth if there's a chance your mum is alive.'

'I love you.' He sighed in defeat. We had lasted our whole relationship without arguing, that defiantly wasn't the time to start.

Billy looked down at the phone and then back up at Liam apprehensively. 'Shit, Liam, shit!'

The room was filled with bodies again, just like it was supposed to be. It was nice to see everyone back together, even if it wasn't under better circumstances.

When are we ever gathered under good circumstances?

I passed around bottles of beer, studying everyone's baffled and uncomfortable expressions as I did so.

Billy and Liam were sitting together on the smaller sofa with Billy's super-duper laptop close to hand.

Neil and Carlos were standing by the open patio doors, chain smoking and discussing something in secret.

Probably how they murdered Ric. I grimaced.

Chris was sitting on the larger sofa with Jamie perched on his knee. They smiled at me kindly as I passed them a bottle.

Jamie and I texted everyday — but I hadn't seen her since she'd moved out the week before. The thought of drifting from my best friend made a tear appear in my eye. I made a point of sitting with her and Chris instead of lingering by Liam. I received a warm smile from Jamie, I knew she appreciated the gesture.

'What's it like being back at home?' I smiled back.

'It's nice.'

I took a slurp of my cold beer and eyed her. *That's it? 'It's nice.' Maybe we had already drifted more than I'd realized.*

'She misses you.' Chris rolled his eyes. 'She talks about you all the bloody time. I'll leave you two ladies to have a catch up, before I have to endure another night of Brooke this, Brooke that.' He winked, kissing Jamie on the head before sliding from underneath her and walking over to join Carlos and Neil for a smoke. Jamie watched him leave with the same hopelessly in love, gooey-eyed expression I probably gave Liam all of the time.

222

'It's nice to see you so happy.' I smiled genuinely as she scooted closer to me.

'I am. And you?' She glanced over to Liam, 'I know we could be on better terms me and him, but I know his good to you.'

'I'm happy. I promise.'

She sighed deeply. 'Thing is, we should already know that about each other, we shouldn't be having a *catch up* we should just be there when things happen, like we always have been.'

'Yeah, you're right.' I sighed too. 'Things have just been…' I was at a loss. There were no words to describe how things had been, and there were certainly no words in the world to describe how things were about to get.

'Crazy. I know.' Jamie stated, after a moment of silence. She grabbed my hand and squeezed it. 'When this is all over we will go back to the old Jamie and Brooke. We can't lose each other, that's not happening.'

'That will never happen.' A few more tears gathered. I swallowed them back. *Be strong for Liam. Be strong.*

'So we've managed to trace the number that messaged Liam.' Billy announced after a few hours and far too many beers between us.

'Of course you have.' Neil snorted in amusement.

Carlos narrowed his eyes. 'Is it her?'

'There's no way of knowing if it's Liam's mum for sure. The IP address isn't accessible, so whoever sent the text knows what they are doing. But it did come from Italy. A town called Portofino, southeast of Genoa city to be exact.'

Everyone gaped at Billy in a mixture of awe and fear.

What have we got ourselves into? I can't go to Italy! This is crazy!

You're only just having doubts now? A bit late isn't it Brooke? You've already killed two men. A reminded me.

My heart was beating triple its usual speed and the contents of my stomach were making their way to my dry throat.

So you're going to leave Liam to go on his own? You've got two choices, dump Liam, or go with him and meet a human trafficker. A sneered at me.

I can't leave him... I can't go to Italy... I can't do this...

A punched me in the stomach. Hard. She was back with a vengeance.

'Brooke, you okay?' Jamie whispered from next to me. 'You've gone pale.'

I nodded. Words failed me.

'Panic attack?'

I nodded again.

'Oh dear.' Jamie sighed. Pulling me up off of the sofa and into the garden so that I could throw up without anyone seeing.

'I thought these had stopped?' she frowned at me as we sat on the crooked bench at the back of the garden.

'On and off.' I shrugged, wiping my mouth with the back of my hand and inhaling deeply. The warm evening air felt good on my clammy skin.

'Better?'

'Better.'

'I'm coming by the way.' Jamie stated.

'To Italy? Why?' I was surprised, she tolerated Liam at the best of times.

'Wherever you go, I go.' She smiled. 'Besides, if this is how ill you get from just thinking about going, what are you going to be like out there?'

I pondered this question for a second — my heart rate began creeping upwards.

Oh no, not again.

XVI

So there we all were, boarding passes and passports clutched tightly in our hands, waiting eagerly to board the plane.

After Billy had found out everything he possibly could from that one text message, we determined that the likelihood of it being Liam's mum was very thin.

We knew we were most likely walking into a trap from Guedo, or Mr. Daniels, or Seven himself. But we decided to go anyway because quite frankly, I believed after everything that had transpired, we had all gone totally and utterly mad.

I still couldn't quite comprehend that it was actually going to happen; we were potentially meeting a very dangerous man and we were all standing there with suitcases like we were going to have a lovely holiday.

I laughed quietly as I thought about how for a group of smart people, we were acting stupidly naïve.

Laugh while you still can Brooke. A niggled away in my stomach, working her way up to my chest and into my throat.

Please, not on the plane. I gulped down the nausea and inhaled deeply.

I knew we were in way over our head, even with Carlos and Neil by our sides, but still I went on, for the sake of Liam.

I glanced up at my beautiful, curly haired boyfriend and sighed, like I said, I would have followed him to the ends of the earth if I had to, and it was most likely going to get me killed.

225

Or kidnapped and sold on the sex market. Don't forget that possibility. A reminded me.

As the queue started to edge forwards, I watched as Billy disappeared into the plane door first, followed by Neil and Carlos. Eventually it was our turn.

We were greeted by an overly cheerful air stewardess wearing the brightest shade of red lipstick I had ever seen on her huge lips. 'Oh hello there, let me see your boarding passes, oh perfect, you are in D2,' she rambled on, fluttering her eyelashes at Liam as she spoke.

Hands off bitch, I don't have long left with him.

'D for doomed.' Jamie remarked from behind me, 'I'm the window seat, you guys sit together.' She barged past Liam and me and slumped herself by the window, leaving her suitcase in the aisle for Liam to put in the luggage holder. She was still angry with him for the Matt saga, no surprise.

Jamie had insisted on accompanying us, to the detriment of her relationship almost. Chris was adamant that we were all maniacs and he and Jamie had argument after argument about her coming with us. I tried to talk her out of it, but her mind was made up.

Seems Chris is the only sane one out of all of you. A sneered.

Well that doesn't offend me, I've never come under the sane bracket now have I?

Good point. She agreed as she tugged at my beating heart once more.

After twenty minutes or so of fidgeting in my seat and listening in on trivial conversations between the happy travelers around us, the plane began its assent.

There was a couple going on their honeymoon to the village of Nervi. They were disgustingly in love and wanted everyone

226

on the plane to know about it. The woman, with her bleach blonde hair and low-cut camisole, constantly planted inappropriate, never ending kisses on her Greek God like newly-weds.

I mocked them inwardly, they had nothing on mine and Liam's love story.

'I'm living my own love story.'

My heart grew wings every time I thought back to those beautiful words. I just hoped our love story didn't have a tragic ending. Little did I know.

I glanced to my right at Jamie, already sleeping soundly against the window. She'd pulled her silky hair into a messy bun on top of her head and her eye mask was still acting as a head band. I gently pulled it over her eyes, careful not to disturb her. Her phone buzzed for the hundredth time that morning.

It was Chris again.

From: Chris <3

04/07/2018

7:42am

I'm so glad you called before you took off. I only got annoyed because Liam has dragged enough of us into his mess. But I get why you're going. I love that you are a good friend to Brooke. I get that you worry about her. I worry about Liam too.

Be safe. Call me when you land. Can't wait to have you home. Miss you already.

Your C xx

'Oh, that's where she disappeared to earlier…' I thought out loud as I remembered her disappearing for ages as Liam and I were having a cigarette. I switched her phone to airplane mode and placed it gently in her bag.

'Huh?' Liam frowned at me.

'Nothing… Just glad that Jamie and Chris have sorted things out.'

'Oh, have they? That's good.' He replied half-heartedly as he fastened his seatbelt firmly and leaned back in his chair.

'We're going to be okay.' I whispered, but I wasn't sure if I was trying to convince him or myself.

After landing in Italy at around ten am, we made our way to the village of Portofino. The fresh air blew through the taxi window, hitting my cheeks as it did so. I watched admiringly as the pastel colors of the houses whizzed by. I wished with all of my being that I was there under different circumstances, and that Liam and I had just been a normal couple going on holiday together.

There could be worse places to die I guess? I sighed.

The hotel was beautiful, it overlooked the sparkling blue sea. I wanted to strip off my clothes and my worries and run into it with Liam by my side.

My stomach churned with nerves once more, it was as though A was attempting to pull me back to England. To the comfort of Jamie's double bed where we lay giggling about the fit boy on the TV and getting ready for Christmas.

How did we get here?

Too late to wonder that now, Brooke.

We made our way up to the top floor of the hotel and lugged our suitcases into the large room.

Liam looked at me, and then nodded towards the double bed which had been perfectly made with fresh white bedding for our arrival.

I rolled my eyes and blushed. 'Do you ever stop?'

He gazed at me with the same intense, bare-into-my-soul expression he always did and I melted a little more inside.

Maybe it was the impending death threat that turned us on, but whatever it was, the electricity between us was as intense and world consuming as ever.

'I will never stop wanting you.' He broke the electric silence as he pulled me on the bed with him.

It was late afternoon. We were famished, thirsty, and quite honestly I needed to come up for air. We decided to take a walk around the village.

'Let's act like we are on a normal holiday.' Liam grinned, taking my hand and speeding us out of the hotel lobby.

I giggled. 'I like the sound of that.'

'Shall we pretend we are a normal couple too?' He laughed. He looked beautiful in his white linen shirt and matching shorts. His hair was scraped back with some black sunglasses. The sun sparkled majestically against his gorgeously tanned skin.

Wow.

I grinned back at him. 'I don't think we could be a normal couple if we tried.'

'No. You're right. We're Liam and Brooke, that's much better.'

We spent the sunny afternoon strolling aimlessly hand in hand, giddily in love and in our own world.

It was as though Liam hadn't pulled me out of 'Brooke Land.' Instead, he'd entered it with me, casting love and light throughout the whole place, and it was only us two, just how I liked it.

We strolled past the high-end boutiques and pretty pastel colored houses. Liam treated me to an ice cream as we perched on the harbor wall, watching in awe as the huge yachts bobbed up and down.

'Wow.' I gazed at the majestic view. The sun was low in the

sky and glistened over the clear blue sea like glitter.

'I know. Wow.' Liam agreed through licks of his ice pop.

Later, we followed a pathway and stumbled upon a museum named *Castello Brown*, there was an art exhibition taking place there.

As we wondered through the countless pieces of art work I couldn't help but say what I had been keeping in ever since Liam had received that dammed text message.

'Can't we just have a normal life, without all of this trauma and death around us? Isn't this enough?'

I spun around pointing at all of the amazing paintings and happy art-lovers surrounding us.

Liam looked at me wistfully. 'Brooke, don't ever think that all of this...' He held my hand and spun me around again. '...Isn't enough for me. Because it is. it's more than I could ever have imagined.'

I sighed, knowing what was going to follow that perfect sentence. 'But it's your mum, I know.'

'Brooke, if you're scared I can do this alone.' He assured me for the thousandth time.

I shook my head in refusal. 'Not happening.'

We walked around the village some more, the evening air grew brisk and the moon shone brightly above the endless sea, shining down on him. My beautiful Liam.

I grasped his hand in to mine and lent my head adoringly onto his shoulder as we approached a crowd of people gathered around a man playing the piano. We stopped to listen as he finished his gorgeous rendition of Unforgettable.

There were a few soft applauses from the crowd as he shuffled in his chair and prepared for his next song.

'How amazing is it here?' Liam gazed around with the look

of a giddy child on Christmas morning painted upon his face.

'Amazing.' I agreed as the magical sound of the piano echoed around the cobbled street again.

As if Liam's face couldn't light up any more, he turned to me and grinned widely as he heard the notes being played at the start of the song.

Of course, just as we stumbled across the piano man, he would play a song from 'When Harry Met Sally.'

For a brief moment A seemed to vanish into thin air. All that she left behind was happiness and love.

Maybe everything will be okay.

'I think this is the universe's way of saying that we are where we should be.' I smiled at Liam, and in that moment I believed it with all of my beating heart.

'It had to be you, it had to be you...' The ruggedly handsome man playing the piano began to sing as Liam took my hand once more, parading me around in a circle before pulling me towards him and holding me in a perfect ballroom like stance.

I giggled loudly.

He held his hand to his heart and threw his head back dramatically. 'That sound. I love hearing you laugh. I love dancing with you. I love *you.*'

He swayed me side to side as he sang along. 'It had to be you, wonderful you, it had to be you...'

He sang so loudly that the crowd seemed to part in the middle, right where we were dancing.

'Oh, abbiamo degil piccioncini qui stanotte,' Piano man said through the microphone as he smiled at us. We stared at him with blank, apologetic expressions on our faces.

'Sorry, we're English!' Liam shouted over to him.

The man carried on playing the tune and laughed at us.

'Sorry, sorry, English. I see we have some lovers out here, yeah?' he translated.

'For nobody else gave me a thrill...' he continued the song. I blushed as everyone was staring at us now.

'Better give them a show Brooke, they're waiting,' he said as he carried on dancing.

'Guess we better.' I laughed lovingly back at him, allowing him to spin me around as he continued to sing.

Even his voice is beautiful.

We carried on dancing around the cobbles as everyone clapped and the happy crowd grew larger in size.

My eyes glanced around as we danced. The moonlit sea, the piano, the song, even the strangers staring at us; and him, *oh him.*

Everything was perfect.

'For nobody else gave me a thrill, with all your faults, I love you still. Baby it had to be you, wonderful you. It had to be youuuuuu.'

The Piano man and Liam both stopped singing and the crowd erupted with applause and cheer.

'Ay, you got a bigger cheer than me for those moves.' piano man bowed towards us. 'God bless you both.'

God isn't going to help these criminals!

Aaaaand she's back. I sighed.

I took my rightful place on Liam's chest as we threw ourselves onto the bed in our hotel room and nested tightly into him.

'What a day.' Liam exhaled. 'I'm so happy with you.'

'I love you.' I whispered through the lump in my throat.

'Hey,' he said, tilting my chin upwards so he could look me in the eyes. 'Don't be sad about it, everything is going to be fine, we get to be in love and happy like this for the rest of our lives.'

'However short that may be.' I added.

'I love you too.' he sighed, obviously too tired for an argument, or maybe deep down he knew I was right.

I opened my eyes a few hours later. We were still lying in the same positions on the bed, fully clothed. I squinted at the bright alarm clock and saw that it was only one am.

I still have a good few hours before we have to go back to reality.

Sighing, I glanced up at Liam, whose chest I was still rested on. I knew exactly how I would want to spend quite possibly my last hours on earth.

'Liam,' I whispered, kissing his neck gently. He squirmed and sat up suddenly, throwing me sideways.

'Sorry, sorry, everything is fine.' I assured him as I wrapped my legs around his waist and ran my fingers through his soft, curly brown hair that I loved so much. 'I love you,' I whispered. I looked into Liam's perfect face as he held mine in his hand. 'Whatever happens, I love you.'

He nodded slowly as he woke. 'I love you too.' He smiled at me crookedly, before sliding us both to the edge of the bed and reaching for a bag that was hidden in the shelf of the bedside table.

'What's that?' I wondered as I repositioned myself on his lap, not wanting to ever let go.

'I was going to wait until tomorrow night... take you for dinner... but... what the hell... close your eyes.'

I did as I was told. I heard the rustling of the bag as he retrieved something from it and the sound of the lamp above the bed being switched on.

Wait for what? I breathed heavily in anticipation.

He took a deep breath in before saying, 'okay, you can open

them.'

It took a second for my eyes to adjust to the light; Liam was examining my face closely as he waited for a reaction.

I glanced down, and there in his hand was a tiny box that had been opened, showcasing the sparkling diamond ring that was sitting inside.

I looked at the ring and then back at his wide-eyed, hopeful face. I pulled myself off of his lap and stood in front of him, shocked to my core. 'You do think we're going to die!' I exhaled, tears pouring from my eyes.

He perched himself up onto his knees and pulled me close to his warm body with one hand, the other still clutching the jewelry box. 'No I'm not going to let that happen, Brooke. Just, just shh for once and let me do this properly!'

He beamed as he clambered off of the bed and placed himself down onto one knee.

Oh wow. Liam is on one knee in front of me! Am I dreaming?

He quickly attempted to tidy his head of curls and straighten his wrinkled clothes. Although he looked pretty perfect to me.

My eyes glistened with tears as he started to speak again. 'I've always loved films, especially romance, you know this about me right?'

I nodded. 'Of course, of course I know that.'

He laughed sleepily. 'Of course you do. Yeah.

Well since the moment I met you I've felt like my life has just been one big romantic film... no... it's been *better* than a film.'

I giggled at his attempt to remember the speech he'd clearly been rehearsing. 'Even better than The Notebook?'

'Brooke, you're even better than the Notebook.' His eyes were filled with excitement and passion. *Wow.*

'All these quotes I've collected in my head over the years, all those films I've watched and loved, I never really *understood* them. I thought things like that didn't happen in real life. Especially to people like me. I thought that it just happened in the movies...

And then I met you, oh *you...*' he let out a happy sob.

I dropped to my knees so that our tear-filled eyes were level with each other, clutching his wrists as his shaky hands attempted to hold the ring box still.

He placed a kiss on the tip of my nose and chuckled. 'I can do this. I just wasn't expecting to do this right now.'

I smiled adoringly back at him. 'Take your time. I'm not going anywhere.'

'So, I met you, and from the word go, that night on the bench, and then the bar, and then Primrose Hill. I kept looking at you like, wow, just *look at her.* I was *dumbfounded* by you. Still am.

I'm mesmerized by you and I have been since that first little sneeze...' he kissed my nose again. 'I understand what he meant in Sleepless in Seattle when he said the first time he touched her it was like coming home. The first time we kissed, Brooke, I knew *you* were home. The home I've been looking for my whole life it seems.

I get why in A Fault in Our Stars, Augustus said it would be a privilege to have his heart broken by Hazel, because my God, you are a privilege to love Brooke. And if I die tomorrow then it will be a privilege to die having you love me.'

I let out a loud cry, but he continued excitedly.

'You had me at hello. If you're a bird, I'm a bird. To me, you are perfect. Here's looking at you kid. All of it, it all makes complete sense to me now.

In When Harry Met Sally he says that when you meet the person you want to spend the rest of your life with, you want the rest of your life to start as soon as possible. And I understand that now. We haven't known each other long, I know that. But it doesn't matter. I know what I want.

This is the rest of our life Brooke, being married, being happy, and I want that to start as soon as possible. What do you say? Will you marry me?'

He breathed for the first time it seemed in that whole minute.

I wanted to stay in that moment for eternity. His words echoed throughout my mind, body and soul. *Will you marry me? Wow.*

'Yes.' I whispered.

'Yes?' he repeated. 'You'll marry me?'

'Yes I'll marry you!' I shouted. 'Yes!'

He laughed joyously. 'You said yes!'

'Of course I said yes.' I shook my head, sobbing uncontrollably by this point.

He slid the ring effortlessly on my finger, as if it was made to be there.

'It's beautiful.' I smiled, tears now pouring down my face and dropping to the floor before I could stop them.

He cupped my cheeks with his hands and kissed each tear away. 'You're beautiful.'

'Life is not the amount of breaths you take, it's the moments that take your breath away, right?' I smiled. It seemed like the right thing to say for the situation we were in.

He laughed 'Ooooh, she's quoting Hitch now people. She's wifey material.'

Jumping up, he pulled me with him and span me around in the air. 'I love you, I love you, I love you.'

He placed me down on the floor, his arms still wrapped around me. I looked up at his ridiculously happy smile and I knew mine reflected his.

That moment right there, my future husband laughing and loving me so intensely. That was a moment I would never forget.

That moment would for sure, always take my breath away.

XVII

'We'll tell everyone later,' I whispered as we walked towards the café that Billy had told us to meet him at. 'Let's just get this out of the way first.' I swallowed nervously.

Carlos, Neil and Billy were all waiting for us outside a quaint café on the street.

'Where's Jamie?' I shouted down the pavement at them.

'She's in there.' Billy pointed across the road at what looked to be a little corner shop. 'You know, just in case they blow this place up one of us has to keep the memory of the gang alive.' He joked as we stopped next to him, but I wasn't amused.

Liam and I had stayed up all night celebrating our good news, and spent most of that morning doing much of the same. I didn't want to waste a single second of lying in that bed with him sleeping, I wanted to have him all to myself as much as I could before we pressed the un-pause button and went back to the reality that was looming over us.

'So what's the plan?' I grimaced. 'Why are we here?'

I really don't want to know.

'I put an alert on the phone number that messaged Liam. Although I still couldn't access the IP address or any more information, I thought it might come in handy if they receive any more messages. One pinged up about nine this morning. Whoever sent the message is having a meeting here today.'

'What did the message say exactly?' Liam asked, still clutching onto my hand.

Billy looked down at my left hand and smiled knowingly,

nothing got past him. 'Er. Just this address and see you there tomorrow.'

Liam frowned. 'Seems a bit convenient that the whole address is in the text, don't you think?'

Carlos grunted.

'That's what we were thinking. Last night while you were gallivanting off seeing the sights, we were in the bar sorting things out and talking about possible outcomes. Being set up was definitely up there on the list.' Neil remarked.

'Set up?' I frowned. My heart dropped. The happy bubble had well and truly been popped.

'I mean, it's possible they know I've tracked the phone and sent that message as a trap. Like it's possible that the original message was a trap too. But we've said this from the outset.' Billy eyed Liam warily.

Liam nodded. 'Look, before we go inside…' Liam began, but Carlos interrupted him.

'Liam don't even say it, none of us are changing our minds, none of us are scared, if Georgina is in there, we're going in and if she isn't, we're still going in because we're not leaving you alone with fucking scum of the earth Guedo okay?' he boomed, he was a man of few words, but when he spoke, people listened.

'Okay,' Liam murmured. 'Thank you.' He held onto my hand so tightly I thought my blood circulation would stop. I was thankful for the much-needed support — if it wasn't for him, I'd be curled up on the floor in a ball.

'Don't get all emotional on us boy,' Carlos said as he ruffled his hair. 'I didn't raise you like that.'

I glanced at the shop across the street, hoping to catch a glimpse of Jamie before I entered the unknown.

Please God. Keep us safe today. I begged.

Like I said before. God isn't going to help you criminals. A snarled as she donkey-kicked my stomach so hard I nearly curled over.

We stepped inside the cozy little café and chose the table in the furthest corner to sit.

It wasn't busy, there were two other tables, one with an elderly man who was tucking into a large breakfast and a strong smelling cup of coffee. He wore an aged brown suit with matching dress shoes. His eyes glistened blue like they held a million stories of a young Italian boy living the dream.

A few seats away from him sat a teenage boy and girl sipping on milkshakes and giggling innocently to each other. I smiled wistfully at how simple their lives looked and hoped that after that day mine would be equally as easy. *Pfft. Keep dreaming Brooke.*

We ordered some drinks, and then all we could do was wait.

Liam's leg shook nervously under the table.

Carlos and Neil were as apprehensive as I'd ever seen them, and Billy's eyes shot suspiciously across the room at anyone who made a movement.

Me? Well I was full of dread.

I wanted whoever was coming to just be a no-show so Liam would go back to being the happy care-free person he had been the night before.

'I love you.' he mouthed to me as I glanced over to him.

'Love you too.' I smiled reassuringly back.

After a while, the bell on the door jingled, breaking the sickening silence.

A woman wearing a pair of oversized sunglasses confidently strolled in. She was dressed in a clean, nude-coloured suit and had her long, dark hair slicked back into a perfect pony tail.

'She looks like she's in meeting attire…' I hissed, turning back around in my chair to face the others.

All of their jaws had dropped.

'What?' I frowned, spinning back around to face her again.

She was strutting across the cafe to our table. 'Hello boys, long time no see,' she said with conviction.

Then, she took off her sunglasses and I knew exactly who she was.

'Mum?' Liam croaked. 'How, how…'

'How, how, how?' She mimicked him mockingly as she scraped over a chair and placed herself down next to me at the table.

'Hello, you must be Brooke?' she held out her hand for me to shake, I starred at her hand and back up at her in disbelief.

'You shake it sweetie, let's not get off on the wrong foot now.' She smiled. But it wasn't a friendly smile.

I quickly shook her hand. 'Sorry, hi. I just, I've always known you to be dead,' I rambled.

She laughed. 'Well at least this one can string a sentence together, anyone else?' She looked over at the others, studying them intensely.

So that's where Liam gets it from.

'Carlos, Neil, you're looking *gorgeous* as ever, and I'm guessing you're Billy?' She tilted her head towards him. 'They said you'd be the runt of the litter.

And then there's my Liam baby.' She smiled again.

Why is her smile so unnerving?

Liam looked angry, his leg was still shaking and his fist was clenched, the pit in my stomach grew, something didn't feel right at all.

'What the *fuck?* How are you sitting in front of me right now with your Prada sunglasses on looking like *that?*'

'Let me explain…' she leant forwards. 'You probably have a lot of questions…'

Carlos snorted and bellowed above her as she spoke. 'I second that. For someone who is being held captive by her abusive boyfriend and a bunch of human traffickers you look pretty good to me. Because that's the only reason you would have disappeared and left your four-year-old son isn't it, George? Not by *choice*. Surely not.'

Georgina flipped her ponytail jokingly and winked at Carlos. 'Why thank you. You look pretty good to me too darling.'

My stomach flipped and I suddenly felt the urge to run.

'I understand you've been trying to find me?' she raised her perfectly plucked eyebrows.

'All my life.' Liam's voice cracked.

Oh, my beautiful Liam. he looked so *hurt*.

'And you've stumbled across a few things lately. No thanks to this one?' she elbowed me playfully. I tried my best to offer her a smile through my nausea. 'You want answers?'

'Would be nice. We've come all this way.' Neil snapped. Billy stared at her completely bemused, still not uttering a word.

'Why do you care so much? You thought I'd died right?' she directed her question to Liam, he nodded. 'So if I was dead, why not accept it and move on?'

Liam's eyes widened in shock. 'Because you're my mum? I wanted to know what had happened to you.'

'You still want to know?'

'You're still my mum, aren't you?' he replied quietly.

Georgina studied his broken-hearted face for a moment.

'So you found out about Guedo setting up Rebecca?'

'That's true?' Neil shouted. 'I'll kill him.'

'You'll do no such thing.' Georgina glared at him menacingly.

'Still putting him first over everyone I see.' Carlos murmured.

Georgina ignored him, continuing her line of questioning. 'And you know about Marylyn Daniels' involvement?'

His name is Marylyn? I would never have guessed.

We all nodded slowly.

'And you know who Seven is?'

'No! No! We know nothing about that.' Liam rushed his words frantically. 'We got caught up in that by accident. Brooke's friend was somehow involved. I didn't know it had anything to do with *you*. I'm so confused. You work for Seven?' he gulped at the prospect.

'So you're telling me that you knew all about Guedo killing Britney, about Guedo setting up Rebecca. About your *friend* knowing all about Seven, finding out about Marylyn being involved, you knew *all* of that, and you didn't link any of it?'

I coughed nervously to clear my throat. 'Yes. I did,' I squeaked.

What are you doing Brooke? Keep quiet!

'So one of you has a brain.' She smirked. 'So what's your take on this? I'm intrigued.' She leaned back in her chair and studied me.

'Er… I think that Guedo works under Seven. And I thought, *we all* thought, that you'd got caught up in it somehow and that's why you were killed. We thought Guedo had killed you. Or that if you weren't dead you were too afraid to leave. I think that's why the boys are really shocked that you are, er, doing okay…'

I paused and studied her face. I could see where Liam got his good looks from — he was her double.

243

He had inherited her dark chocolate eyes and tanned complexion. I guessed from her long curled eyelashes and thick hair that she most probably shared his natural curls when it wasn't styled and straightened to perfection.

It led me to wonder what his dad looked like, he must have got his height and build from him because she was a very petite woman.

'Er…' I continued cautiously. 'I think that Guedo setting up Rebecca was his way of tying up loose ends, protecting himself from anyone that may draw negative attention to him, that kind of thing. And killing your friend Britney, we thought maybe that was a warning to you?'

Georgina cackled in amusement. 'My *friend*? Oh you really have got the wrong end of the stick there.

Say Brooke, if some *whore* decided she was going to give Liam her number while you two were dating, would you want that bitch dead?'

'Er, I wouldn't like her.' I mumbled, shrugging my shoulders.

'You say not liking her, I say wanting a bullet to go through her skull, same difference,' she retorted.

'*You* killed her?' Liam asked. 'What about the note, from Guedo?'

'Guedo left me a little love note after *he* killed her for me, so romantic. It was when we'd decided to leave and elope.' she gushed.

'You're *married* to him?' Liam gasped.

'When did you become so fucked up George?' Carlos questioned sadly.

She shot them both an unnerving look. 'We're getting off topic here, continue.' She aimed at me.

'Okay. Er, I know that Mr. Daniels was being blackmailed, quite possibly by Seven, to keep the NCA far away from the organization. And I think that Matt and Harriet were threatening to blow up the whole thing, so Seven was keeping tabs on them, that's why they were so scared. And…' I breathed heavily, eyeing the five sets of eyes goggling me intensely.

'And?' Georgina prodded.

'…And I think that the biggest mistake you ever made was leaving your incredible son to go along with that scumbag. You've missed out on getting to know him and watching him grow into the amazing man he is today. The man I'm going to marry.'

I flinched as she shot up in her seat.

'Brooke…' Liam hissed apprehensively, his eyes filled with worry.

'You stood up to my mum so I'm trying to do the same.' I shrugged. He nodded in reply. It wasn't the time or place for a domestic.

'Well done for that remarkable take on the whole situation. But you still haven't *quite* got it.' Georgina stated, her dark eyes glared at me sinisterly. 'Wow. You really do love each other aye. And what about Ric?' she ordered. 'What happened to him?'

The boys shot me a concerned look before answering her. 'Ric's dead, we had to save Jamie that night, I mean they fucking took a twenty-four-year-old girl for no reason…' Neil snarled emotionally.

'…Oh, there are lots of reasons why someone would take a twenty-four-year-old girl.' Georgina remarked sinisterly.

Of course they killed Ric. Why had I even considered another alternative?

Neil looked at my guiltily, noticing my internal turmoil. 'Ric

245

said he was going to hunt us all down and kill us, we didn't have a choice.'

Georgina shrugged. 'Guess you didn't have a choice then. Ric was an idiot anyway, no loss there.'

How is she so blasé to death?

There was a moments silence, the tension at the table was so thick you could cut it with a knife.

Billy was still muted; I think he had gone into shock. Carlos and Neil's anger was visibly bubbling through their huge bodies, causing their faces to turn red.

And I couldn't even look at my poor, heartbroken Liam in the eyes. Then, the silence was over and the nightmare began.

Pulling a gun out from the waistband of her suit trousers and slamming it on the table, Georgina called to the waiter who had served us our drinks.

'You. Lock the doors. Now.' She clicked her fingers.

Panic stricken, he ran to the door, ushering the customers out as he did so.

The teenagers' milkshakes went flying as they fled and the elderly man jolted up in his chair and followed them as fast as his unsteady legs would allow him to. The waiter slid across the locks and changed the sign to 'closed' before turning back around to face us.

What is she going to do?

She's going to kill you all. A shrugged. *'Bout time I had a break, you're exhausting Brooke. It's a full time stint with you.*

'Go in the kitchen and don't come out, even if you hear gunshots.' Georgina instructed him. He sped past us and disappeared into the kitchen.

'Mum, why are there going to be gunshots?' Liam asked slowly.

246

'You're still calling me mum?' She chuckled nastily. 'Even though I'm pointing a gun to you all, you're still holding onto the silly hope that I'm going to pick you up and squeeze you tight and tell you everything's going to be okay because mummy is here. Well in answer to your earlier question, no, I am not your mother and I haven't been since I left. That part of my life is dead and gone, you with it.'

Liam's eyes filled to the brim with tears, I could tell he was holding them back with every ounce of his being.

'Anyway, relax, I'm not going to kill anyone today, I don't want blood on my new suit.'

She sighed, leaning back in her chair once again but still gripping onto the gun that was placed on the table. 'As long as you all agree to my terms, then nobody is going to get hurt.'

'What terms?' Neil growled.

Billy was shaking uncontrollably, Liam was too. I wanted to scoop them up in my arms and take them away from that horrendous woman. They were too precious. *They can't die.*

'You quit your job or you'll end up like Harriet.' Georgina snapped at me. 'And the rest of you, give up. Move away. Don't contact each other, we'll know. You don't look for me or Guedo or anyone ever again. Understand?'

'What did you do to Harriet?' My voice cracked. *Oh no. Not Harriet too.*

Georgina shrugged as if it didn't matter. The red lava that I had only ever experienced when talking to Ric, began to boil through my body once again.

'What. Did. You. Do. To. *Harriet?*' I repeated, more aggressively that time.

'Oh she's got fire; I like her for you.' She said to Liam before facing me again.

'See, you don't even know what happened to your pretty little friend. If you must know, Harriet and Matt had decided that they were going to turn us all in. And then *strangely* Matt disappeared.'

She raised her eyebrows and patted her nose knowingly. How did she know what had happened to Matt? We thought we had hidden that terrible day up so well.

'She couldn't live with herself through the grief, she knew he wouldn't just leave her, so she thought *we* had killed him.

She decided that enough was enough, she had to finish what they had started. She went to Marylyn and told him everything they knew. Silly little girl.' Georgina paused and rolled her eyes. 'So I killed her.'

I wailed. I wanted to be sick. *Harriet! Oh my god! No!*

'More details? Ok… Well Marylyn sent her a text to meet him a day or so after she had told him everything, of course she jumped at the chance. She thought that she'd finally caught us.' She sniggered. *She's sniggering at Harriet! That bitch.*

She really is a bitch, and that's coming from me! A agreed. She was surfing on the red waves this time, coming prepared after she had nearly drowned in the lava before. The waves were growing larger and hotter inside of my body. I wanted to explode.

'Then we pulled her into the car and kept her locked up in one of the houses we have going at the moment. Eventually though that annoying girl got rather loud, crying and calling for help so I slit her throat and threw her into the nearest river I could find.

Then I moved out here because Marylyn had told me they were closing in on Seven at the NCA. After that idiot Spence got arrested. I couldn't keep getting my hands dirty.'

I cupped my hands over my mouth, feeling as though I could

throw up at the thought of poor Harriet and how scared she must have been. I just wished she'd involved me in what she and Matt were planning; maybe we could have helped them.

'You keep saying we?' Liam frowned. 'She thought *we* had killed him. A house *we* have going on at the moment… you're not just Guedo's girlfriend, you're not being blackmailed or too scared to leave. You're *involved* in all of this. You do it on *purpose.*'

It was his turn to cup his mouth with his shaky hands.

Georgina smiled. 'Getting closer.'

'Let them out of here, this is between me and you. No one else.' He sniffed.

'Liam, no!' I argued. 'We're not going anywhere.'

'She's right, they're not.' Georgina cackled. 'I'm not that stupid. Anyway, this isn't just between you and me because *you* got all of these poor people involved.' And without a second thought she lifted up the gun, grabbed me and pointed it towards my head.

Liam jumped up in his seat in sheer panic. 'NO!' he screamed.

'I know I said no one was going to die. But you know a lot more than I initially thought. *She* is more clocked-on than all of you put together.'

'Please. No. Not her. Shoot me.' Liam begged.

Carlos, Neil and Billy were watching me in shock. I noticed Carlos and Neil both had their hands placed inside their jackets.

How did they smuggle guns here? Then I thought back to Neil's earlier remark. *'Last night while you were gallivanting off seeing the sights. We were in the bar sorting things out…'* At least that was a glimmer of hope, we had some sort of defense prepared.

249

She pressed the gun harder against my head and dug her nails into my shoulder. I looked at Liam; I wanted him to be the last thing I saw if this unhinged woman decided to blow my brains out.

'Don't even think about pulling a gun on me. I'll shoot her as soon as you do.' She hissed.

Their hands slowly made their way back to the tabletop, both their fingers were twitching in anticipation ready to grab them again. It was like witnessing a wild western show down.

Weirdly, with a gun pointed to my head, it was the calmest I'd felt all afternoon. The choice had been taken away from me, it was in her hands now. There was nothing I could do to change that.

'We don't know anything important. We don't know who Seven is, we don't know where you and Guedo live. I don't care anymore, after meeting you I don't want to know another thing. Just let her go. *Please.*' Liam pleaded.

Carlos narrowed his eyes at Georgina and sighed. 'She's not letting any of us go Liam.'

Liam shot him a frantic look. 'Of-of course she is!'

Carlos leant over and grabbed Liam's shoulders as he shook uncontrollably. 'There's something we know now that we didn't before though, right? We didn't know your mum was a crazy bitch involved in the whole thing. Shit sounds like she's bloody *running* it!'

He turned slowly to face her, one hand still clutching Liam.

Georgina laughed hysterically, she really was deranged. 'He's right my darling, I never had any intentions of letting you walk out of here alive. You see, you remember me as mummy dearest who worked so hard to provide a better life for you. But that was never the case. Guedo and I are in love and I would have followed him anywhere.'

'He brainwashed you mum.' Liam couldn't hold back the tears any more. 'You were a good mum at one point.'

Georgina snorted. 'What do you remember? You were a toddler when I met Guedo. He loves me and he wanted me to come with him. I finally had a place in this world. Look at me.'

She swung her hair over her shoulder once again, the part of my head where she had been pressing the gun for some time now was pulsating agonizingly.

'I look great, I'm powerful, people listen to me, people are *scared* of me and these silly girls that get themselves taken should take a leaf out of my book before becoming so pathetic and weak.'

'So you're going to kill your own son for a bit of power.' Liam sniffed.

I closed my eyes and attempted to drown out the conversation they were having; it was only prolonging the inevitable.

We were all going to die here.

I kept my eyes firmly shut as I processed all of the new information. It was all beginning to make perfect sense now.

She was a lost cause long before she went missing; Guedo had made sure of that. Being in an abusive relationship had led Georgina to make some awful decisions. She didn't care about Liam, she only cared about Guedo.

She wasn't on the CCTV footage of the incident with Rebecca because she had helped to set that up, Rebecca had spoken out against Guedo and she had to be sorted out.

She wasn't included in the line-up on the board in Matt's house because he had never seen her before, she wasn't a victim or a disposable employee like Matt and Mr. Daniels... She was

251

the person in charge… Georgina was Seven.

'G, the seventh letter of the alphabet.' I whispered. 'It's been right under our noses the whole time…'

'Clever girl!' Georgina shrieked, finally pulling the gun away from my head and pushed me forcefully towards Liam. He jumped up and stood in front of me, it was like being in Matt's house all over again.

She walked over to the front door, unlocking it — for a split second I thought she was going to let us out — but then I saw him walking towards the café, dragging Jamie along with him.

I didn't think my heart could sink any lower, but it did.

'Hey baby.' Georgina gushed as Guedo stormed through the door, a few of his minions followed after him dressed head to toe in black.

'My mum is Seven?' Liam sobbed as I grabbed onto his arms from behind.

'Liam, we need to get out of here now.' I whispered shakily. I watched as Guedo threw Jamie to the floor. 'Jamie! Don't hurt her, please…' I begged, but no one was listening.

Guedo clicked his gun and pointing it towards her head. 'This one was hiding across the street.' His gruff voice bellowed throughout the tiny room.

Georgina knelt down to her level and pulled Jamie's chin up to face her. 'Hello sweetie, so you're the one that got away?' She studied her face for a moment. 'Well you're very beautiful aren't you? There's going to be lots of men who are going to *love* you.'

She smiled menacingly.

Jamie looked at me with a powerless expression painted across her pale white face before turning back around slowly and spitting in Georgina's eye.

'Fuck you! Fuck all of you!' She screamed.

Georgina stood up and shrugged. 'Shame, we would have made a lot of money with her.' she nodded to Guedo while wiping her eye with the back of her hand.

Before I could let out a cry, the sound of Guedo's gun pierced through the air. Jamie's body fell lifelessly forwards as her blood covered the entirety of the surrounding area.

My knees dropped to the crisp, solid floor with a painful thud, Liam tried to pull me towards him, but I was frozen on the floor.

From that moment on it was as though everything around me was happening in fast forward, whilst I was stuck in slow motion.

I watched through tear-filled eyes as Carlos and Neil grabbed their guns. Carlos took the first shot, hitting a surprised Guedo in the chest. He fell to his knees and grasped the wound while shooting aimlessly around the room, attempting to catch Carlos and Neil with one of his bullets.

The gunshots pierced continuously through my ears. Neil had taken care of the three other men who were in the room on his own as Carlos strolled over to Georgina and Guedo.

Bodies were draped over the tables where less than an hour ago people were sitting, happily sipping milkshakes from.

Georgina was attempting to pull Guedo out of the café as he grew weaker, but Carlos wasn't going to let that happen. He violently yanked Georgina away with one hand as he pointed the gun at Guedo's head with the other.

Guedo managed to pull himself up slightly onto his elbow. 'You don't want to kill me; you won't find anyone.' He smiled smugly at Carlos.

'You just killed Jamie! Of course I want to fucking kill you.' Carlos shouted back and before Guedo could say anything else a bullet met the middle of his forehead.

Georgina let out a chilling scream. 'NO!' she cried as she frantically tried to pull away from Carlos' tight grip.

Neil ran over to Liam and me, shouting over the cries of Georgina. 'We've got to get her out of here Liam!'

I could just about hear him — the ringing of the bullet that had entered Jamie's head was still screeching in my ears.

Somehow Georgina had managed to grab hold of Guedo's gun. Carlos let out a bellowing wail as she shot him in the leg before charging towards us.

'Big mistake!' she screamed. Carlos managed to pull her back which gave Neil just enough time to pick me up and run me out of the building — he threw me to the pavement as he flew back inside towards Georgina and Carlos who were battling it out on the ground.

I could see Liam tugging on Billy's arm, who was sat frozen in the seat he'd been perched on since we had entered the café.

'Billy, Liam!' I screamed. 'Please come out of there!' Liam looked out the window at me as if he was apologizing.

I knew what he was about to do.

I scrambled to my feet and ran to the door, but he had already reached it. He slammed it shut and locked it.

I let out a measly cry as I banged my fist on the glass repeatedly, 'Liam, please, no!'

'I love you!' he shouted through the smudged window to me. 'I love you so much!' he placed his hand on the glass and I mirrored him as I sobbed.

Then his hand disappeared.

'Liam, we're meant to be getting married!' I screamed as loudly as I could. 'Come out here now!' I watched as he hurdled towards Georgina and grabbed a chunk of her hair, pulling her off of Carlos.

I carried on banging the glass frantically, sobbing and screaming. 'I love you, I love you.'

As I watched Liam drag his mum away and pull her into the kitchen area where no one could see him I remembered what he had said the night we met.

'He wants to die a hero, if he had to die, he'd want it to be saving the people he loves most...' I sniffed as I wiped the tears from my eyes and stepped backwards. Carlos and Neil were using all of their strength to pull open the back door that Liam had obviously locked behind him.

'BILLY! I screamed. 'Billy let me in!' I pleaded, but Billy was still frozen to the chair, staring emptily at the bodies in front of him.

I heard some voices from up above and stepped backwards some more to have a clearer view, somehow Liam and Georgina had made their way to the roof of the building.

Some passersby muttered something in Italian at me as I had stepped into their walkway. They were oblivious to what was happening.

The street was quiet and the sun was at its highest point in the sky, making it hard to see onto the rooftop.

I could make out Liam holding a gun towards Georgina's head, I sighed in relief. Maybe he would come back to me after all.

I heard the click of the gun and closed my eyes in pure alleviation, but after a second another click followed, and another, each time no gunshot was made.

'Shit!' Liam's voice echoed down to me, my heart raced and I opened my eyes.

Georgina was laughing that hysterical laugh again and I heard her say in a smug voice, 'good job I have this.'

There were some shouts of which I couldn't make out, some screams and then a deafening cracking sound rang through the street.

No, no, no, no! He cannot die as well!

I threw myself against the door once again, screaming for Billy to open it or for Carlos and Neil to get through the door and save Liam, but I knew in my heart they would be too late.

He was gone.

'Let me in!' I screamed one last time; Billy jumped up in his seat as if he had just awoken from a trance and ran over to me, finally unlocking the door.

I pushed him out of the way angrily and ran to Neil and Carlos. 'Something happened! I can't hear them anymore; they were on the roof!' I screeched, throwing myself at the door they were trying to push open still.

'It's useless!' Carlos panted through the pain of his bullet wound. Neil had managed to break a hole in the door with the bottom of a fire extinguisher, but it still wasn't big enough for any of us to fit through.

'You keep trying. There must be another way to get up there.' I shouted as I fled outside and studied the surrounding area. 'There's an alley, maybe that leads round the back!' I called to them, but before they could join me I was gone.

I ran to the back of the building and raced up the metal steps that led to the roof of the café, but there was no one there waiting for me.

The roof was empty.

'Liam!' I screamed over and over, but he wasn't there, I knew he wasn't. He wouldn't just leave me like that.

The sound of a car engine echoed loudly and I peered over the edge of the rooftop to see if I could spot the vehicle that was most probably Georgina's getaway.

And there it was.

A pool of blood had been smeared off in the direction of the road beside us, and in it was one of Liam's worn out trainers.

My Liam. My beautiful Liam. No, no, no, no...

I fell to the floor and let out a bloodcurdling scream.

My head hit the concrete as I lay drably at the edge of the roof. I didn't care if I fell off. In fact, I wanted to.

Two of my best friends and the love of my life were gone; it didn't matter if I died too.

I faintly heard Neil's voice behind me as he attempted to shout over my screams. He placed his hand on my shoulder, but I shrugged him away. Police sirens wailed in the distance, but there was nothing they could do now. He was gone.

He was gone and there was no reason for me to get up because there was no reason for me to live any more.

XVIII

My feet were blistered and my clothes drenched. But I didn't notice things like that anymore. I was numbed to most feelings and most sensations.

The only thing I felt was pain.

My headphones were firmly in; they had been playing 'It Had to be You' On repeat for god only knows how many hours as I walked around London aimlessly.

'When a man is tired of London, he is tired of life...'

Liam's words rang through my body.

I was wearing his green coat. The one I loved so much. It smelt like sweet aftershave. It smelt like him.

I'd told him this coat was my favourite thing about him, why had I said that? Why hadn't I said his voice, his hair, his chocolate brown eyes, his kind heart? What about his kiss? I ran my fingers along my lips, remembering how often he had been there. *Oh, Liam.*

Why hadn't I met him sooner?

Why was he gone? And why was *I* still here? A million and one questions like that had ran through my head every day since we'd returned from Italy.

I was too tired to think of any answers.

I looked at the time on my phone, my stomach hurled as I realized it was already 3:15 pm.

They're burying her now. My poor Jamie.

I wasn't allowed at the funeral. Her family and my family had made that very clear.

'Thank god we have each other, B.'

'When this is all over we will go back to the old Jamie and Brooke.'

I curled over in agony as the familiar agonizing stab of pain shot through my heart.

A had left me alone, leaving my head unbearably silent. I'd assumed it was because I had no fears, no anxiety and no worries left.

I wasn't scared because I just didn't care anymore.

I walked in the pouring rain until I ended up at the bench outside my work. The place that was currently under immense investigation for corruption and misconduct, thanks to us.

When we'd returned home I couldn't face the painful reality of what had happened, it was too much to bare. So I threw myself head first into putting forwards a case to present to the Anti-Corruption department of the NCA.

Billy, Neil, Carlos and I were broken and lost, we were in a haze of grief and pain and still couldn't see a way out. Occupying ourselves in something useful was the only way we could even have hoped to get through the first week home. That first dreadful, horrendous week.

It had already been three weeks of coroner's inquests on Jamie's body, police investigations both in London and Italy, and interview after interview, re-hashing that earth-shattering day over and over again.

I shuddered.

There was currently a police search attempting to find Mr. Daniels, Georgina and… and my Liam's body.

The stab of pain was there once more. 'Argh.' I cried as I clenched my chest with both of my hands.

Panting from the pain, I sat on the bench and stretched my legs out, just like he always had. The beautiful voice suddenly stopped singing our song as my phone battery died. Sighing, I wrapped the headphone wire around it and shoved it in a pocket.

I looked at the space beside me.

I could almost *see* him.

His curly hair was blowing in the winter breeze. It was cold the night we'd met. It was constantly cold without him.

He was tired. I'd wondered why.

'Bless you.' He'd said as his aftershave had made me sneeze. I sniffed his coat hoping for the same effect, but no luck. It wasn't as strong now. I knew one day the smell would disappear altogether.

My heart wrenched.

'Do you want to come with me?' He'd held out his hand, towering over me.

I took his invisible hand and walked with him, the same route we had taken to the crummy little bar in Camden. He was laughing, so was I. I tried to remember the last time I'd laughed.

Oh that's right, we were in our hotel room in Italy, he'd just proposed. I looked down at the sparkling ring on my finger, I knew I would never take it off.

He was spinning me around in the air, I'd just said yes. *I love you, I love you, I love you!'*

'Oh Liam. I love you too.' I whispered.

I remember thinking that I'd never forget that moment, that it would always take my breath away. How right I was.

I clutched a nearby lamppost as the pain surged through me once more. It was as though tiny bits of glass were jabbing at me from all angles, especially in the center of my heart.

'Miss? Are you okay?' a passerby asked from under their orange umbrella. I couldn't see their face; the rain was hammering down too hard for me to look up.

I winced and managed to croak out a reply. 'I'm fine. Thanks.'

They walked away, I wanted to call them back and scream that I wasn't fine. That I'd never be fine again. But I was alone with my pain once more.

'Come with me?' He'd asked me again as we'd left the bar. I peered up at the sign, it wasn't switched on so I assumed they weren't open yet.

Maybe it's still the afternoon then? I wondered. Although it didn't really matter anymore.

I followed him once more until I came across Primrose Hill. It wasn't as breathtaking without the moon and lights sparkling against the night sky. Without him.

I lay down on the wet grass, looking up at the grey clouds of the rainy summer's day.

He was lying next to me, clutching my hand.

'I'd want to die a hero. I'd want to die for a cause or for the people I loved. I'd want my last seconds to be so filled with love and purpose, you know?'

'I know Liam, and you did. You got your wish. You will always be a hero.' I sobbed, my tears meeting the raindrops that were already rolling down my face.

'It's been very nice meeting you, Brooke. I think this is the beginning of a beautiful friendship.'

'Casablanca.' I replied through my sobs.

Eventually, I peeled myself off of the grass. It had stopped raining and the sun was peeking around the clouds. There was a faint rainbow in the sky. I didn't care. The world shouldn't be allowed to have sunny days and rainbows, not while people like Liam, Jamie and Harriet were dead.

I lugged myself towards his house. The heaviness of his wet coat was slowing me down, but I refused to take it off.

As I reached his front door, I felt in his pocket for the keys. He had a keychain with a picture of me on it. I hardly had any photographs of us. Why didn't I take more? I sighed achingly.

I trudged up the stairs and into the bathroom, peeling my wet clothes off one by one as I ran myself a hot bath. I was shivering.

'I'm glad you're here.' He'd said as he'd undressed me.

I reached out to stroke his cheek with the back of my hand, but my fingers met emptiness, that was all that ever surrounded me now.

I lowered myself into the bath. It was probably way too hot to sit in, but the burning sensation didn't register to me. I closed my eyes and lay myself backwards, covering my forehead, my eyes, my nose and then my mouth with the water.

I just want to sleep.

There's nothing left for me up there.

I allowed the darkness to take over as it became harder to breath.

Peace at last.

I gasped heavily as I sat up. It was like I'd been violently pulled out of the darkness.

No, No, NO! I just want to sleep.

I could almost feel his fingernails digging into my arms and his panicked voice asking me what I was doing.

'Everything is going to be okay.' He'd whispered. He hadn't

let me sleep before, but he wasn't here now. Why did he care?

Why can't I just sleep?

'Just let me sleep! Please!' I begged.

I closed my eyes and hugged my knees to my chest. I could feel his lips kissing mine, his warm hands running across my body, his legs holding me in place, surrounding me and keeping me safe.

'I just miss you so much.' I cried.

The water had turned cold and my tears had dried on my cheeks. I somehow found the energy to lift myself out of the bath. It was nighttime now; I knew that much.

That meant Jamie was now 6 feet under and I would never see her again. I fell to the cold, tiled floor and heaved at the memory of my beautiful best friend being murdered before my eyes.

Get up Brooke.

I jumped. 'Who are you?'

Get up!

I stood up slowly. The voice in my head was female, but it wasn't A.

'Jamie?'

Get dressed Brooke. I shivered as the goose bumps covered the entirety of my skin. I did what the voice told me to do, I pulled myself out of the bathroom, throwing on one of Liam's tops from the laundry basket.

Oh, that smell. I breathed in heavily and sneezed. I waited for his voice to say 'bless you,' but of course there was no response. I was alone.

I wandered into the movie room. I had spent every night in that room since returning from Italy without him.

Switching on the projector I inserted 'The Notebook' and

curled up on one of the beanbags, throwing a blanket around my shoulders.

The smell of scented candles, popcorn and him, oh him, was the only comfort I had left. As the film started I thought back to the many nights we'd spent together in that very room.

Once 'The Notebook' had finished, and I'd cried for a while, I placed it back on Liam's favourite shelf, and replaced it with 'When Harry Met Sally.'

'Dance with me?' he'd asked as the film ended. I held out for his invisible hand once more and listened as the beautiful melody began to play over the credits.

We danced around the room, and as I closed my eyes I blissfully forgot my heartbreaking reality. I felt his arms around my waist as he pulled me towards him. The odor and warmth smelt like home. He would always be home to me.

'...and the movies that we know, they're all just passing fancies that in time may go...'

Long after the song had finished, I opened my eyes and the tears began to roll out of them again.

'Back to reality,' I croaked.

My throat was dry and my stomach ached with hunger, but I couldn't bring myself to eat anything, I couldn't remember the last time I *had* eaten anything.

Well that's just stupid.

The voice spoke again. I ignored it and chose another film to drown out the painful silence. And then another after that, and another after that one.

And then, like every other night, I cried myself to sleep.

XIX

'Brooke?' Neil's voice broke my straying thoughts about joining Matt at the bottom of the Thames.

'What?' I frowned.

'Do you want to say a few words?'

'Oh. Er. I guess I should…' I stepped forwards towards the flowers Billy had placed delicately under a towering tree.

We were standing on Primrose Hill, the sun was shining brightly in the sky and passersby were enjoying the heat of the English Summer. But I felt cold, I felt cold and empty and lost.

I stared down at the funeral flowers in front of me. Harriet's name was written with an assortment of pink and white orchids, Jamie's with rainbow carnations and Liam's with white Chrysanthemums.

They looked beautiful, but it felt so wrong. Their names shouldn't be associated with *funerals* and *death.*

My stomach churned.

'You don't have to, we'll understand.' Chris sniffed through his tears.

His face had almost turned grey from the lack of sleep and food, I guessed I looked the same, although I hadn't seen my reflection in a mirror for a while.

I waited for A's sarcastic comment about how terrible I really looked, but there was still no sound. I missed my anxiety, at least back then I could feel things other than heartache.

'I'm okay,' I lied. I'd already established that I would never be okay again.

I gazed around at the small group of people we'd invited. Katrina the waitress and her equally gorgeous fiancé were standing hand in hand a few feet away from me. She was sobbing and blowing her nose with a silk handkerchief. I thought back to our first date in her cozy little pub and how it was obvious even then that he was perfect for me.

Carlos, Neil, Dale and Billy were standing the opposite side of her, shifting uncomfortably on the spot as they tried to contain their emotions.

Chris had his arm wrapped around my shoulders, tears rolled down his lovely face. *Oh Jamie, he loves you so much.*

Auntie Veronica was there too. Standing alone, her long, black skirt blew slightly in the summer breeze. She looked as beautiful as ever. I was glad she'd made an appearance.

'Er. Thank you everyone for coming. I wasn't allowed at Jamie's funeral…' I gulped as I said those words. *Jamie's funeral.* I still couldn't believe she was gone. '…And we haven't found Liam yet…' I held my head in my hands at the thought of my poor Liam out there somewhere. The ache ripped through my heart even more.

Chris squeezed my shoulder. 'You can do this.'

I inhaled deeply and wiped the tears from my eyes. If there was one thing I knew I had to do, it was to say goodbye to the people I loved the most.

'…So, a few words… Er. Harriet…' I inhaled again. 'Harriet was one of my closest friends in the world. She was kind, caring and loyal. She wanted the world to be a better place, and I won't let her down with that. I'll finish what you started Harriet. I promise.' I blew a kiss to the sky.

'Jamie…' I croaked, holding back the next flood of tears. 'Jamie was my best friend, my sister, my soulmate. I can't believe you're gone. I miss you so much. I love you. I'm so sorry…'

Chris broke down next to me, falling to his knees.

'Chris…' I knelt down next to him and grabbed his hand.

He glanced sideways at me and nodded. 'I'm sorry, carry on.'

I squeezed his hand and stayed on the floor with him. I didn't have the strength to get back up. 'Liam…'

You can do this Brooke.

'Liam you were the love of my life. You always will be. It's been a privilege to have my heart broken by you…' I smiled through the tears as I thought about how he'd used that quote in his proposal. I made a mental note to watch A Fault in Our Stars that night.

'Goodbye, until we meet again,' I added. Planting a kiss on my index finger and reaching forwards to place it on Liam's name.

'I'll love you forever.'

I perched on the bar stool in Katrina's buzzing pub, gazing over at the corner table that was set for two people.

'Brooke my darling, how are you doing?' Veronica asked as she passed me a large glass of red wine.

I gulped the wine, still staring at the table. Our table.

'Everywhere I go is haunted by him,' I breathed.

'Oh, darling. But someday you will be able to see them as happy memories. It won't always be this hard.'

I shot her a disapproving look. 'Why does everyone keep saying that? *It gets better Brooke. It won't always be this way Brooke. You'll meet someone else Brooke.* I don't want to get over him, then he really *will* be gone!'

Veronica sighed and gave me her most sympathetic, annoyingly patronizing look.

'Don't look at me like that, *please* Ron. I just don't understand how life will ever be normal again, they are all gone and I'm the only one left...' I gulped the rest of my wine down and nodded to the adolescent girl behind the bar for a refill.

'You're not left on your own. You have us, your family.'

I snorted. 'My *family?* Since when?'

'Jamie's mum and dad will come around; they are just grieving. And your mum...' Veronica sighed again. There was no way she could justify Claire Hamilton. Not this time. 'You should come and live with us.'

I shook my head. 'I have a home.'

'You can't live in his house forever, Brooke.' She frowned.

'I can and I will.

Where's my wine?' I shouted to anyone that would hear me.

The bewildered teenager ran back over like a dog being called to heel. 'I'm sorry miss. I'm not old enough to serve alcohol yet, I just need to find Gary but I think his on his break... I'm just here as an extra pair of hands because Katrina was at some funeral.' She rambled.

'*Some* funeral?' I scraped the stool backwards and jumped up. 'Don't be so fucking disrespectful. Forget your wine, I'll get some from the shop. I'm leaving.'

'Brooke…' Veronica called after me as I headed for the exit.

I span around so fast it made me dizzy.

You really need to eat. The new voice scolded me. I preferred A, at least she didn't boss me around.

'No Ron!' I shouted. 'I'm leaving. *Don't* come after me.'

'Brooke what's going on?' Katrina wiggled through the front door.

'Maybe you shouldn't employ *children* in a pub. Just an idea.' I snapped as I brushed past her and out onto the cobbled street where I fell to my knees and sobbed once more.

XX

'I'm so sorry you're going through this. That must have been so hard having to hear all of that again,' Nyema said cautiously as she perched on the end of Mr. Daniels' old desk.

I was standing by the floor to ceiling windows, peering down at the road ahead, at the bus stop, at the cars speeding past, at our bench.

'Thanks,' I croaked as I turned to face her. 'And thanks for everything you've been doing here. I couldn't have done it without you.'

'Don't mention it, it's the least I could do. I just can't believe Mr. D... all this time...' she shook her head in astonishment.

We had just returned from Mr. Daniel's court hearing. He had been found guilty by all twelve jurors on all charges and sentenced to life imprisonment without bail. We were one step closer to bringing down the whole organization. It was the only thing keeping me going. The only thing keeping me from doing something really, really stupid.

The hearing had answered a lot of troubling questions for me.

Rebecca was completely innocent and finally exonerated of all charges after the CCTV footage of Guedo, Georgina and Rebecca entering the pub together was found, along with the text messages between Georgina and Rebecca proving that they were friends and Georgina was the one involved with Guedo, not Rebecca.

It seemed that at the last trial Rebecca's defense lawyer was a part of the whole organization, and that's why significant evidence that would have proven her innocence was never brought forward.

The bulletin board and journals we had found in Harriet's house was her way of linking together enough evidence to bring forwards to Mr. Daniels. From reading through the notes in her journal, it seemed Matt had wanted out of the organization for some time, but was in so deep that he didn't know how to leave. Harriet had decided to use her resources in the NCA and his knowledge of what went on to build a case of all of the events that had and were going to happen. That's why she had skipped so many days at work; she was leading an investigation of her own.

From the timeline that Mr. Daniels had described while on the stand, it seemed that Harriet had come around after being knocked unconscious by Matt not long after we'd left their house on that horrific day.

She fled straight to Mr. Daniels. Obviously she'd seen Matt's dead body and thought that the police were her best bet for help. She must have *hated* me. The thought made me want to hurl.

Of course neither Harriet nor Matt could have known that Mr. Daniels was involved in it all, he had to keep that knowledge as quiet as possible. Mr. Daniels testified how she was bruised, bloody and hysterical when she showed up to work. He said she spilled everything she knew, and that he recorded it and sent it straight to 'Seven.'

I felt sick to the core at the thought of poor Harriet hopelessly looking for help in all of the wrong places, I wished she had come straight to us — then maybe she too wouldn't be dead.

'He really tried to play the victim didn't he?' Nyema sighed.

I nodded.

It turned out that Mr. Daniels had decided to resign in an attempt to get away from Georgina and the organization, after they apparently *forced* him to kidnap Jamie.

But it wasn't that easy. Georgina still had him doing her dirty work by threatening to tip off the police that he had been compromising the investigation for all of those years. He was found attempting to flee the country. The coward.

'He got what he deserves,' I stated coldly. I had no sympathy for him whatsoever.

'Yep, you've got that right.' Nyema nodded. 'And all of those girls have been saved and returned home now. Thanks to you, Brooke.'

I shook my head. 'No. it was a team effort.' I managed a smile in her direction.

I told myself constantly that Liam and Jamie didn't die in vain; if they hadn't died there wouldn't be evidence tying Georgina and Guedo to any criminal activity, hence not being able to prove Mr. Daniels' guilt. It was a small comfort, but one I needed.

'You have a good team on your hands, you know, the ones who don't work here. Your secret team.' She tapped her nose knowingly.

'My secret team are the best,' I agreed.

Billy was fired at work for using their resources without permission, but he said it was worth it. He constantly reminded us of how we should be proud of our achievements as a group of misfits and amateurs.

'So, what happens now boss?' Nyema asked as she slurped

on her iced coffee.

'Boss. That still sounds so strange.' I smiled half-heartedly at her.

'Well, get used to it, boss.' She grinned.

I was now head of the NCA department after a thorough inquest had been carried out.

I knew that Georgina was still out there somewhere, probably aware that we were coming for her whole organization, but I chose to ignore her threat to quit my job.

I didn't care about threats to my life or safety any more. I had come to the conclusion that if I were to be killed it would be a kindness; it would stop the constant heartache that I felt every waking moment of every day.

'What happens now...' I repeated. 'Good question.'

'Well, obviously we have to find out what happened to Matt. That would link them to another murder and be more evidence against Seven. Er. Georgina even...'

I attempted to hide my discomfort. I knew at some point Matt's mystery disappearance would be bought to attention, I needed to steer the investigation away from that at every chance I got until we had created a solid story.

'First things first, a drink?' I changed the subject. 'I think we deserve it.'

'Sounds good, but can I say something before we go?' She glanced at me warily awaiting my response.

I nodded.

'I can't even begin to imagine how you're feeling, and I know you've mentioned before that you don't get along with your family...'

I raised my eyebrows at her, thankful that she hadn't mentioned Matt again. 'Yeah, you could say that.'

'Well all I'm saying is I don't want you to feel alone. I know you have your friends, but they were there, they are grieving too. If you want someone to speak to, I'd like to think of us as friends, so I'm always here. Just wanted you to know.'

Tears filled my eyes as I tried and failed to smile at her. 'A friend sounds good.'

'Drink.' She nodded as she retrieved her bag.

'Lots of drink.' I added as we exited the room.

DECEMBER

182 DAYS AFTER...

THE BEGINNING AND THE END.

After sitting in the drab, frosty waiting room for what seemed like forever, an unfamiliar voice broke the silence, 'Brooke, Dr Daw will see you now.'

I followed the plump receptionist down the corridor until we reached the oh-so familiar office of my counselor.

I wondered what had become of dreamy Daniel.

I slumped down on the cream leather sofa, opposite Dr Daw who sat royally in her arm chair.

'Hi, again.' I smiled half-heartedly.

'Brooke, it must have been over a year since our last session. What brings you back?' She asked in her song-like voice.

'It's pretty fucked up,' I stated, 'I wouldn't know where to start...' I shuffled in my seat, the thought of explaining what had happened that day all over again was enough to make me want to hurl.

She chuckled at my brutal honesty. 'Well we can only start at the beginning...'

I breathed in, still unsure whether I wanted to delve into the deepest darkest parts of my life, to tell her the whole painful, horrendous truth, but I was sitting in that room again and there was no turning back now.

'Right, the beginning...'

'Take your time.' She smiled.

'Liam and Jamie are dead,' I whispered, wiping the smile clean off of her face. She took a moment to compose herself before asking me what had happened.

'We were trying to find Liam's mum...' I began.

'I remember you telling me about this, did you find her?' Dr

275

Daw interrupted as she placed her notepad and pen on the table next to her.

I nodded, wincing at the memory of Georgina's piercing laugh. 'We found her, and she was linked to the human trafficking organization I have been investigating at work.' Again, Dr Daw's face dropped a little more.

'We went to Italy; Liam was so desperate to meet his mum, but she-she...'

'Do you want to tell me what happened?' Dr Daw asked quietly.

I shook my head. 'I've told so many people what happened recently, I don't think I could go through it all again. I just need to say how I'm feeling out loud. I haven't spoken to anyone about how I really feel...'

She nodded in response, encouraging me to continue.

'It's been 6 months since we came back from Italy... 6 months and it's still not any easier than the day it happened...' I inhaled deeply as my chest began to ache even more.

'...I have relentlessly tried to find out what happened to him. I've carried on paying his phone bill just so I can ring and text his mobile every day in the hope that it isn't real, that one time he is going to answer my call and tell me everything is okay...'

'So you didn't see what happened to him?' Dr Daw asked, attempting to make sense of my scattered explanations.

I shook my head.

'Okay. But you know for a fact he passed away?'

'There was blood, his shoe...' I closed my eyes as the cracking sound of Liam's body falling from the roof echoed through my brain. It was a sound I knew I would never forget. It was a sound I heard in my nightmares every single night.

'...There's just been no closure, no body, no explanation,

there was no goodbye.' I paused and composed myself as my chest grew tighter from the pain. 'Instead it's like he never existed, he has just been taken away from my life as fast as he arrived in it. All I have left of him is his little home, and for the past 6 months I have spent every single night in his movie room watching his favourite films on the projector, cuddled up in his woolen blanket that he used to wrap me in when I fell asleep.

Every night I send him a text with the name of the film I'm watching and his favourite quote from it.'

Dr Daw smiled sympathetically at me. 'What was last night's one?' she asked.

'Last night was Sleepless in Seattle, it was like coming home, only to no home I'd ever known,' I answered. 'I know deep down that Liam isn't seeing these text messages and that me sleeping in my dead fiancé's house spending the nights exactly the same way we used to a year on isn't healthy, but what else am I supposed to do? Accept that he is dead and move on? I don't think that is ever going to happen, Dr Daw. How could I forget someone who gave me so much to remember?'

'You were engaged?' She asked. I nodded. 'And Jamie, what happened to her?'

'She was shot.' I stated bluntly. Dr Daw winced.

'I hardly sleep, but when I do all I see is them. Jamie's body lying on the floor in front of me, and Liam falling from the sky. It's like his fall is never-ending. And Harriet too, I see her...'

'Harriet?' Dr Daw raised her eyebrows. 'Your friend from work?'

'She's dead too...' I whispered. 'I don't have my best friends to help me grieve; I don't know what I'm supposed to do without them...' I grabbed a tissue from the table in front of me and attempted desperately to wipe all of the tears from my face.

'Do you have anyone to speak to, anyone around you?' Dr Daw broke the silence after a minute or so.

'Auntie Veronica constantly calls me, asking me to move in with her, so does my dad, wanting me to see the twins,' I replied.

'But you don't want this?' Dr Daw asked as she took a sip of water.

'I don't want to see my parents, or my auntie, or my brother and sister. I don't want to see anyone. I'm not the person they once knew; I wouldn't even know how to act around them anymore. They are better off without me in their lives anyway.'

I shrugged the thought of my little brother and sister away as quickly as it had entered my mind, there was no way I could start thinking of anything else that made me sad, my heart couldn't break any more if it tried.

Dr Daw held up her hand and shook her head before walking over to me and placing herself next to me without making a sound, she often reminded me of Auntie Veronica and how she floated through life.

'Brooke I have known you from a little girl, I have watched you grow through all of the turmoil and upset you have endured, I have watched you come out the other side as an intelligent, strong young woman and for a while there you seemed like you were very happy...' she spoke softly.

I looked up at her, 'I was happy, I was so happy.' My voice cracked and the tears continued to flood down my face. I pulled at the tissue anxiously as I felt Dr Daw watch my every move. 'People keep saying that I will be happy again, but that's not fair. They don't get to be happy, so why should I?'

'Oh darling. I know that you didn't come here today for me to say something profound, and there are really no words or answers I could give you that will change how you're feeling. You *came here for a familiar face to talk to, a friend, didn't you?'*

I nodded. 'We, we were going to get married, we had the rest of our lives ahead of us.'

I smiled at the memory of Liam's nervous proposal in our hotel room. I wanted to go back to that moment; I wanted to go back there so desperately. I wanted to wrap my arms around his neck, run my fingers through his curly brown hair, look into those beautiful brown eyes and listen to his joyful laugh. I was wrong — my heart could break some more — I felt my chest tighten and the pain flew through it as I realized I was never going to experience any of those things again.

I sobbed, I wailed, I screamed until I couldn't breathe, all the while Dr Daw held onto my trembling shoulders.

XXI

I had been situated on the uncomfortable bench for some time, the crisp air whirled around me as I clicked my lighter on and off repeatedly in an attempt to warm my hands. The road in front of me had grown busier as time passed; headlights glistened against the evening sky.

I glanced down at my phone; the time said 19:26, my stomach flipped in anticipation. I knew it wasn't long to go, but the minutes seemed like hours and I couldn't wait any longer.

I glanced back up at the rotating doors that I had been watching like a hawk for the past hour, knowing that one of the times they spun round the minute would finally be here. Also knowing that I didn't have a clue what the hell I was going to do when that minute came.

Would she be angry? Would she have moved on?

Maybe she was happier now.

Then, that minute I had been so nervously waiting for finally arrived. The steel doors rotated and there she was. My heart felt as though it skipped a beat. Just like before, her pure existence made me melt.

She paused under the shelter of the building and lit up a cigarette, blowing the smoke so elegantly into the air. I watched in awe as the wind gently blew her long, chocolate hair and her pink, silk scarf over her shoulder.

I closed my eyes for a second to remember the times she

would lay on my chest and I would nestle my face into her hair because she smelt just like coconuts.

She strutted to the edge of the road in her thigh high boots, cigarette in one hand and a rolled up newspaper in the other. *Oh you haven't changed one-bit girl,* I smiled to myself.

I knew attempting to explain what was happening wouldn't be easy, and that asking her to mess up her whole life again for me was selfish in so many ways. But I had waited eight months for this; two hundred and forty-three days had led me to this very moment and I didn't want to spend another moment without her, however crazy things were about to get. Surely as long as we were together again nothing else mattered? *Oh I hope she feels the same.*

I let out a deep sigh and stood up slowly, waiting for her to notice me as she crossed the road. I stared eagerly as she drew closer and then, she realized, and time stood still.

Our eyes met and the whole world ceased to exist, the only thing I could see was her.

Her perfectly shaped silhouette sparkled majestically against the starry sky; her long hair blew beautifully and her face was still a picture of absolute perfection in my exhausted eyes.

To the outside world we appeared to be nothing more than two strangers walking towards each other, but in our world we were so much more than that. We were the reconciliation of secrets and inside jokes, of anguish and pain, of happy days and even happier nights, of unconditional love, of undying passion and lust. All of those things were meeting again for the first time in two hundred and forty-three days and our eyes told the story of how we felt about that.

We were frozen in time for what felt like eternity before Brooke broke the silence with a whisper so quiet that only we, in our world, could hear.

'Liam?'